NEPTUNE
AVENUE

NEPUNE
AVENUE

A Jack Leightner Crime Novel

Gabriel Cohen

MINOTAUR BOOKS
NEW YORK

This is a work of fiction. All of the characters, organizations, and events portrayed in this novel are either products of the author's imagination or are used fictitiously.

A THOMAS DUNNE BOOK FOR MINOTAUR BOOKS.
An imprint of St. Martin's Publishing Group.

NEPTUNE AVENUE. Copyright © 2009 by Gabriel Cohen. All rights reserved. Printed in the United States of America. For information, address St. Martin's Press, 175 Fifth Avenue, New York, N.Y. 10010.

www.thomasdunnebooks.com
www.minotaurbooks.com

Map by Jeffrey L. Ward

Library of Congress Cataloging-in-Publication Data

Cohen, Gabriel, 1961–
    Neptune Avenue : a Jack Leightner crime novel / Gabriel Cohen. — 1st ed.
        p. cm.
    "A Thomas Dunne book for Minotaur Books" —T.p. verso.
    ISBN-13: 978-0-312-38061-8
    ISBN-10: 0-312-38061-5
    1. Leightner, Jack (Fictitious character)—Fiction.   2. Police—New York (State)—New York—Fiction.   3. Murder—Investigation—Fiction.
4. Brooklyn (New York, N.Y.)—Fiction.   I. Title.
    PS3603.O35N47 2009
    813'.6—dc22

                                                            2008045680

First Edition: May 2009

10   9   8   7   6   5   4   3   2   1

For Tim, Tracy, Carmen, and Jackson

BROOKLYN

NEW
JERSEY

Manhattan

Hudson River

East River

Queens

Fulton Fish Market

Brooklyn Heights

Boerum Hill

Red Hook

Crown Heights

New York Bay

Brooklyn

Midwood

Mill Basin

Bensonhurst

Jamaica Bay

N

Brighton Beach

Coney Island

Rockaway

Atlantic Ocean

0 *Miles*   5

0 *Kilometers*   5

2001 Jeffrey L. Ward

NEPTUNE
AVENUE

She carried her beauty like a burden.

She was slim, with high cheekbones and almond eyes and fine, feathered blond hair that reminded him of some eighties disco queen, an impression furthered by her silky black blouse, laced with metallic stripes. Yet she seemed far more serious than her fashion sense implied.

When she turned, he saw that a scar notched the edge of her jaw. Somehow, the mark only enhanced her looks. Even her sullenness was oddly attractive. Yet she didn't seem arrogant or vain. Perhaps she bore a touch of self-consciousness about the scar, mixed with the self-protection of a woman who unintentionally drew the attention of every man she passed.

What I would really like, he couldn't help thinking, would be to give this woman a good reason to smile.

CHAPTER ONE

The rookie didn't faint or lose his lunch. Detective Jack Leightner supposed he ought to give his new partner some credit for that.

A patrol officer met them outside the crime scene, an abandoned row house on the edge of Crown Heights. The uniform looked a bit pale. "It's not pretty in there," he said. "The body wasn't found for a few days."

Jack just glanced at the crowd of scowling locals standing beyond the yellow tape, out in the brutal August heat. "Keep an eye on my car," he said, then turned to his partner. "You ready for this?"

The young detective from the Seventy-first Precinct nodded in a show of eagerness. "Let's do it." It was Kyle Driscoll's first time as primary detective on a homicide. He was in his late twenties, and he had burnished brown skin and the confident good looks of a professional athlete.

The body was on the second floor, but its odor met them downstairs, as soon as they walked into the dark front hallway, starkly lit by a floodlight one of the Crime Scene techs had planted to guide the way. The smell was god-awful and sickly sweet. Thousands of years of evolution had prepared human beings to hate this particular scent: it meant *Avoid this spot. Bad things happen here.*

The young detective swallowed. "Should we do that thing with the Vicks VapoRub?" He was still doing his best to act enthusiastic, but the smell was clearly getting to him.

Jack tried not to grin. As a veteran with Brooklyn South Homicide, it was his job to temporarily pair up with local detectives and assist them with their murder investigations. "What thing?" he asked.

The rookie squirmed. "Don't you smear it under your nose to cover up bad smells?" Even real cops were susceptible to false information from TV shows; in Jack's experience, it took several years to mature beyond all that.

He shook his head. "We don't do that—all it would do is burn your nose. Don't worry, you'll be fine."

The rookie nodded. The young man had earned his detective's shield, but he'd spent his first few months on robberies and assaults. He wanted to prove that he was ready for the big show.

The house was an empty shell waiting to fall in on itself, but Jack noticed some elegant architectural details—crown moldings, a dusty, gap-toothed chandelier—from an earlier era. The rookie pulled up short as they reached the top of the staircase. Through the first doorway on the left—a bedroom, judging by a dingy mattress on the floor—they could see a whirlwind of activity. The plywood in the windows blocked any natural light, but the Crime Scene Unit had lit the place with more floodlights on stands. Jumpsuited techs crouched down searching for evidence, a photographer was snapping photos, and the Medical Examiner's investigators bustled back and forth. In the heart of the maelstrom, as always, was a terribly lonely and still center. In this case, the body was that of a young black woman, hanging by a rope attached to a chain that had probably once supported another chandelier. She was half dressed, in a shorty negligee; she wore her orangey hair straightened and it looked almost shellacked; her light brown legs were purpled with the blood that had settled within. Despite her current puffy condition, Jack figured that she had been a pretty young woman.

He turned and caught the rookie staring. He'd wanted to see, to become privy to this dark knowledge, and now he probably wished he hadn't.

"The M.E.'s guys control the body at the scene," Jack explained. "That guy in the white shirt is Anselmo Alvarez, head of the C.S.U."

The rookie stared up at the corpse; Jack didn't know if he was even registering the commentary. Having him around was disconcerting; he reminded Jack of his own early days with the NYPD. He recalled the shock of his first few bodies. And he remembered farther back, his first memory of a corpse, when he was a little kid: the sudden jolt of adrenaline he'd felt after almost stepping on a dead squirrel on a sidewalk, its wiry body splayed and stiff, its little watermelon-pit eyes staring up, accusing. There was something terribly unnatural about any creature with its animating spirit gone, and sensible people did everything they could to avoid looking at such things. Jack saw himself and his colleagues through this rookie's naïve eyes now, and thought something he rarely bothered to think anymore: *What a weird goddamn job.*

He squared his shoulders. There was no room for emotion here, or philosophy: this was just a puzzle that needed to be solved. He turned to the kid. "We're going to have to wait a few minutes until we can get inside."

The rookie nodded, doing his best not to look relieved.

Anselmo Alvarez stepped out into the hallway. He and Jack had become friendly over the years, two fairly small men in a world of big cops, and two relative outsiders, a Dominican and a Jew. Alvarez was the best forensics man in Brooklyn. He started to offer a prelim, but Jack waved him off. "This is Kyle Driscoll from the Seven-one. I want him to look at the scene fresh, without any preconceptions, and see if he can tell us what happened." He had a son a few years younger than the rookie. Though he had never felt right talking about the job with Ben—or with his ex-wife—he liked to mentor young detectives, to reach them before the job made them jaded or cynical.

The photographer had finished his work, and it was time for Jack and his young partner to go in. The rookie hesitated before they stepped over the threshold, but this time it didn't seem to be fear or distaste that was holding him back.

"Something on your mind?" Jack asked.

The rookie squinted. "Um, *yeah*. If this woman killed herself, then why is Homicide here?"

Jack nodded. "That's a good question. Let's see if you can answer it."

The room was sweltering; Jack felt his shirt cling to the small of his back. As they moved inside, his own questions began to pop like firing nerve synapses, but he kept them to himself.

The Crime Scene crew had left a stepladder next to the vic, and he climbed up for a look at her neck. Then he moved down and examined her fingertips. Finally, he turned to the rookie. "You all right with a closer look? There's something up there I want you to see."

The rookie nodded. He climbed the ladder gingerly, as if he were ascending a gallows himself.

"Look at the neck and see if you notice anything," Jack said, patiently.

While the young detective followed his suggestion, Jack turned away and surveyed the rest of the room. Even without the corpse, it would have smelled bad. The place was a mess, with junk-food wrappers strewn about, a pile of dirty clothes over by the window, an open Domino's box sitting next to the soiled mattress, revealing a half-eaten pizza. A bitter odor, faintly detectable under the overpowering scent of the body, gave away one reason for the human presence here (crack cocaine), and an economy-size box of condoms half tucked between the mattress and a dusty baseboard gave away another. Jack noticed one unrolled, forsaken condom lying next to the bed, and he crouched down for a closer look. Then he straightened up and motioned toward the door. "That's enough for now."

THEY STEPPED OUT OF the house and into a blast of humid summer heat, but the fresh air still felt good.

Beyond the little concrete front yard, several radio cars and a Crime Scene van were pulled up to the curb. Across the street, another small crowd had gathered: not resentful black neighbors, but dour, bearded white men. Despite the heat, they wore black suits and black hats. Crown Heights was home to three main population groups: African-Americans, black immigrants from the West Indies, and these ultrareligious Hasidic Jews.

The rookie breathed deeply. Jack gave him a moment to recover, then turned his attention to the matter at hand. "*So:* why wasn't this a suicide?"

The freshly minted detective frowned in concentration. "There was something weird about the neck. It looked like there was another mark across it, instead of just from the rope."

Jack nodded. "That's exactly right. In a hanging, the ligature mark would rise up behind the ears, but here we have a mark that goes straight across, which would indicate strangulation. And it's thin, with a double groove—probably caused by an electrical cord." He leaned back against the stoop's iron railing, then noticed flakes of rust coming off onto his sports jacket, and moved away. (Despite the often grubby nature of his job, he was a bit fastidious.) "Did you notice the condom next to the mattress?"

The rookie frowned again. "Um, I think so. It was unrolled, right?"

Jack nodded. "Yeah, but what else?"

The rookie squinted. "I don't know."

Jack crossed his arms. "It was dry and empty. Now why would there be an open condom lying there with nothing in it?"

He watched the detective struggle to work through the implications. "Whoever was using it didn't, um, finish what he was doing?"

Jack nodded. "You're doing good. Let's try to re-create the scene. Someone else was in that room with the woman. A john, or maybe her pimp. He unrolls a condom but can't finish his business. Or can't get started. Maybe she says something about his manhood, or maybe she doesn't even have to; either way, he gets enraged. He reaches out and there's some old appliance lying there and he strangles her with the cord. Did you notice that I looked at her fingernails?"

The rookie nodded uncertainly.

"What do you think we might find there?"

The rookie squinted. "The killer's DNA? Like, what if she scratched him as she tried to pull his hands away?"

"Actually, we often find the victim's *own* tissue under her fingernails: she digs into her skin, trying to pull away the cord. So anyhow," Jack concluded, "the perp calms down and sees what he's done, and then he tries to cover it up by making it look like a suicide. Luckily for us, like most criminals, he's not a rocket scientist."

The rookie sank down onto the stoop, took out a hand-kerchief, and wiped his face.

THEY SPENT THE NEXT couple of hours canvassing the neighborhood for witnesses. Fruitlessly. Nobody wanted to step up and get involved, not the distrustful black locals, not the sour-looking Hasidim. They checked with a local Vice team to see if the victim was a known hooker, but no luck there. They showed a photo to some working girls—nada—and then ran it by some informants on the local drug scene. Nothing. And then their tour was over.

"Don't worry," Jack told his new partner. "We'll have an I.D. soon. We'll get a match on her prints. Or we'll find out who was selling her drugs...." He certainly hoped he was right—the odds of solving any homicide dropped drastically after the first forty-eight hours.

The rookie was quiet for the first part of the drive back to the Seven-one house. As they passed a bunch of little kids dancing around in the spray of an open hydrant and then rolled by clusters of old folks sitting on folding chairs right out on the sidewalk, Jack left him alone; the young detective had plenty to think about.

"You got any questions?" Jack finally said.

The rookie chewed his lower lip. "Does, ah, does it get to you?"

"The bodies?"

The rookie nodded gravely.

Jack leaned back and dropped his forearm on his armrest.

"We do this every day. We kick into an investigative gear as soon as we hit the scene. If we got emotional or took it personally, there's no way we could do the job."

The rookie frowned but didn't speak.

"What?" Jack said.

The rookie chewed his lip.

"Something bothering you?"

The rookie shrugged. "I was wondering why everybody didn't wear Tyvek jumpsuits. I thought that, after O.J. and all, we were supposed to be more careful about dealing with possible evidence."

Jack glanced at him. The rookie was looking straight ahead, as if he was embarrassed. "Well, law enforcement all across the country *has* been more careful since the Simpson thing, but that doesn't mean that we're gonna have a perfect textbook setup for every single investigation. If you watch some of these TV shows, you'd think that every murder gets solved by forensic evidence, but in real life that's pretty rare. Most cases still get solved because we found a witness or because the mutt confessed."

The rookie still frowned.

"What?"

The rookie looked away. "I was just wondering if maybe there would have been a more textbook setup if, you know—if the victim hadn't been *black.*"

Jack resisted an urge to swerve to the curb and throw the car into Park. "Listen," he said. "You've been on the job long enough to know that every case gets its own priority. And yeah, the killing of some crack-addicted hooker is not generally the highest-precedence type of situation, as far as the brass or the press are concerned. But if you're suggesting that we might do a shoddy job because of the color of her skin . . ."

At the next red light, he turned and stared at the young detective. "I don't hear you complaining about the fact that the victim was a *woman.* Or that somebody cold-bloodedly murdered a *prostitute,* because he thought nobody would give a shit . . ." Despite all his talk about professionalism and detachment, he pictured the girl hanging so helpless in that dismal room and he felt a deep flash of anger toward whoever had done this to her. "That girl wasn't able to protect herself, and now she can't speak for herself, and we're damn well gonna stand up for her."

The young detective looked only slightly chastened, but enough so that Jack didn't feel a need to point out that if the case *had* been high priority, the rookie would never have been given responsibility for it. He was here to encourage the kid, not bust his chops. And so he added, decisively, "And you know why we're gonna put some extra mojo into this case?"

The rookie shook his head.

"Because this bastard thinks he's smarter than the NYPD."

CHAPTER TWO

At home later, Jack tossed his keys on a side table and headed back to the kitchen to see what he could scrounge up for dinner. He hated the way his footsteps echoed in his front hallway. He knew he should have been glad to be free from foul odors and grim sights, but the fact was that he would have been happy to stay on the job all the livelong day. Hell, he would have been willing to work around the clock, but ever since a precipitous drop in the Big Apple's murder rate, the golden days of overtime were gone.

He stood holding open the door to his near-empty fridge for a minute before he realized that he wasn't even paying attention to what was inside. He wasn't very hungry anyhow—at least, not enough to try to cobble together a meal from a block of cheese, a jar of peanut butter, and the remains of some Chinese takeout. He cocked his head; as always, he could hear his landlord's TV blaring upstairs. He told himself that the old man could probably use a visit, but then shook his head—who was he kidding? They could keep *each other* company.

Upstairs, he found Mr. Gardner sitting in his murky front room, in his duct-tape-patched recliner, watching the local news. The old man had always been short and stocky, but the weight had melted off after his stroke a couple years back, leaving behind a shriveled, bespectacled garden gnome. Jack handed him a can of Schaefer and then dropped down onto the spavined, nubbly couch.

On the TV, a massive old console that had probably once displayed the original *Honeymooners*, a reporter with starched blond hair was delivering a report about a pothole in Forest Hills, intoning so gravely she might as well have been describing the aftermath of a volcanic eruption. Jack shook his head. Where did they find these people, these puffed-up androids?

During a commercial for maxi pads, both men instinctively turned away from the screen's blue glow. Mr. G trained his thick eyeglasses on his tenant. "Hey, whatever happened with that lady friend of yours, that . . . what was her name? I ain't seen her around for a long time."

Jack stared down at his beer, working up a fib. "She, ah . . . she got a job out in California."

Thankfully, Mr. G—easily distracted—had returned his attention to the TV, where they were showing footage of a factory explosion in Tennessee. (Which had nothing whatsoever to do with local news, but fulfilled the station's mission of constantly providing viewers with something to gawp at.)

Now that they had gotten past the one subject Jack didn't want to discuss, they sat in a companionable silence. Jack glanced around the dimly lit room: a shelf of knickknacks collected by Mr. Gardner's long-deceased wife, a bookcase holding rows of Reader's Digest Condensed Books, a pair of shriveled leather slippers lying on the worn carpet. Mr. G lived a lonely life, enlivened only by visits from his health care aide or much rarer visits from his uptight son. Jack thought of his apartment below: was his own home life so different? He had been divorced for more than fifteen years, had settled into a comfortable bachelor routine where he didn't ask for anything outside of his work—and then romance had given him a whole new life. He had become spoiled, and it had blown up in his face. He was learning to accept less all over again.

When the local news gave way to "entertainment news"—celebrities falling in and out of rehab, making babies, then bailing out on their childish marriages—his tolerance meter pushed too far into the red. He rubbed his hands on his knees and stood up.

Mr. Gardner turned away from the TV, its light reflecting sideways on his thick bifocals. "You okay, Jackie?"

Jack frowned. The old man *knew*; he didn't miss a trick. He reached out and squeezed his friend's shoulder. "I'm fine, Mr. G."

Downstairs, he heated up the remains of the chow mein and ate it on his kitchen table with *The Daily News* spread out in front of him. He couldn't focus on the words tonight. He rose, placed his dirty plate in the sink, then walked through his empty apartment. He had done his best to remove all traces of Michelle: some lotion she had left in the bathroom cabinet, bobby pins on his dresser, the earplugs she had used when he snored . . . Wincing inside, he went to his small office at the front of the apartment, sat at his desk, and reached under a stack of medical papers. (He'd been shot in the chest two years before, after an ambush on a dark street in Red Hook. His insurance company had supposedly covered his surgery and hospital care, but the bills kept coming.)

There was one romantic memento left, this snapshot he now held in his hands, taken by his friend and colleague Gary Daskivitch. The big young bear of a detective had introduced him to Michelle in the first place, had set up their original blind date. Occasionally they had all gone out together, Jack and Michelle, Daskivitch and his cute little red-haired wife.

He stared down at the picture. Wood paneling in the background, light glinting off rows of bottles. Monsalvo's bar, a local dive he'd frequented for years, for a quick draft after work. Both couples had sat in a back booth, laughing, when they weren't gathered around the jukebox—Dolly Parton singing "Crimson and Clover," Sinatra crooning "The Way You Look Tonight"—or waltzing across the ancient linoleum floor or playing a new video bowling game old Monsalvo had (shockingly) installed, trying to keep up with the times. In the picture, Jack sat with Michelle leaning against him, her head on his shoulder, her black hair shining faintly in the dim light, eyes closed, a beautiful, soft look on her face. He had cupped her cheek in his palm and gazed down at her, heart full of love. . . .

He sighed. Enough of this crap. He had worked hard to harden himself, just like he did at work. *Nothing personal*, that was the credo. He carried the picture into the kitchen and lit a burner on the stove. *I'm through with romance*, he said to himself, and lifted the photo toward the flame—but he couldn't do it. He couldn't give up this bittersweet vestige, this last sadly pleasurable source of pain.

BROOKLYN SOUTH HOMICIDE WAS headquartered in Coney Island. When Jack stopped by early the next morning, he noticed two things in quick succession.

First, he veered into the back room, where he discovered that—pet peeve—nobody had bothered to refill the old Mr. Coffee maker that sat on one of the storage shelves.

And then he came back into the squad room, glanced up at the wall, and stopped short. A big erasable bulletin board held the names of all of the victims in current homicide cases. A new name jumped out at him. And he knew that his claim about taking every case impersonally was about to get shot to hell.

CHAPTER THREE

Daniel Lelo.

He had hoped there might be another Brooklynite with the same name. Even as the attendant pulled out the drawer, he held on to that slim chance. The morgue was freezing, especially after the August heat outside, but now a deeper chill ran up his spine.

The victim had a bullet hole in the center of his forehead, and undoubtedly the back of the head would be a pulpy mess, yet the stern, round face was easily recognizable. Jack noticed powder burns speckling the skin, which indicated that Daniel had been shot from a distance of less than eighteen inches. Killed in his car, the report said. On Neptune Avenue.

Jack stared down at his friend. Daniel had been a big man, with a body like a seal's; it was hefty, but you sensed that there was plenty of muscle underneath. And here was his tattoo: a mermaid drawn crudely on his left shoulder.

The man had been lying down when Jack had first seen him two years ago, when they had been in the hospital together, but warm blood had coursed through Daniel's veins, and his eyes had been able to move, at least enough to follow an overhead TV. . . .

AT FIRST, JACK HAD been given a private room. He'd felt like a dog hit by a car: he just wanted to curl up and sleep. Across the hall, though, lay a wounded gangbanger who shouted and complained all night long.

"Gimme some morphine!" the kid whined. And "Where are my goddamned Mar'boros?"

Jack wanted to march over, put a stop to the noise, and give the poor nurses a break. But he couldn't even sit up.

The racket went on. At 2 A.M. he managed to reach the call button. While he waited for someone to come, he fingered the bandage on his chest. The entry wound beneath it was only the size of a dime. As a veteran homicide detective, this didn't surprise him—he had seen more bullet holes than he could remember, and they were often modest. Inside, though, the burning metal had passed through his lung and a fragment had lodged in one of his vertebrae—its heat had shocked his spinal cord, causing temporary paralysis from his chest down.

He lay waiting in the dark. Finally a nurse arrived, a calm Filipina.

"Everything okay?" she asked. She leaned over to check a burbling tube they had inserted between his ribs.

"I'm all right," Jack croaked. He paused to draw another breath. "Is there any way I could get moved somewhere else?"

The nurse sighed. "I'd like to help you, but it's Saturday night." They both knew what that meant. A New York City hospital was a zoo on even the slowest nights.

"Yo, bitch!" the gangbanger shouted. "I need some morphine!"

The nurse shook her head. "The young men act so macho when they start a fight, but when they get shot they turn into the biggest babies." She gave Jack a sympathetic look. "I'll try to move you, but I can't promise another private room."

"That's all right—I'll take anything."

She patted his hand where it lay on top of the covers. "I'll see what I can do."

And so, the next morning, he found himself lying in a double room, across from Daniel Lelo.

His new roommate didn't shout. In fact, he would barely talk. Jack tried to strike up a conversation several times, but the man just muttered—with a strong Russian accent—that he didn't speak much English. He lay in his bed by the window, staring up at his TV. Jack was not surprised by the man's terse replies: Russian immigrants often distrusted the police. It didn't help that the room was visited all day by a steady stream of cops, from fellow detectives to headquarters brass, paying their respects to one of their own.

The roommate spent much of his time on his cell phone; Jack lay back, listening idly. His own parents had come from Russia, and he could recognize an occasional word, but not nearly enough to make sense of the talk. From what he gathered from overhearing the hospital staff, the man was a gunshot victim too, one of several innocent bystanders caught up in some sort of outdoor shooting in Coney Island.

That afternoon, the man set down his phone and immersed himself in a book.

"What'cha reading there?" Jack asked.

"Chekhov," the man muttered. "Stories."

Jack nodded, though he didn't know anything about the

author. At least the guy had answered. He tried to keep the conversation going. "Wasn't there a guy on *Star Trek* named Chekhov? My son used to love that show."

The Russian just frowned.

Jack turned away. He wished he could get up and take a hot shower, but that wasn't an option: nearly a week of bed rest had lowered his blood pressure so much that even raising his head made him feel faint, as if all his blood had taken a quick elevator ride south. The doctors had a fancy term for it: *orthostatic hypertension.*

Late in the day, the Russian put down his book and turned on his TV. Static filled the screen. The man raised his remote again. The field of static was replaced by another, then another. The Russian muttered a curse, one Jack's father had used when drunk.

"Too bad about your set there," he said, giving the neighborly thing one last chance.

The Russian just scowled.

A few minutes before dinnertime, the hospital chaplain poked his head in the doorway.

"Jack Leightner?"

"That's me."

"I'd like to invite you to our services on Sunday."

"I'm Jewish. And I doubt that I'll be up and about, anyhow."

The chaplain frowned at his clipboard. "Sorry about that." He went on his way.

Jack turned and found his roommate staring at him. The man's face seemed less forbidding.

"You are Jewish? You don't look it."

Jack shrugged.

"And your first name," the Russian said. "Like President *Kennedyee.*"

Jack smiled. "I guess he wasn't very Jewish. What's your name?"

"Danylets. In this country, people call me Daniel. Where you are from?"

"Originally? Russia, believe it or not. My father came from somewhere near Leningrad and my mother's family was from Kiev."

The man actually smiled. "Ukraine! Myself also."

Jack nodded uncertainly. Ukraine—was that part of Russia? With all the recent chaos in that part of the world, who could keep track? "What do you do?" he asked.

"In my country, I was brain surgeon. Here, I am taxi driver."

"You were a surgeon?" Jack said, eyebrows raised.

"No." The Russian grinned hugely. "I heard this on TV. You like?" His face was transformed—he looked boyish, a sunny cherub.

Jack smiled. He wasn't much of a joker, but—like all cops—he appreciated wit under pressure.

The Russian stroked his thinning hair. "*Ekshully,* I am in business. Import-export."

Vague phrase. It made Jack think of knickknacks, like the brightly painted Russian doll his mother had kept on her dresser when he was a kid—he had loved to discover the smaller dolls nested inside. Smaller, smaller . . . he'd keep going until he reached the last tiny one.

A knock at the door.

"Dany?"

The Russian turned to Jack. "My wife."

A woman stood in the doorway. Maybe thirty, she was

slim and stunning. She wore a silky black blouse, covered in metallic diagonal stripes. *Brighton Beach,* Jack thought; the neighborhood was on the south shore of Brooklyn, full of immigrants from Soviet Russia. Their fashions trended to an earlier era.

The woman didn't smile; she looked as though maybe she never did. She came in and set down a shopping bag.

"This is Eugenia," the Russian told Jack. He turned to her. "Zhenya, this is Zhack. From Kiev."

"Very nice." The wife nodded, with no change of her gloomy expression.

Jack noticed a short, deep scar on one side of her jaw. Somehow, it only accentuated her beauty.

"Actually," he said, "I was born here. My mother came from there."

The Russian shrugged. "No problem. You are still a *landsman.*" Jack recognized the word: Yiddish for "countryman."

The woman turned to her bag and started pulling out Tupperware. Jack couldn't help looking at her, but he caught himself: here he was, thinking about another man's wife. He was glad that he would soon see his own lovely visitor, Michelle.

"You must eat with us," Daniel said to him.

"Thanks, but I already ordered my dinner."

A couple of minutes later an aide, a big, cheerful Jamaican man, came in to deliver Jack's tray. "What smells so good? That can't be from our kitchen."

"Have some," the Russian said. His wife started spooning food onto paper plates.

"Just a little taste." The aide accepted a plate covered with little dumplings. "What is this, ravioli?"

"*Pelmeni.*" The Russian watched him take a bite. "You like?"

"Man, this stuff is *nice*. Thank you."

The Russian beamed.

Jack did his best not to stare at his new friend's wife.

AND NOW HERE WAS Daniel, or what was left of him, lying in a refrigerated drawer.

Shot *again*, Jack mused.

What were the odds?

CHAPTER FOUR

Back in his car, he pulled out his cell phone and called Kyle Driscoll about their Crown Heights case. "Listen," he told the young detective, "I've got something I need to take care of. Why don't you check in with the M.E. and see if he's got any kind of I.D. on our victim? And then, I guess, keep going with the neighborhood canvass, and I'll meet up with you as soon as I can."

He hung up, feeling a bit guilty after his big speech about priorities. He made another quick call, then dropped the phone into the cup holder next to him. As he drove away from the Kings County Morgue, he thought about the man who had become his hospital comrade. Outside the car, Brooklyn residents limped down Linden Avenue in the blistering heat, but Jack barely saw them. He was focused on another scene, in his mind's eye.

The rehab gym had been like a strange dance hall; the patients sat with their wheelchairs in a row, waiting for the physical therapists to take them for a whirl. The long, sunny room was crowded, and everything was forcedly cheery, from the lite rock on the radio to the brightly colored exercise balls stored in nets over the mats. The more mobile patients gritted their teeth and did their best to walk the length of a set of parallel bars, to lift small weights, to keep their balance while standing on yellow DynaDiscs. Others were lucky if they could wiggle their fingers.

Jack and his roommate had begun working out together, sharing the aches and pains, giving each other encouragement. He remembered an afternoon when he had sat in a wheelchair, curling a small dumbbell. Next to him, Daniel breathed heavily between his own sets. He gave Jack a frank, open look. "Do you remember what it was like when you was shot?"

Jack rested the dumbbell in his lap. He couldn't recall much about his own shooting—the shock had been overwhelming—but a physical memory came through. He touched his chest. "It was like a hammer. No—a chisel. Sharp."

"For me, it was like the bite of a bee."

"The sting."

"*Steeng*, yes." The Russian ran a hand across his broad face. "I never think that one little piece of metal can make life so changed."

Jack looked at the Russian and knew exactly what the man meant. Before his shooting, he had been unaware of his belief in an invisible membrane that protected him from the world. He realized it only after that membrane had been brutally ripped apart. Normally, Jack would talk only to fellow cops about his on-the-job experiences; they understood him in a way that even his ex-wife never had. But getting shot was something cops didn't really understand, even though they witnessed violence all the time. It wasn't something doctors really understood, either, though gunshot patients were often rolled into their wards. Having a bullet slam into your flesh was not just a physical annoyance, as it seemed in the movies, where a cop might take a hit in the shoulder and then just jump up and run after the bad guys. No—it was a profound psychological disturbance, a violation, a deep emotional trauma. After the incident in Red Hook, Jack had crossed over into a different universe, the world of victims, and this stranger seemed to be the only person who could really appreciate how he felt.

MOST OF THE PEOPLE who traveled to Coney Island in search of a little summer fun had no idea what the neighborhood was like just a couple of blocks away from the amusement parks and the beach. Here, where the year-round residents lived, there was very little public fun—it was a gritty little working-class backwater, a reminder that the nearby resort had fallen on tough times. Mermaid Avenue, the main shopping strip, had a busy street scene, populated by hard-faced, hard-drinking skels in bleached denim, do-rags, tractor caps, unlaced sneakers. Next to the elevated subway tracks that traversed the neighborhood stood an abandoned little building with a fitting name: Terminal Hotel. (It was easy to imagine some boozer or junkie settling in there to die.)

As if matching the general tone, the sky was overcast today; the clouds looked like dirty mattress stuffing. Jack glanced up at a second-floor sign advertising the Salt and Sea Mission, a Bowery-like project for the redemption of those whom the street had not entirely claimed. As he drove, he kept picturing Daniel's face, so animated in the rehab gym; in the morgue, a lifeless lump of clay. They hadn't kept in touch for long after they left the hospital: a few trips to the Brighton boardwalk (to walk together for physical therapy), a few afternoons sharing a couple of beers. And then things had petered out. They didn't really have enough in common, beyond their shootings. It was like being comrades with someone in the army; for a while you were intensely close, but after you got back to your old surroundings, you drifted apart.

A block north, on Neptune Avenue, the street carnival thinned out, and the smells of salt air and fried food gave way to that of spilled motor oil. Along this industrial stretch, Neptune was home to automotive shops, gas stations, and—just up the way—a big repair facility and storage yard for subway trains. Jack parked in front of a Chinese takeout place and stepped out into a cool morning. Across the street, in front of a block presided over by a body shop, an auto glass place, and an auto parts emporium, scraps of yellow crime scene tape fluttered in the breeze. The car Daniel had been driving when he was killed was already gone, hauled off to the NYPD's vehicle facility for further inspection.

Jack got out and crossed the busy avenue to the far corner, where a broken umbrella lay sprawled across the curb and scraps of paper littered the sidewalk—and his Homicide colleague Linda Vargas stood waiting. She was a short, wry Puerto Rican. The first thing that men tended to notice about her was that she had soccer-ball-sized breasts. If they made a pass, though, or condescended to her in any way, she could swiftly make them feel as if they were staring up at her from the curb. Underestimating her was not a mistake that anyone—perps or fellow cops—was likely to make twice.

Vargas's finely plucked eyebrows went up. "You trying to steal my case?"

Jack shook his head. "Nope. It's just that I met the vic a few times. Back in the hospital, after I got shot." (Having some familiarity with a victim wouldn't automatically disqualify him from helping with a case, not unless there was some sort of major connection that might foul up later legal proceedings, but he didn't want to seem unprofessional in his interest.) "Who caught the case for the Six-oh?"

Linda pulled out a cigarette and lit up. "His name's Scott DeHaven."

"How's he doing?"

She blew a puff of smoke over her shoulder, in consideration of the fact that Jack had stopped smoking since the hospital. "He's all right. He's over at BCI." The Bureau of Criminal Information.

Jack nodded. He had to wonder whether the precinct detective might find Daniel's name in any records over there.

Vargas moved into brisk business mode. "*So:* the vehicle was found here in the right lane—evidently it drifted into the curb after the deceased was capped. The angle made it look like a shitty parking job, which is probably why nobody called it in right away."

Jack frowned. "How long was the body sitting here?" It felt a little weird calling a friend *the body*, but he knew he'd have to keep his feelings out of this.

Vargas shrugged. "The M.E. says maybe a couple of hours."

Given the steady flow of passing cars, it seemed incredible that no one would have noticed, but Jack knew that they were looking at a time of death of midnight or 1 A.M. The avenue would have looked a lot different at that hour. All of the security shutters in front of the auto shops would have been rolled down. And the Chinese takeout place and the pizza parlor? Closed. He glanced at the red and yellow awnings of the nearby businesses; their bright colors would have been muted in the night. *In the dark, all cats are gray.* In front of a big liquor store on the next block, three life-size statues of pirates stood sentinel. Jack wished that they could talk.

"What'cha thinkin'?" said Linda Vargas.

Jack scratched his cheek. "The guy was shot at very close range, so where would the shooter have been?" He answered his own question. "In the car next to Lelo, or right outside his window. Did Crime Scene find powder on the seat next to him?"

Vargas shook her head. "Not much. It looks like the shooter was outside."

Jack nodded. "I guess he couldn't have just driven up next to the vic, because he would have been on the left side of the other car. Unless there were two of them . . . Or maybe he was on foot and walked up from across the street when the car was stopped at a red light? Maybe an attempted robbery?"

Vargas nodded. "Sounds good, only we found his wallet still in his pocket, and his cell phone on the seat next to him. I mean, it could've been a robbery gone bad, and the perp freaked out and took off before he grabbed the dough, but that doesn't seem likely. . . ."

"Have you gotten the cell phone records yet?"

"They're on the way."

Jack stared into the empty space where the car would have been stopped. "Hold on," he said. "Maybe there's another option. Instead of being on foot or in a car, what if the shooter came up right beside him on a motorcycle or a bike?"

Vargas nodded. "I can see that."

"Any bullet casings?"

"Nope. He cleaned up after himself."

"Witnesses?"

She shook her head. "He picked a nice spot for a quiet killing." She pointed up the avenue. "The only open business within sight would have been that gas station down there, and it's a bit too far for a real I.D., even if someone had been standing out front. And there are only a couple of residences within the sight lines." She pointed across the street, at a couple of little

apartments above the Chinese takeout place and the pizza parlor. "We've got an old guy says he heard a pop in the middle of
the night, but he didn't get up or even look at a clock. That's it.
No other drivers, no foot traffic, no calls to nine-one-one."

Jack frowned. What did they have? No leads, as yet. Not a
robbery. A random shooting, perhaps, but the odds of that were
highly unlikely, especially considering the fact that Daniel had
already been caught in one such incident. No, this had the ear-
marks of a premeditated, execution-style murder.

Oh, Daniel, he thought, shaking his head. *Who did you get
yourself tangled up with?*

He looked at his watch, thinking that he really ought to
return to Crown Heights, but then—picturing some silky,
feathered blond hair, picturing a sexy scar—he couldn't help
making one more personal stop.

CHAPTER FIVE

Even more than the back of Coney Island, Brighton Beach was a separate pocket of Brooklyn, and a self-enclosed universe.

If you continued east from the crime scene, moving along the shore, you'd see the old Parachute Jump rising up over the boardwalk, a defunct ride that looked like the skeleton of a giant steel mushroom. Then a couple of small amusement parks, just a grubby reminder of the resort's former glory, but still crowded in the summertime. The Coney boardwalk was an incredible melting pot, all kinds of working-class New Yorkers coming out to the beach as they had for decades, seeking relief from the broiling concrete and asphalt of the city. Hip-hoppers and salsa enthusiasts, Pakistani car service drivers and big Mexican families, Italian-American deli countermen in bleached jean shorts and wifebeater shirts—they thronged the boardwalk in a pulsing river of city life.

Walk fifteen minutes along the weathered gray boardwalk, though, and everything changed.

As a boy, Jack had come to Brighton Beach several times a year to visit his uncle Leon, who always had a box of saltwater taffy ready for his nephews. Back then the neighborhood had been different, filled with European immigrants. In the past few decades the Russians had taken over. You heard the language everywhere, as Jack did when he emerged from his car on Brighton Beach Avenue, the neighborhood's main shopping artery. It was like passing through some kind of Star Trek transporter machine. The place was known as Little Odessa, because so many people from that region had emigrated here, and they had done their best to re-create a world of seaside cafés and glitzy nightclubs. They filled the avenue, buying foods from home and cheap, flashy clothes. There was something elemental and doughy about them; they had grown up on meat and potatoes, and potatoes alone when there was no meat. The old women looked like little plump doves, their men like bare-knuckles boxers who hadn't been very good at protecting their faces.

The sun had broken through the clouds now, and the day was warming up. Jack turned onto a quiet side street, where he passed a row of old apartment buildings designed like Tudor castles—if Tudor castles had fire escapes running down the fronts. Ahead stood the boardwalk, and beyond that, a bright blue strip of ocean.

Up on that boardwalk, Jack remembered, were a couple of cafés, where a line of sun-leathered old women sat on benches facing the sea, hands folded over round bellies. Some of them might mill around a wizened little woman selling knockoff designer scarves out of a shopping cart. Another might offer something else, little packages that disappeared rapidly into the shoppers' bags.

"Medicines from Russia," Daniel Lelo had explained once, smiling at his cop friend's suspicion. "For foot care, for headache. They miss the things from home."

Daniel had led him a little farther down the boardwalk, where a bunch of men sat playing chess. Each pair was surrounded by a huddle of spectators, old guys in sporty caps who stood with their hands behinds their backs, watching intently and offering advice—*kibitzing*. No one spoke English. Daniel could become completely absorbed in some strangers' match. And when he sat down to play, he surveyed the board with impressive cool, made his moves rapidly—and won. "I am not an addict to vodka, cigarettes, or coffee," he had said. "But every day I must have my chess."

Jack had asked if the NYPD was having any luck finding the shooter who had put him in the hospital. The Russian shook his head. "I hev mostly bad luck. My family is famous for this. Half of my relatives was killed by Stalin. Of the ones still alive, half was killed by the Nazis. We are specialists in being in wrong place in wrong time." He smiled at Jack. "Do you like jokes?"

Jack had shrugged. This seemed like an odd segue, but as a cop he knew that humor was one of the only ways to deal with the worst things in life.

"Okay," Daniel said. "A communist, a fascist, and a Jew is walking down a road. From sky comes voice of God: 'For each of you, I give one wish.'

"The communist says: 'I wish all fascists will be destroyed from face of earth.'

"The fascist says: 'I wish all communists will be destroyed from face of earth.'

" 'And you?' God says to the Jew.

The Jew thinks a minute, then he says, 'If you will give their wishes, then I will just hev a nice cup coffee.' "

Jack smiled grimly at the memory as he marched toward a big brick apartment building.

THE FOURTEENTH-FLOOR HALLWAY WAS a pale minty green that reminded him of the ruffled tuxedo shirt he had rented for his high school prom. He had been nervous then, gearing up to meet his date's parents, but that was nothing compared to the unsettled feeling he had now. He reached out and rang the bell.

The door opened. Eugenia Lelo stood there in a black dress; she looked as if she hadn't slept since her husband's body had been found.

He quickly stuck out his hand. "Mrs. Lelo, I'm Jack Leightner. You might not remember me, but I was in the hospital with your husband a while back." He cleared his throat. "I don't know if your husband told you, but I'm with the New York Police Department."

Eugenia—or *Zhenya*, as Daniel had called her—brushed a wisp of hair from her eyes. As always, there was a distance to her, a willed remove. New York was full of attractive, haughty women, but her somber face was that of someone who had grown up in a harder world, and her recent news had certainly compounded that gravity. Today, though, Jack sensed something vulnerable about her. She looked faintly bedraggled, like a cat caught out in a light rain, and he found himself oddly moved by a little gap between her front teeth.

He took a step forward. "Would you mind if I come in?"

The woman frowned. "Other police come already. Yesterday."

Jack nodded. "I know. I'm just here to help them, and it would help me if I could talk to you."

She stared at him thoughtfully for a moment, with pale green cat eyes. She seemed to decide that there was no point in arguing, and stepped aside. Jack had been here before, to pick up his friend for their walks together, but he'd never seen the inside of Daniel's apartment, and he figured that Eugenia had likely been responsible for this lack of hospitality—she had never shared her husband's decision to open up and relax.

Though small, the place was lavishly decorated. A chandelier hung above the front hallway, which was lined with shelves of ornate porcelain figurines: little lords and ladies, shepherds, swans. The woman's taste was over the top, in Jack's opinion, but he told her it was a beautiful apartment—he was trying to melt the frost.

She led him quickly through the dining room. A black cloth was draped above the mantelpiece; Jack figured that it probably covered a mirror. He didn't know much about what these new immigrants did when they were alive, but he knew about their funeral practices—and those of the Chinese, Yemenites, Pakistanis, and other groups who had swelled Brooklyn's population. A Jewish death would be followed by a week of *sitting shiva*, a time when mourners would be comforted by visits from family friends. He felt a twinge of hurt that he had not been invited, but shrugged it off.

Several sandwich platters sat on the dining table, along with piles of cookies and cakes. The only visitor at the moment was a squat little woman with an ancient, sun-dried face. She bustled around rearranging the food; with her air of grave authority, she reminded Jack of a little bishop.

He nodded hello as Eugenia led him on, into the living room, where the walls were covered with bookcases. Daniel, Jack remembered, had been a voracious reader: novels, science, history, poetry. A sectional white leather sofa faced a big picture window and a balcony overlooking the beach. Eugenia waved her hand, inviting Jack to take a seat.

"I'm very sorry about Daniel," he said.

Eugenia didn't respond. "Would you like some tea?" she said instead. It sounded like she was reciting from a phrasebook.

Jack nodded—maybe this little act of hospitality might relax her stiff façade.

While she was gone, he stepped out onto the balcony and raised a hand to shade his eyes. Way down on the beach, the late morning sun glinted off a lounge chair; farther on, heads bobbed out in the choppy ocean. A steady stream of old-timers shuffled along the boardwalk. Directly below stood a big fat man who looked stark naked; as he moved away, Jack was relieved to see that his giant belly overhung a tiny bathing suit.

Across the way, a swanky new condo complex dominated a huge plot of beachfront property. For most of the century, the site had been home to the Brighton Beach Baths, a private club where members could swim, whack a handball, play a round of canasta. Jack's family would never have been able to afford the membership. When he was little, at home in Red Hook, he didn't know they were poor, but he remembered coming here to visit his uncle; he would stand on the boardwalk and look on wistfully as the club's laughing families drank pink lemonade and relaxed under shady umbrellas. Maybe that was when he had first learned that the wealth of the world was not equally shared.

Daniel's wife came out and set down a teapot and two glass cups in filigreed metal holders. As she bent over to pour the tea, he glanced at the scar on her jaw and noticed a bit of soft blond down at the back of her neck. It puzzled him that his outgoing friend had married someone so glum, but if he had learned one thing in life, it was that marriages were often difficult to understand from the outside.

Eugenia's body shifted under the black silk of her dress; even with its conservative cut, it was clear that she had a fine figure. Maybe sex had provided her marriage bond. There *was* something very appealing about her sulky face, her pouting lips. Jack blinked: it had been a long time since he had felt any real attraction to another woman, after the way his last relationship had ended. . . . He looked away. *Get a grip*, he told himself. This is a murder victim's wife you're looking at. Your dead friend's widow.

He sat in a rattan armchair, and the woman handed him a cup of tea. He blew across the top to cool it, then took a sip: it was very strong. Eugenia sat too, though she perched on the edge of her chair, uneasy.

"How are you doing?" Jack said.

She looked at him as if he had just inquired about the weather on Pluto. "My husband is dead."

He cleared his throat again—evidently, she was not in the market for comforting. Not from him, anyhow . . . "Could you pass me the sugar?" he said. The bowl was just a couple of feet away, and he could easily have picked it up himself, but he wanted her to pass it. It was a technique he had used many times when questioning recalcitrant people: getting her to cooperate in such a small way might subconsciously lower her resistance to his questions.

Eugenia complied.

He leaned forward. "I'm sorry to have to ask about this, but we really could use your help. Do you have any idea why someone would have done this to your husband?"

She shook her head, but he thought he noticed a slight hesitation. He could have been wrong, but he had spent a long career honing his interview skills. . . . "Do you know why Daniel was in Coney Island that night?" Though the two neighborhoods were right next to each other, he knew that residents of

Brighton Beach tended to stay close to home, among others who spoke their language.

Eugenia shook her head.

"The shooting happened late—did he say anything about where he was going?"

She shrugged. "He sayed he must have meeting with business client."

"Do you know who it was?"

She shook her head.

"He stayed out late?"

She nodded. "This is not unusual. You know: men, drinking . . ."

He thought for a moment. "Was there anybody at work he was having problems with?" In the hospital, Daniel had mentioned his import-export business. As it turned out, the man had not imported knickknacks at all, but something quite different: fish. The business had sounded mundane until Daniel explained that he wasn't talking fish sticks; he dealt mostly in sushi-grade product. He boasted that his company was becoming involved in the new global markets. *Black cod caught off the U.S. West Coast might end up in Tokyo,* he'd said. *Pollack served as fish-and-chips might come from the Bering Sea.* He said a single high-quality bluefin tuna could weigh six hundred pounds and cost tens of thousands of dollars, making it the most valuable fish in the world.

Now Jack thought about all that money. And he thought about the crude, macho world where the fish were sold: the Fulton Street market, next to Manhattan's South Street Seaport. The place had long been notorious for Mafia involvement. A D.A. task force had supposedly driven the mob away, but he wondered how complete the eradication had been. . . .

He leaned toward Eugenia. "Was Daniel having any trouble with competitors?"

Her face remained opaque. "Dany does not tell to me his business."

He sighed. "We're trying to help you, Mrs. Lelo. It would be great if you could help us too. Any little thing might be useful—a phone call or letter that might have upset your husband, somebody he might have mentioned . . ."

She bowed her head; it took Jack a moment to realize that she was crying. All of a sudden she didn't look so tough. "What you want from me? My husband is dead." She curled up, sobbing.

Jack considered putting an arm around her, but didn't think she would accept any comfort from him. After a moment, he stood up. "I'm going to go now. I'm very sorry about your loss." He pulled out his wallet and handed her his card. "If you think of anything that might be useful, please call me. At any time." He started to leave but turned back to the young widow. "I want you to know that I'll do everything in my power to catch whoever did this to your husband. That's a promise."

OUT ON THE STREET, he called Linda Vargas.

"The wife said that just before the murder, Lelo was having a meeting or drinks with some business client. Did you find the guy?"

"Yeah," she said. "Witnesses saw them having what looked like a very friendly drink in a sports bar in Coney Island, and then Lelo left, alone. The client stayed in the bar for a couple of hours after he left. He said they had just met for the first time that evening."

Jack frowned. "Okay, thanks."

As he walked back to his car, he wasn't thinking about

this apparently innocuous client; he was musing about his interview with Daniel's wife. There had definitely been a little flicker of oddness about the exchange. Something the woman was holding back . . . He would definitely have to pay her another visit.

He flushed, despite himself.

The thought of seeing her again was not displeasing.

CHAPTER SIX

"If you don't mind, I'll do the talking here," he told Kyle Driscoll.

The young detective shrugged as if he didn't care much one way or another, but Jack wasn't fooled. This was probably the worst part of the job, and even the most gung-ho cop wouldn't wish to take the lead.

He straightened his tie, then reached out and rang the doorbell.

Kyle took out his handkerchief and mopped his brow. The day had warmed up again, but it wasn't just the heat that was causing him to perspire.

The block was a bit seedy, with scraps of trash blowing along the sidewalk and random crap—piles of trash bags, discarded furniture, broken children's toys—littering some of the little concrete front yards, but this old brownstone was immaculate, with a well-tended little garden and a well-swept stoop.

Jack stood there with his hands folded respectfully in front of him, waiting. He nodded to his partner. "You did good with the I.D."

Kyle's expression barely changed, but Jack could tell that he was pleased. The M.E. had fingerprinted the homicide victim from the day before, but there'd been no match in the system, which indicated that she must have been new to her harsh lifestyle. But the young detective had kept showing the photo around this morning, and he'd found a patrol officer who recognized the victim from their high school days.

The door opened a few inches and a middle-aged black woman peered out. She had a fleshy, placid face, sprinkled with freckles. Carefully permed hair. "May I help you?"

As planned, Jack was the one who answered. "Mrs. Walters?"

The woman nodded. "Yes?"

Jack held up his badge. "We're with the NYPD. Would you mind if we speak with you for a minute?"

The woman's brow furrowed. "What is this regarding?"

Jack kept his voice steady and calm. "I think it might be best if we discuss it inside."

The door swung open. The woman was on the heavy side; she wore a pink pantsuit and looked as if she might have been on her way to church.

The front hall was dark, with polished wainscoting and a big picture of Jesus hanging over an antique side table. Mrs. Walters led the detectives into a front room, an old-fashioned parlor with crocheted antimacassars, a stack of magazines fanned perfectly across a spotless glass coffee table, and lots more religious imagery. The place had a faintly bitter, lemony scent: furniture polish. The woman gestured that the detectives should sit on a wine-colored couch, and then she perched on the edge of an uncomfortable-looking high-backed armchair. She touched a hand to her face. "Is this about Celia?"

Jack nodded. "Yes, ma'am, I'm afraid it is."

Mrs. Walters's face tightened, and he sensed that this

was hardly the first time she had heard bad news about her daughter.

"Is anyone else home?" he asked. "Your husband or another relative?" The woman was going to need some support.

"Please—just tell me what this is about."

Jack sighed. "I'm afraid we might have some difficult news." He reached into his pocket for a Polaroid of the dead girl. The C.S.U. photographer had taken the photo after she'd been laid out on the floor, and he'd done his best to get the least gruesome shot.

"We received a report about a young woman who was found yesterday morning. She was deceased. I'm very sorry, but I'd like to show you a photo and ask if it might be your daughter."

A small tremor ran through Mrs. Walters, but she managed to nod. She stood slowly and reached out for the Polaroid.

Jack braced himself. He had seen all sorts of reactions from next of kin. Tears, of course, and shock, denial, anger, even bitter laughter . . .

Mrs. Walters stood there for a moment staring down at the picture. A little puff of a sob escaped her mouth, then her eyes rolled up in her head and she dropped like a log, crashing right through the center of the glass coffee table.

"Jesus!" Jack said, and turned to his partner. "Call for a bus!"

While he checked to make sure that she was still breathing (yes) and for any injuries from the glass (nothing serious), Kyle called for the ambulance, then rushed off and returned with a damp dish towel. They helped Mrs. Walters onto the couch, where she lay, moaning feebly, her whole body trembling spasmodically.

While they waited for the ambulance to arrive, Jack

looked at a framed photo on a side table. It showed a little girl, maybe eight, wearing a high-collared dress, her hair in pigtails, her face sweet and shining. Despite the obvious differences in age and circumstances, he could see the clear resemblance to the woman in the Polaroid.

Whoever had killed Celia Walters had not just killed a crack-addicted hooker—he had robbed this woman of her little girl.

AFTER, JACK AND HIS new partner stopped off at a local deli for some coffee, and then they sat out in the air-conditioned car to drink it.

"Well, *that* went well," Jack said.

Kyle had just taken the first sip of his coffee; he suddenly sprayed it toward the windshield. He held a hand to his mouth, trying to block his laughter, without success.

Under other circumstances, Jack might have laughed too—the job was grim, and sometimes a little black comedy provided the only relief—but he couldn't help picturing the photo of the little girl.

"I'm sorry," Kyle finally said. He wiped his eyes. "I didn't mean any disrespect to those people."

Jack shrugged. "Don't worry about it."

Kyle loosened his necktie. He glanced out the window, then turned to Jack. "Hey, listen, I just want to say . . . about the other day . . . I hope you didn't think I was saying that *you* were some kind of racist or something."

Jack waved a hand. "No problem. Let's just catch the creep who did this." He was peeling the little plastic tab off his own coffee lid when his cell phone trilled. He fished it out of the cup holder and glanced at the little screen. Anselmo Alvarez, head of the Crime Scene Unit.

"What's up?" Jack said.

"I've been going over some interesting results on your Crown Heights strangulation."

"Like what?"

"We found some animal fur."

Jack didn't bother asking how the C.S.U. man knew that it was animal in origin. Animal hairs were usually finer than human hairs. Not only that: under a microscope, the fur of each species looked markedly different. (Cat hair, for example, had distinctive overlapping scales.) "What was it?" he said. "Cat? Dog?"

"Guess again. You're gonna love this."

The morning had left Jack with less patience than usual. "I don't know, for chrissakes. Lion? Muskrat? Give me a break here."

Alvarez chuckled. "You were close with that last guess. I had to show the samples to a guy in the Manhattan lab. We're talking beaver."

Jack sighed. "Are you yanking my chain?"

"No joke. Really. Listen, I don't suppose there are any big ponds in Crown Heights, no beaver dams. . . ." Alvarez chuckled again.

Jack squinted; bright sunlight flashed into his eyes off the hood of a passing car. "Can you think of any reason we'd be seeing something like that here?"

"Well," Alvarez said. "Considering who lives in the neighborhood, I can think of *one*."

Jack frowned, stared out at the street, and then suddenly he got it. "No," he said. "*Please.* This is the very last friggin' thing I need to deal with today."

His new partner watched as he clicked the phone shut. "What was all that about?"

"C.S.U. They, ah, they found something kinda weird." Jack passed on what Alvarez had told him.

Kyle worked here in Crown Heights, and he seemed like a sharp guy. It took him only a few seconds to put it together. "Beaver fur, huh? Like those hats the Hasids wear."

"I suppose." Jack's collar was feeling tight all of a sudden. Despite their insular ways, the Hasidim were very active in their neighborhoods, organizing safety patrols, keeping close tabs on their local politicos. They were vocal citizens, quite ready to express their feelings to the NYPD and City Hall, and then to organize aggressive protest marches if they were not happy with the results. What's more, they often lived side by side with African-American communities in the city—like oil and water. Just what he needed: to set off a big neighborhood commotion at the peak of the summer heat. Still, *someone* had killed that girl, and whoever did it had to pay. . . . He sighed. "This is a pretty tenuous connection. I mean, *beaver fur*—that could come from all sorts of things."

"Oh yeah? Like what?"

Jack frowned. "A coat."

"In August?"

"How about . . . ?" His mind went blank. What the hell else would beaver fur be used for?

Kyle sat up straight. "Well, I guess we should start questioning some of these Hasids."

"What—at random?"

Kyle's face tightened. "Hey, if we'd found something like a piece of street jewelry, like . . . I don't know, a *grill*"—slang for a gold tooth cap—"we'd be bringing some Brothers in off the street, right? Why should this be any different?"

Jack sighed. Here it was again: the *race* thing. And here *he* was: a Jewish cop talking to a black cop about whether a

Jewish perp might have killed a black woman. "Look," he said, doing his best to sound impartial. "I'm certainly not saying that one of these guys *couldn't* have done it."

He couldn't help thinking about a time when he'd been a rookie detective himself, working a robbery detail in the Nine-oh. Sometimes, late at night, cruising along one of the dark, lonely streets near the base of the Williamsburg Bridge, he'd see a streetwalker stepping out of a parked car and notice a black-hatted man in the driver's seat. Take a very strict moral code, throw in some powerful sexual urges, and the result could be a life split in two: the public saint, the private sinner. It happened with people of all religious stripes, from Catholic priests to Pentecostal televangelists.

"I'll tell you what," he said. "Why don't we look up local Hasids who might have been collared for sex crimes?"

And so they did. They searched databases, found several possible suspects, and began to check them out. Every one of them had a rock-solid alibi.

CHAPTER SEVEN

By the end of a long, frustrating, and unproductive shift, Jack was ready for a cold beer and an hour of mindless TV. He drove almost home, but at the last minute he started picturing Daniel Lelo's face, there in the morgue, and so he didn't turn off Coney Island Avenue toward his apartment. Instead, he continued on toward Brooklyn's south shore and a certain McDonald's restaurant.

The outdoor seating area was well maintained, with colored pennants overhead snapping in a stiff shore breeze. Above them, though, Jack saw an ancient plastic bag trapped in a tree, like a shredded ghost marking the spot where Daniel Lelo had been "innocently" caught in cross fire two years before.

Inside, business was slow—the quiet before the dinner shift. "WelcomeToMcDonald's MayITakeYourOrder," mumbled the girl behind the counter. Her eyelids looked as if they might roll down at any second, and stick.

"Hi there," Jack said. "I'll have a hamburger and some fries."

When the food was ready, Jack paid, then flashed his badge. "I'm with the NYPD. Were you here when that shooting happened a couple of years back?"

The girl shook her head, a little more awake now. "I just started last month."

"Is anybody working today who might have been here then?"

She nodded, went in the back, and returned with a short black teenager, name of Tyrese Vincent.

On top of his head the kid wore dreadlocks tied together and standing straight back like a bunch of asparagus. Jack asked to speak to him outside, on the site of the shooting.

"Tell Andy I'll be back in a minute," Tyrese said to the girl. Thankfully he seemed much more bright-eyed than his colleague, who just snapped her gum in response.

It was hot outside, but the kid looked glad to be free for a couple minutes. They sat next to a McDonaldland playground, presided over by a big grinning plastic Ronald. Jack found the character sinister; it reminded him of that famous serial killer who liked to dress as a clown.

He leaned toward the McDonald's employee. "Can you give me a rundown of what happened the day of the shooting? Where were you when it started?"

Tyrese squinted at him, and not just because of the late afternoon sun. "Why you aks about this now? The police already checked this shit out."

Jack dipped some of his fries in ketchup. "I know. It's just that . . . some of our paperwork is not quite wrapped up."

The kid shrugged. Why argue? He nodded toward the side of the restaurant. "I was on break over there, havin' a cigarette."

"How many people were outside?"

"It was lunchtime—we was full up."

Jack looked around. There was seating for perhaps twenty-five customers. "Was there an argument or anything? A fight?"

"Naw, man, it was quiet. Everybody was eatin'." Tyrese turned toward the sidewalk and shaded his eyes, remembering. "Then this white motherf—this white dude came walkin' down the sidewalk over there. He had a backpack and he pulled out a Mac-nine or some such shit."

Jack set his hamburger down in midbite. "How did you know it was a Mac-nine?"

Tyrese rolled his eyes. "I seen movies. If I was some kind of criminal, I wouldn't be workin' at no goddamn McD's."

Jack raised his hands, palms out, and smiled. "So what happened next?"

Tyrese shook his head. "There was a black dude sittin' over there." He pointed to a picnic table in the corner. "He was all dressed in blue; looked like he might'a been a Crip. He saw the white dude and then he pulled out his own gun. Then the white dude pulled off a coupl'a shots."

"Do you think he was going after the gangbanger?"

Tyrese shrugged. "Can't say for sure, but I don't think so. White dude looked all surprised when he saw the other dude's gun."

"Who was he aiming for, then?"

"I 'on't know, man. I kept my head down, you know what I'm sayin'? It went all wack."

"What happened?"

"It was like the dolphin show over at the Aquarium, yo—people all divin' over benches and shit. Then people lyin' on the ground, all blooded up."

"Who got shot?"

"There was this big old lady, got hit in the arm. And this Russian dude, 'bout old as you, he took one in the back."

Daniel.

"Then the black dude pulled off a coupl'a shots, and the

white dude ran off." Tyrese wiped his forehead; Jack didn't know if he was sweating due to the memories or his polyester uniform. "Some crazy-ass shit. All I can say, we get a lot of little kids out here. I'm glad none of them got kilt."

Jack wiped his own forehead. Daniel had been reluctant to talk about the incident; his description had been considerably more spare. "What do you think it was all about?"

Tyrese shrugged. "The cops found a coupl'a witnesses who I.D.ed the black dude. Turned out he'd been busted a bunch of times for slangin' rocks." He looked at his white visitor and decided that some translation might be in order. "*Selling crack*. Cops said the dude with the Mac-nine must've been after him, some kind of drug thing . . ."

Jack rubbed his jaw. "You wouldn't happen to remember the name of the detective who interviewed you back then?"

Tyrese nodded. "His name was Wright. Easy to remember, because I figured he was *wrong*. He didn't want to listen to me—he had his mind made up."

Jack frowned. They were in the Sixtieth Precinct. He knew the detective, Bobby Wright, an old-timer who was just riding out his days until he could take his pension and go sleep on the job as a night watchman somewhere. No Sherlock Holmes—and no civil rights crusader . . .

Tyrese shook his head. "He wanted me to say that the Brother did it, but I kept telling him that the Russian drew first. Typical cop bullsh—"

Jack held up a hand. "Whoa—the shooter was *Russian?*" Daniel had definitely never mentioned that. "How do you know?"

"Yo, mister, I live out here. I know what a Russian looks like. Blond hair, tight-ass face. And he shouted somethin' just before he pulled the trigger."

"What'd he say?"

Tyrese shrugged and raised his open hands. "I'm not no translator—just a burger prep specialist."

Despite the general grimness of the day, Jack smiled again. He liked this kid. "Did they find the gangbanger?"

"Naw. Far as I know, they never caught up with his ass."

Jack stared out across the hot asphalt. "The white guy—what did he look like?"

"He was all skinny, maybe twenty-five . . ."

"Blond, you said?"

"Yeah. With a crew cut." Tyrese pressed his hands against his cheeks. "Thin face."

"Did you see if he had any marks? Scars, tattoos, anything unusual?"

Tyrese raised his eyebrows. "I was runnin' from the motherfucker, not dancin' with him!" He frowned in concentration, though. "He had some kind'a mark on the side of his neck. A tattoo or somethin'."

Jack wrote that down. "What was he wearing?"

Tyrese frowned, struggling to recall. "I seem to 'member . . . he had some kind'a old-school kicks: Fila, maybe, or Adidas, with the stripes. The backpack . . . and blue sunglasses, the kind that wrap around."

Jack turned away for a moment, drumming his fingers on the picnic table. He turned back to the McDonald's employee. "Anything else you remember?"

The kid shook his head.

Jack closed his notebook and stood up. "Thank you, Tyrese. I appreciate it." He handed over one of his business cards. "If you think of anything else, just give me a call. . . ."

Tyrese stood up. "You're welcome. I hope you don't mind my sayin' this, but you best be careful checkin' this shit out."

Jack stopped. "Why?"

"Them Russians are into some nasty business, man."

"What do you mean?"

"I know I just work at McDonald's, but I can still afford a *TV*. They got their own Mafia, yo, only more nasty than the Eye-talians. They all into *chainsawing* people, and shit."

THAT EVENING, JACK CONSIDERED going upstairs to keep Mr. Gardner company, but he just wasn't in the mood. He went for a walk instead.

Monsalvo's bar was a little bunker on the edge of Midwood, an anomaly in a neighborhood characterized largely by another puritanical Hasidic community. As he stepped inside, Jack was welcomed by several old-timers. They made him think of pigeons, the way you could often catch sight of a little flock of them wheeling over some low Brooklyn rooftop, bellies flashing as they caught the light, then returning to home base.

"Jackie L., how they hangin'?" called out Tommy McKettrie, a long-retired bus driver with a wrinkled face that always seemed subject to an extra dose of gravity.

Joe Imbruglia, retired welder, threw a copy of *The Post* down on the cigarette-scarred bar. The old man's claim to fame was that he had helped build the Verrazano-Narrows Bridge. "Jesus, look at this crap!" he said. "Who is this Britney Spears? And why should I give a shit? I remember when we used to have stars who didn't look like kids working the counter of some goddamn convenience store. Remember Rita Hayworth? Remember when you first see her, in *Gilda*, and she throws her hair back and gives Glenn Ford the eye? Cripes, I almost had my first heart attack when I saw that...."

Jack settled onto a stool and ordered a draft from Pat,

the ruddy-faced young bartender. One thing he liked about this place was that it wasn't frequented by cops, and he could talk about other things beside who had gotten passed over for promotion, or the impossibility of making a decent living on the paycheck. He could just sit and stare up absentmindedly at some ball game on the TV, and try to forget the gruesome images of the day. He sipped his beer and watched Pedro Martinez finish off Derek Jeter with a called strike that must have been at least six inches outside.

Soon the old men were embroiled in a lively jukebox-inspired argument about the relative scat-singing abilities of Tony Bennett and Mel Tormé. Jack tuned them out; he nursed a couple more beers, and soon he found himself thinking about Daniel Lelo's widow. Zhenya. He had missed something there, no doubt about it.

Back when his son Ben was little, the boy had gone through a phase of being obsessed with Spiderman. The character had always talked about how his "spider sense" tingled when something was wrong. Likewise, being a good detective was largely about developing a profound sensitivity—not ESP or some other superpower, but an awareness acquired through years of learning how to read subtleties in an interviewee's body language and voice. Learning to recognize lies—and most people stretched the truth even when they didn't have anything to hide. Problem was, as a detective in New York City, you had to deal with all sorts of cultural and ethnic groups, from Dominicans to Senegalese, Poles to Bengalis, each with its own codes and mores, and that made it harder to understand what was really going on. Stepping into someone's personal space, for example; that meant one thing to someone in Sunset Park's Chinatown, something completely different to a Brooklyn Heights WASP. The Russians were a tough group: they tended to hold on to their native tongue, which meant you often needed a translator to deal with them, and they were notoriously wary of the police, perhaps because they thought the police were like the KGB. Even so, Jack reflected, he had gone too easy on the wife, out of consideration for her recent loss. He should have pushed harder.

He exhaled. Enough with the work thoughts; he was off duty. He took out his cell phone again. Thinking about his son had reminded him that he hadn't seen the kid in way too long. It also reminded him why. Jack had gotten divorced when Ben was eight. Ever since then, he'd done his best to stay involved in the boy's life, but his son had turned sullen and resentful. It was only in the past couple of years, after Jack had gotten shot, that he'd started to make some headway at repairing the damage. And Michelle had helped. Ben liked her; he would come over for dinner sometimes, and they'd almost started to feel like a family. When that relationship suddenly ended, Jack got the sense that his son blamed *him*, as if he was just naturally incapable of maintaining a relationship, of holding on to a woman's love.

He called the kid and made a future dinner plan, then put away his cell and sipped his beer. His mind drifted again. *A woman's love* . . . he pictured Zhenya Lelo tucking a loose strand of fine blond hair behind her ear; he thought of that endearing little gap between her teeth.

He frowned.

He finished his beer.

A few minutes later, he stood up and threw some money on the bar.

HE KNOCKED SOFTLY ON the mint green door. He stood waiting. Checked his watch: only nine thirty. Not too late to pay a little official call. He heard a TV murmuring somewhere down the hallway, smelled boiled cabbage. He shifted his feet; he wouldn't knock again. Maybe she was sleeping. Or maybe she was out, being comforted in the home of some friend or family member.

The door swung open just as he was pivoting away. Zhenya, now wearing slacks and a navel-revealing blouse. Barefoot. Somehow, she didn't seem to be quite so surprised to see him this time—and then she surprised *him* by turning away without a word, leaving the door open behind her. He paused on the threshold, then followed her in.

She walked down the hall, hips swaying—it occurred to him that maybe he wasn't the only one who'd had a couple of drinks. She continued on through the dark dining room—he could see half-eaten platters of food still sitting dejected on the table—and led him into the living room and out on the balcony. Sure enough, there was a bottle of Irish whiskey sitting on the little glass coffee table.

She turned. "You will have a drink?"

He shrugged. He had expected to have to press her, and her lack of resistance left him off balance, leaning forward, unsure of how to proceed.

She stepped back into the living room and then came out with a glass for him. Poured him a healthy measure.

He stepped to the railing and looked down: on the boardwalk, old couples with their arms around each other strolled in and out of cones of light cast by yellowish sodium-vapor lamps. Beyond, the dim beige expanse of the beach, and then the gray ocean stretching out into the night...He breathed deeply of the salty air and turned to find Zhenya sitting in one of the rattan chairs, legs tucked beneath her, regarding him coolly. He could see the light from the condominiums reflected in her impenetrable cat eyes. As she reached out for her drink, he saw her nipples press against the soft blouse, and he quickly looked away.

He sipped the smooth malt. He thought of saying something about how he might have expected her to be drinking vodka, but realized how dumb that would have sounded.

Zhenya picked up her drink and took a long pull. He wondered how much she might have already downed.

He rolled his glass between his palms. "I was wondering if you gave some thought to what I was asking earlier. If you can think of someone who might have had it in for Daniel."

She made a face. "*In for?* What this means?"

"Someone who might have been angry with your husband. Someone who owed him money, someone he owed money to . . . ?"

He could sense her tightening up again. She seemed to see him as a bad guy, like an interrogator in some Iron Curtain holding cell. He turned toward the ocean view. Bullshit. He was just trying to find out who had killed her husband—and his friend.

Normally when interviewing an uncooperative witness he might try to rattle her somehow, throw her off base. He could ask if she had a life insurance policy on her husband, imply that she was involved with the homicide. Come to think of it, he *should* check that possibility. . . .

He took another sip of whiskey. If he pushed too hard, she would just clam up. He'd have to come at this from a different angle. He turned back to her. "You don't seem to like me very much. Maybe it's my job, or maybe you just don't like *me*. Whatever it is, it's okay. . . ."

She didn't contradict him.

He sighed. "When I was in the hospital, after I got shot, I was having a tough time. It's hard to explain what it feels like when you've come that close to dying. You feel so weak. It kind of shakes up everything you think you know about life. . . ." He lifted his drink but didn't sip it; just stared down at a faint circle of light shimmering on top of the dark liquid. He looked up at her, in direct appeal. "Your husband helped me get through that time. He pushed me to work harder in physical therapy. He knew what I was going through. And now I owe it to him to find out who did this."

Eugenia scowled. "You are policeman. Police only helps police."

He shrugged. "Okay, so I'm a cop. That doesn't mean I'm not here to help you. Don't you want to know who did this to your husband?"

Her eyes clouded up, and she rubbed them angrily. "Nothing can bring him back. You do not know how it is like to lose someone."

He looked down at his drink again and was silent for a minute. When he finally spoke, his voice was muted. "You don't know anything about me. My younger brother was killed when he was just thirteen." He winced. This was something he never talked about. Was he bringing it up now as some sort of cheap way to earn her cooperation—or to win something else from her? He stole a quick glance: her face had softened a little, but not enough.

"Was you ever married?" she asked.

He chuckled bitterly. "Funny you should ask . . . Would you like to hear a little story?"

She just stared at him, still wary.

He cleared his throat. "Just before I got shot, I had started going out with a woman. You know what that means, *going out*?"

She nodded.

"All right. *So*—even though we had just met, she came to the hospital all the time after the shooting. I can't remember if you saw her or not. Anyway, when I got out, she moved in with me. I *had* been married, a long time before, but I was divorced. And I hadn't been with someone—*really* been with someone— for a very long time. And I fell for this woman pretty hard. I bought her a diamond engagement ring, I planned out how to surprise her with it. . . ." He glanced at Zhenya, who was re- garding him now with much greater interest. He paused. It was an old interview trick, talk about yourself a bit, make your- self seem vulnerable, get the interviewee on your side so you wouldn't seem like the Big Bad Cop. . . . Was that what he was doing? Or was it just the alcohol talking? The stuff seemed to be having a greater impact on him tonight than he'd thought.

He looked at her for a moment more, then turned away. Maybe he wanted to open himself up to this sad, lovely woman for reasons of his own.

"What heppened?" she asked quietly.

"It was New Year's Eve. A year and a half ago. I made reservations at a fancy restaurant. I was all nervous, waiting for the right moment." He chuckled sourly again. "You know what I was thinking about? Which knee to get down on when I asked her to marry me . . . And so the time came, and I pulled the ring out of my pocket, and I popped the question. And you know what she said?"

Zhenya shook her head, and he knew he had her full at- tention now—she was like a rapt kid, eager to hear the end of some bedtime fairy tale.

He snorted. "She told me that she was having an affair with someone else. And then she ran out of the restaurant." He finished his drink and set the glass down heavily. "Don't tell me I don't know anything about loss."

They sat in silence for a couple of minutes, looking out at the dark ocean. Jack was embarrassed and felt a little guilty about using his personal stories. What Zhenya was thinking, he had no idea, though he could tell that the air between them was considerably less strained.

He sighed. "You know what I think? I think that somebody might have tried to kill your husband two years ago. And maybe it was the same person who succeeded the other night. You know what else? I think you know something about this, something you're not telling me."

Zhenya sat in silence, a silence that lasted so long that he thought she might not say anything at all. Anxious, the woman ran her palms along the armrests of her chair. She kept her eyes averted, but finally she began to speak. "Where I come from, we do not use police to help our troubles. Where I come from, police *is* our troubles. But you was my husband's friend." She cleared her throat. "There was a man. For some times, my husband knows him. But then they was having some kind of *arg*..." She struggled with the word.

"Argument?"

She nodded.

"What about?"

She shrugged. "I told you: my husband does not tell to me his business. But some weeks ago, I see him talking to this man. And I think Daniel is very *aff*..." Again she struggled with the word.

"Afraid? Daniel was scared?"

She nodded nervously. "This man is very bad. I am afraid also."

Jack was careful not to look directly at her; he didn't want her to stop talking. It all clicked into place. Her weirdness during the first interview. Her edginess around him. It wasn't hostility, after all—it had been fear.

"Do you know his name?"

She chewed her lip. "You will not say to him that I am the one who told you? You must make promise."

He nodded gravely. "You have my word on it."

She stared at him. He could almost see the gears of worry turning in her head.

But she told him the name.

When he stood up to go, she led him through her dark apartment, and they stood for a moment in her little foyer, a moment when time stretched out, full of something he could not name. "I'm so sorry about Daniel," he said again. And then he took a risk: he held out his arms. For a moment, she just stood looking at him, and he thought that maybe she was offended or that she had just gone back to being cold, but she stepped forward and gave him a quick hug.

After the door closed behind him, he stood out in the hallway for a moment, remembering the feel of her lithe body, pressed close to his heart.

Out in his car, though, he slumped back in his seat. What the hell was he thinking? This woman was in a period of *grief.*

He resolved to let Linda Vargas handle any future contacts—and to make sure that Daniel's widow would receive any necessary police protection.

CHAPTER EIGHT

The room was shaped like a huge wood-paneled fish tank, and it was chilly, with an antiseptic smell. The ceiling was high; if it were lower, the proceedings might have felt too human, hardly the desired effect here in Brooklyn Supreme Court. Jack slipped into the back row of the public gallery, an uncommon experience for him. (He had been inside such courtrooms many times, but he usually sat up on the witness stand.) Now—here on the first day of his two days off—he had the time to take in random details, like the scuffed linoleum floor and the back of the pew in front of him, covered with graffiti scratchings: *Cherry. Poppa D.* And that great old standard, *Fuck You.*

The jurors were not dressed for a noble proceeding: they looked as if they'd been plucked off a Brooklyn sidewalk. The judge, a tall, handsome black man, sat back in his leather throne with one hand splayed over his face as if he was getting a bad headache, perhaps inspired by the schleppy defense attorney, who stood next to the jury box anxiously shuffling his notes like an actor who had forgotten his lines.

At the prosecutor's table sat the assistant district attorney Jack had come to speak with; all he could see now was that she was tall and that she had gracefully graying hair. He had looked up the name given to him by Eugenia Lelo and found that this woman had prosecuted the man three years ago. Jack was eager to confront him, but he knew it was better to do some homework first.

The witness on the stand was a patrol cop, a young guy with gelled, spiky hair who sat up at full attention, like some kind of wary woodland animal. As his testimony proceeded, Jack learned that he worked the Sixty-second Precinct—Bensonhurst—an Italian neighborhood with a growing population of Asians and Russians, one of whom sat in the loneliest seat in the house. The defendant was a small Russian man with a bald spot and no visible neck—that was all Jack could see from behind.

The charge was fraud. The cop had been driving on the Shore Parkway when he came upon the defendant, parked at the side of the road in a rear-ended car, which also contained three other Russians. Behind it sat a crumpled car occupied by a frantic Korean woman. The Russkies claimed she had been negligent in her driving.

The defense attorney searched for his next question. The judge asked a court officer to lead the jury out. Then he scowled down from the bench.

"Counselor, I spent part of my weekend looking over the papers for this case. I don't know what you've been doing, but you're wasting the court's time. I'm going to adjourn until tomorrow morning, and I hope you'll have a better handle on your case by then."

The lawyer started to sputter an excuse, but the judge cut him short and stomped out. As soon as he was gone, the lawyers and court officers abandoned their serious faces; they got all cheerful and buddy-buddy, even the defense attorney and the prosecutor, who Jack was now free to approach.

ANNETTE O'DEA WAS A tall woman, handsome, in her midfifties. She wore a navy blue business suit, not too fancy—it wouldn't do to make a jury think the prosecutor was hoity-toity. Around her neck sat one of those kerchiefy things that was supposed to be the equivalent of a man's tie. She looked prim—until she opened her mouth.

"The poor bastard went out and got himself some cheapo shyster instead of going to the usual firms," she said in a gravelly voice, shaking her head as she and Jack stepped out of the elevator.

He nodded. The Russians had the lawyers they went to, the Dominicans had theirs, and so on through the tribes.

They came around past the X-ray security check and walked out of the building into a fiery hot afternoon. Despite the blast of heat, the prosecutor lit up a cigarette and inhaled as if the thing contained emergency oxygen. Over the tops of the old stone buildings that huddled together in downtown Brooklyn, thunderclouds were moving in. O'Dea looked up and snorted.

"The judge just wanted to wrap things up in time to beat the rain home."

Jack smiled. Decades of dealing with the legal system had taught him how the supposedly grave, impersonal courts were actually administered by a bunch of very human, crotchety individuals.

They crossed a stone plaza filled with pigeons and office workers sneaking cigarette breaks. Jack hurried to keep up as the prosecutor strode across busy Court Street. She navigated through the heavy sidewalk traffic and veered onto Montague Street, the main commercial strip of Brooklyn Heights. She turned to him. "I almost feel sorry for the defendant, but I don't."

"Because he's guilty?"

"Right you are. He's guilty as the day is long. He's a crook and he's incompetent enough to let me prove it. He's a *schlimazel.* You know the difference between a *schlemiel* and a *schlimazel?* A *schlemiel* is a guy who spills his soup. A *schlimazel* is the guy he spills it on. Jesus, how do I know these things? I'm Irish Catholic for chrissakes."

She stomped on her cigarette, turned off the sidewalk, and pushed into a fancy pub. "This okay? I hope you don't mind me eating, but I had to skip lunch."

"It's fine."

They took a back booth, surrounded by gleaming gold railings. The prosecutor ordered white wine and a cheeseburger, then spread her napkin on her lap. "This is one advantage of eating at a nice place—I hate those cheap napkins that get lint all over your clothes. Anyhow, this defendant is a real chump. He'd have to be, to lose one of these cases."

Jack nodded. The law said you were automatically in the right if you got rear-ended—it was just made for fraud. The perpetrators of these scams had no fear and no shame. They'd pack a car with fellow citizens in need of a little extra cash, then go find a slow car inhabited by an elderly person or a woman, someone juries might stereotype as a bad driver. They'd pull in front of it and jam on the brakes. After the "accident," everybody went to the doctor. The bill went to the government or the insurance company, and the settlements went to the perps—with a kickback to the collaborating doctor.

O'Dea took a gulp of her wine. "This is what I've learned in twenty-three years of fraud cases: the defendants never say they were wearing high heels when they tripped on the sidewalk. They were never alone in the car, and they'll never have sex again." She scoffed. "Last month I had a case, the defendant actually said, 'Because of the accident, I can only do it doggie-style with my wife.' Mind you, they're both in their sixties; he claims they were having sex seven times a week. I ask him, 'Who's the doggie—you or your wife?' He says, 'I can't discuss this in front of a lady.' I said, 'You can tell me—I'm not a lady.'"

Jack laughed. They traded shoptalk until their food arrived. The prosecutor dipped a steak fry in ketchup. "Mind you, I don't wanna knock these people. A while back I hurt my hip and had to take a car service to the hospital every week. Most of the drivers were Russian immigrants; they'd been engineers, doctors, professors. . . . They come here, they have a hard time finding work, so they end up driving a taxi, working two jobs—and they still put their kids through college. You gotta admire that."

Jack nodded. His own father had been one of those honest, hardworking Russians, a stevedore on the Red Hook waterfront. (The old man had been an abusive hard drinker, too, but that was another story.)

"Even so," O'Dea continued, "they came from a place where you had to learn some hustles to stay alive. Some of them developed a two-tier moral system. Everybody knew it was wrong to steal from a friend or neighbor, but it was okay to get what you could out of the State."

She glanced at her watch, and Jack decided to start in with his questions. "What can you tell me about my Russian?"

The prosecutor made a face. "Semyon Balakutis. *Lovely* human being."

Jack leaned forward, eager to hear about the man who had argued with Daniel Lelo. Maybe killed him.

"First of all," O'Dea said, "he isn't Russian. You gotta remember that the Soviet Union was made up of about fifteen different republics."

"Which one was he from?"

"I don't remember. He might have told us, but at least half of what he said was bullshit. He would lie about stuff that didn't even matter. These people like to do that to Westerners; they call it 'hanging spaghetti over our ears.'"

"Do you remember what he was like? I know you've worked a lot of cases since then. . . ."

The prosecutor set down her cheeseburger as if she had lost her appetite. "This one, I remember. He came into town from Detroit. When I picked up his case, I made some calls to the D.A. there. There were all kinds of nasty rumors floating around about the guy, but he only got charged a couple of times. One was for attempted extortion, a liquor store owner. The other was for assault; apparently he beat some girlfriend almost to death."

Jack frowned. "How many convictions?"

"That's the thing: *zero.* Witnesses tended to drop out. Like the girlfriend. And listen to what happened with my case here: Balakutis walked into a bridal shop on Kings Highway that was owned by a Russian and told the man he'd cut his ear off if he didn't pony up for some protection. As it happened, the owner was friendly with the local beat cops, and he figured that this kind of shit wasn't going to happen to him in America. He told Balakutis to take a hike."

The prosecutor grimaced. "One afternoon the desk sergeant at the Six-one is doing some paperwork, and he looks up to see the guy stagger in holding a wad of paper towels to his bloody ear. What was *left* of his ear. The guy was all primed to testify. At that time I was doing some work with an Organized Crime task force. We pulled Balakutis in; the shop own-er picked him out of a lineup. Open and shut case, right?"

She pushed her plate away. "We get to trial, and the own-er's up on the stand, and Balakutis is staring at him, and the guy starts shaking, literally shaking. Out of the blue, he says that he accidentally got his ear caught in a window fan. A freaking *win-dow fan.*" The prosecutor shook her head, remembering. "We brought in the desk sergeant, who testified that the man had fingered Balakutis. We got a medical expert, who said there was no way the shop owner's injuries could be consistent with damage caused by a fan. We threatened to charge our wit' with perjury. Nothing helped; he wouldn't budge."

"What'd you end up doing?"

"What could we do? We dropped the case."

Jack sat for a moment, digesting this information. He leaned forward, resting his elbows on the table. "Let me ask you something: in the course of putting it together, do you remem-ber if the name Daniel Lelo ever came up?"

The prosecutor shook her head again. "Why? Who's he?"

Jack pulled out his wallet to pay the check. "Somebody who might've run into a bigger window fan."

CHAPTER NINE

Doughnuts.

Hundreds of them, arrayed in rows. Sprinkled with jimmies. Dusted with powdered sugar. Glazed with icing. Crusted with coconut. Crullers. Bear claws. Doughnut holes. Jelly doughnuts. Chocolate doughnuts. Old-fashioneds. They looked as if they might get up and dance, like extras in some old musical.

"It's lucky we're not in uniform," said Linda Vargas. They stood in a short line, scoping out the environs.

Jack turned to her with a puzzled expression. "Why?"

His colleague nodded toward the big glass cases full of doughnuts. "I'd hate to reinforce a stereotype."

This was the last place Jack had expected to find Semyon Balakutis. He was not given to romanticizing hoodlums, not after decades as a cop, yet he would have expected to encounter the man in some more impressive environment. A gloomy lair of an office; two big goons in the background, one lone lamp casting a circle of light on a massive old desk... He glanced around. The store, just off Kings Highway, could not have been brighter, more forcedly cheery. Pink everywhere. And orange.

Vargas shook her head. "I still say you're crazy, coming

in today. I'll tell you one thing: if this was *my* day off, I'd be out at the beach with my honey and a big pitcher of sangria."

Jack just shrugged.

Vargas eyed him. "How's your social life these days?"

Jack thought of Michelle—sour memory—and then he thought of Zhenya Lelo, the other night. "It's slow."

The girl behind the counter was a skinny little thing dotted—like a doughnut—with bright pink acne. When the last customer paid and moved away from the register, Vargas stepped forward and addressed her. "We're here to see Mr. Balakutis."

The girl pushed back her little polyester cap and frowned. "Um, I think he's at the bank? But he said he'd be back soon?"

Vargas turned to Jack and shrugged. They got a couple cups of coffee, then sat at a corner table to wait.

"Where's your new partner?" Jack still hadn't met the precinct detective assigned to the case.

Vargas shrugged again. "He's got a court appearance today. He seemed happy about it. I bet he wishes Daniel Lelo had got himself whacked over in Sheepshead Bay."

Jack nodded; that would have put the homicide in the jurisdiction of the Sixty-first Precinct. He couldn't blame the detective for not wanting the case; sometimes Brighton Beach felt so confusing that you might as well have been trying to work a case in a foreign country. With his own background, he reflected, maybe he should have known more about the Russians, but the neighborhood was as opaque to him as to everybody else on his squad. Luckily, despite all the hoopla about Russian mafia, the murder rate was very low, and it had dropped by half in the past decade. Of course, this was no consolation to Daniel Lelo.

He stared at the racks of doughnuts and found himself

singing a tune. "Sugar, uh-uh uh-uh uh-uh, aw, honey, honey."
He squinted. "Tommy James and the Shondells?"

Vargas shook her head. "The Archies. Jesus, don't ever tell
my daughter I knew that—she already thinks I'm the squarest
thing since Lawrence Welk." She looked at Jack over the top of
her coffee cup. "So tell me, how well did you know this Lelo
guy?"

Jack shrugged. (It was a shruggy kind of afternoon.)
"We used to work out in the hospital gym."

"Nice fellow?"

He nodded, but changed the subject. "Did you check on
whether he had life insurance?" He prided himself on doing
the right thing; in homicides of a married person, you wanted
to check if the spouse might have hidden motives. Despite her
evident grief, Eugenia Lelo shouldn't get a free pass.

Vargas nodded. "He didn't have any."

"How much money in the bank?"

She shrugged. "Not much. His business seemed to be doing okay, but the guy wasn't much on savings."

Jack nodded, relieved, but then was annoyed at himself
for his reaction. *Let's keep this strictly professional, people. . . .* He
turned sideways, regarded another glass case. "I didn't know
they had ice cream now, too."

Vargas dabbed at her mouth with a napkin. "It's a new
thing. Combining businesses. They figure they get morning
customers with the doughnuts and coffee, afternoon and evening traffic with the ice cream. All in one store. Makes it more
profitable."

Jack raised his eyebrows. "How do you know that?"

"My husband was thinking about taking out a franchise.
He's getting fed up with cranky clients and all that bidding

shit." Vargas's husband was an electrician, a scrawny little guy. She was crazy about the man.

"He gonna do it?"

Vargas shook her head. "I know these places don't look like much, but it's not so easy to get in on this business. The parent company expects each franchisee to develop five different stores."

"How much money do you need?"

Vargas sighed. "They expect you to have seven hundred and fifty K liquid, and a net worth of at least one point five mil'."

Jack whistled in surprise. "This looked like a pretty silly business for a bad guy to be involved with, but now I'm thinking, it would be a great way to launder some money."

Vargas held up her cup of coffee. "I'll tell you what's criminal: they sell this stuff at a markup of almost two thousand percent."

The door swung open and a stocky man came in. The detectives recognized him from his driver's license photo. Mid-fifties, wearing a black polo shirt with a white stripe down the left side. Short-cropped hair, hooded eyes that drooped to the sides, a small, tight mouth. He had a cocky, rolling walk. *Prison yard strut*, thought Jack. Maybe the guy had not done time in the U.S., but that didn't mean he'd never been behind bars.

It was Vargas's case, so she was the one who stepped forward and badged the man. "Semyon Balakutis? We'd like to ask you a few questions."

Balakutis barely blinked. "There is problem? I hev all licenses, back in office." His teeth looked oddly small, like Chiclets, and he seemed to have too many of them. His accent was thick, but at least they probably wouldn't need to come back with a translator. Jack stared, wondering if this was the man who had killed his friend.

"Why don't you show us?" Vargas said. Jack stood next to her with folded arms. They had no interest in the store's paperwork, but it couldn't hurt to start things off by demonstrating who was in charge.

Balakutis led them back to a little office, where a pale, storklike man in a polyester brown shirt and orange tie sat doing some paperwork. Balakutis muttered something in Russian, and the man jumped up and edged out past them.

There was hardly room for all three of them inside. The ventilation seemed poor back here, and the sugar smell was so intense that Jack couldn't imagine working in it every day—it would definitely put an end to a sweet tooth. Balakutis went around behind the small desk and gestured for the detectives to sit in two molded plastic chairs in front of it. He reached out to the corner of the desk and picked up a manila file. Jack noticed the man's flashy watch: either a Rolex or a damned good knockoff. The Russian immigrants had something in common with the black gangsta rappers of East New York or the South Bronx: a love of *bling*, a fervent belief that one's worth could be measured by externals like jewelry, cars, and clothes.

Balakutis opened the file and turned it around so his visitors could see. "All licenses. Very correct."

Vargas didn't even look down. "Semyon," she said. "Is that Russian for 'Simon'?"

The man just shrugged, like he couldn't be bothered to answer.

Vargas didn't react, just glanced around the office. "Nice business you have here. I guess you must get all the free doughnuts and ice cream you want."

Jack watched carefully. His partner would make small

talk for a minute so they could see how the man dealt with in-nocuous queries. Then they could compare how he reacted to the real business at hand.

Balakutis smiled, but no warmth reached his eyes.

"Good coffee," Vargas said. "Starbucks must be worried."

Balakutis kept silent; just smirked. Tough guy. He crossed his arms and his biceps stretched the sleeves of his polo shirt. Jack found something almost chemically unpleasant about the man. He had the sour cockiness of a playground bully—something Jack, as the son of immigrants and as a child who had been small for his age, had known about all too well. It seemed amazing that such a physical impression could mat-ter, when they were all adults here. But playground bullies grew up, and sometimes their threats turned into action; they kept the homicide squad in business. Movies tended to glamor-ize such thugs, to present them as clever or even admirable, but they made Jack's skin crawl. They fed off one essential, deeply ugly proposition: that it was okay to forcefully rob someone else of their hard-earned money or their health or their sense of safety in the world. Such people were not clever, not even slightly admirable; they were lazy and selfish, and what they did was profoundly unfair, and it needed to be stopped.

"How long ago did you open this store?" Vargas asked.

Jack watched carefully. He tended to rely on intuition, but Vargas was big on scientific interview techniques. She had just asked a question requiring simple recall. When answering such questions, suspects had to access their brains' memory centers, and their eyes tended to move toward the right.

And Balakutis's eyes did so as he prepared to answer. "Six months."

"Is it fun owning a doughnut shop?" This question

required cognitive thought; the eyes tended to move up or to the left.

Balakutis's eyes drifted briefly left. "It is a good business."

Vargas looked on with satisfaction, and Jack had to give her credit. When she asked for the man's alibi on the night of Daniel's murder, she would watch carefully to see if the answer seemed to require memory or a more creative thought process.

Balakutis shifted impatiently in his seat and picked up his folder again. "As I say, all licenses are correct."

"That's very nice, but we're not with the licensing department." Vargas waited a moment to increase the pressure. "We're with Homicide."

"Homicide?" For the first time, the man's composure slipped. "What is this to do with me? I am businessmen."

Vargas pulled her chair closer, crowding the man's space. "Why don't you tell us what you were up to on Thursday." The day of Daniel's murder.

Balakutis scowled. He started to pull a calendar out from under a pile of papers, but Vargas put out a hand and stopped him. "Just remember." She didn't want him reeling off some written alibi.

Balakutis's eyes suddenly moved right, but that—unfortunately—was because his office man had just stuck his head inside the door. Jack knew that his partner was silently cursing the interloper.

"Excuse me," the man said. "I need some tens for the register."

Balakutis was not happy with the interruption. He snarled something Russian, and the guy got even paler. He darted into the office, opened a drawer, grabbed the bills, and scuttled out.

When the detectives looked back at Balakutis, the man's

claws had retracted, and he had replaced his scowl with a be-
nign look. "On Thursday morning I was here in office." His
eyes moved right—remembering. "In afternoon, I was talking
with contractor for new store, and then—"

Vargas held up a hand. "Tell you what: why don't you
start with the end of the night, and then go back in time."

Jack enjoyed watching her work. She had just pulled
another arrow out of the new investigative quiver: studies
showed that experienced liars liked to list alibi events in neat
chronological order, but the challenge of working backward
could throw their smooth preparation out of whack.

Balakutis's eyes shifted hard left. Time for a little creative improvisation? His hand drifted up and over his hair.
Jack glanced at his partner. Grooming behavior—along with
fidgeting or licking the lips—was another possible indicator
of deception.

Balakutis leaned back and affected an air of casual curiosity. "If you tell me why you are asking this questions, perheps
I can help you more."

Vargas ignored him. "Late at night Thursday. Start
there."

Balakutis shrugged, but his eyes shifted right. "I was in
my house. Sleeping."

"Is there someone who could testify to that?"

He nodded. "My wife."

"And before that?"

He licked his lips. "We had dinner."

"Where?"

"At my home." Balakutis ran his hand over his hair again.
"Before that?"

"I telled you. I talk to contractor."

Jack stood up and then sat down on a corner of the man's

desk, crowding him further. "You didn't happen to visit Coney Island that night, did you?"

Balakutis looked confused—or did an excellent job of feigning it. He shook his head.

"How long have you known Daniel Lelo?" Vargas asked.

The man's eyes shifted back to the other detective. "Who? I do not know this name."

Vargas chuckled. "You sure about that?"

Balakutis nodded.

"That's funny," Vargas said. She made a show of consulting her notebook. "We have a witness who saw you talking to him. Very reliable."

Jack restrained a wince. His partner had not mentioned Zhenya's name, but he wished she had said less.

Vargas took out a photo of Daniel and held it up. "Does this refresh your memory?"

Balakutis suddenly reached for the top drawer of his desk.

Jack held up a warning hand. "*Easy*, now."

Balakutis frowned. "I need my glasses."

Jack and Vargas exchanged looks, then nodded, watching the man carefully. He pulled open the drawer and took out a pair of wire-rimmed spectacles. He put them on, then nodded. "Ah yes, now I recognize. . . ." He shrugged and raised his hands in insincere apology. "You must forgive me. I am businessmen; I speak with many people."

"You had a conversation with Lelo recently. On the boardwalk on Brighton Beach."

Jack winced. He wished he'd told his partner to protect Zhenya's identity more strenuously, but he had not wanted to seem too personally involved.

Balakutis shrugged. "Is possible. Like I say, I speak with many, many people."

"And you argued with him?"

Balakutis glanced toward the door.

"Look at *me*," Vargas commanded. "Did you have an argument with him?"

Balakutis leaned back and crossed his arms again. "I do not remember."

Jack and his colleague exchanged looks. Vargas shrugged very slightly.

Both detectives stood up.

Vargas leaned over the desk. "We'll do a little checking into your story. I really hope you haven't told us anything we might find out is untrue."

Balakutis, off the hook for the time being, regained his confidence. He smiled another insincere smile. "I am always happy to assist police." As the detectives moved toward the door, he called out. "Perheps I can offer you some doughnuts? On the house."

CHAPTER TEN

On the way home, Jack remembered that he was out of milk and toilet paper, so he swung by his local deli. He picked up his items, made small talk with the friendly Pakistani guy at the register, stepped out onto Avenue J, and took a hammer to the heart.

Across the avenue, a flash of silky black hair, a familiar red dress. A woman striding away.

He stood stock-still for a moment, then rushed impulsively out into the throng of pedestrians crowding the sidewalk. He bumped shoulders with a heavyset, bearded man, who cursed him loudly, but he jogged on. He was ten yards behind the woman and couldn't see her face, but he recognized her walk. *Michelle.* What could she possibly be doing here, in Midwood, Brooklyn, unless she had come to see him? His heart raced: did she want to come back? They had spoken just once after that terrible moment in the restaurant, after she had told him about the affair. She had called to say that she wanted to come by and pick up her things. He'd been tempted to hang up and toss them all out in the street, but he had managed a brief, strangled conversation: he arranged a time when he would be out, as far away from home as possible. After, he had come back to find her dresses vanished from the closet, her underwear disappeared from the drawers he had made available in his dresser, her cosmetics gone from the medicine cabinet.

He threaded through the sidewalk shoppers as if tailing some dangerous suspect, not wanting to draw attention to himself in case she looked back, but not wanting to lose her. She stopped with several other pedestrians at a corner, waiting for a light to change, and he caught sight of her face.

It wasn't her. Not even close. He deflated, embarrassed; it took a solid minute before his heart slowed to normal.

He knew it was only a matter of time, though. New York was a city of eight million people, but you still bumped into people you knew. One of these days he was going to round a corner or descend the stairs into a subway station, and, *boom*, there she'd be. And what was he gonna say? He imagined just walking past, ignoring her completely. He imagined stopping to mumble a tense hello. He imagined spitting in her face, though he immediately felt guilty for the thought. He sighed. He'd see her when he saw her, and he'd behave the way he would behave. There was no point worrying about it now.

At home, he stowed his purchases neatly away, then went in his front room and lay down on the couch, disgusted with himself. He was free and clear. He could work as late as he wanted without taking any grief. He didn't have anyone checking up on him, nagging him about bills, yammering away about insignificant bullshit, distracting him from his cases. Hell, he could watch TV in his boxer shorts, drink milk right from the container, stay out all night partying—at least, he could have, if any of those things had suited his personality.

(They didn't, unfortunately, which seemed a bit of a waste.) But he definitely didn't have to deal with any expectations or criticisms, as he had with his ex-wife, didn't have to live weighed down by her not-so-subtly expressed belief that life would be much better if only he were someone different. He was footloose and fancy-free. He should have been enjoying life. Christ, there were plenty of married guys who would have given a nut to be in his shoes.

After he ate dinner, he went up and watched TV for a couple of hours with Mr. Gardner. Two lone bachelors, keeping each other company.

Downstairs again, later, he saw that his kitchen counters were looking a bit grubby, so he took out a sponge and gave them a good wipe-down. So what if his private life wasn't so exciting? Maybe he wasn't rolling in love and sex, but at least things were on an even keel.

His cell phone rang. He wiped his hands on a dish towel and dug the thing out of his pants pocket.

"Zhack?"

A woman's voice. It took him a second to place it, and then his heart was jolted all over again.

"Is this bad time?" Zhenya said. "I am sorry."

"No," he said quickly. "It's fine. I was just—" He looked around his kitchen, embarrassed to admit that she had caught him indulging in his penchant for neatness. "I was just going over some work papers." He glanced at the clock: it was after eleven. Why was she calling at this hour? "Are you all right?"

"Do you . . . do you talk to him?"

Her voice sounded strained. Jack wondered if it was fear or alcohol—or both. "What happened? Did something happen?"

She went silent for a moment.

"Are you at home?" he said. "Stay there."

A SAD-FACED SECURITY GUARD sitting behind a desk called out to him as he walked into the lobby, with its plastic rubber plants and late-sixties chrome and mirrors. When Jack said where he was going, he thought the guard's eyebrows went up a touch, but the man picked up a phone, spoke briefly in Russian, then waved him on. The elevator was air-conditioned, but as it rose he wiped some sweat from his upper lip.

Zhenya met him at the front door but turned away again without a word. Again, he followed her through the dark apartment, out onto the balcony. And there—again—sat the bottle of whiskey. He noticed that she had set out an extra glass. She wore some beat-up jeans this time and a large man's dress shirt. (Daniel's, no doubt . . .) No attempts at fashion tonight; he could imagine her lying on her sofa in this outfit, reading or watching TV.

"What's going on?" he said. "Are you okay?"

Without asking, she poured him a stiff drink, then curled up in her chair and wrapped her arms around herself. She looked as if she might have been crying, but she was not crying now.

She frowned. "Do you talk to him?"

He sat down but shifted uncomfortably. "Balakutis?"

"You told me you will not say my name."

He stared at her. "We didn't. Why? Did he call you? Did he come here?" He thought of Vargas's comments during the interview, a bit too specific in regard to witnesses.

Zhenya chewed her lip. "I am afraid."

Jack's face tightened. "Did he threaten you?"

She grimaced but didn't answer.

Jack thought of the bully's face and imagined planting his fist square in it. He had never gone in for violence on the job, preferring to let his investigative abilities get results, but that didn't mean he never had an urge. He would visit the man again tomorrow, let him know that messing with the NYPD was not like giving a hard time to some poor immigrant shop owner. "I promise you," he said. "He's not going to bother you. You have my word on it."

She turned away, as if to say *I know what that's worth— promises from a cop.*

They sat in silence. There was a soft breeze, and the night air was cooler out here near the water, and ordinarily Jack would have been content to sit and drink and let some of the tension of the day seep out of his bones, but he was acutely conscious of the woman sitting just three feet away. He wanted to reach out and touch her slim shoulder, tell her that everything was going to be all right. Instead, he stood up and walked over to the railing, gazed out past the huge condo building, a crossword puzzle of warm orange and yellow lights, out to the dark beach and even darker sea. He breathed in the moist salt air.

He heard her chair scrape back, and then she joined him at the rail. He looked down at the boardwalk; a few couples were out strolling, even at this hour. He thought of Daniel, thought of saying something about Daniel, but he didn't. He snuck a glance at her and saw a small, wet trail glistening down her cheek. And then—he couldn't say later who moved first—he was holding her in his arms. *I'm just comforting her,* he said to himself, *just helping a woman in distress,* but then she closed her eyes and tilted her face up. The kiss was brief, but it was like tasting a perfect raspberry, exquisite and firm. It was so sweet and so charged that it created an instant craving for more.

Jack pulled back, troubled to find himself trembling. His desire for this woman was not just a potential professional problem, and it wasn't just the fact that she was Daniel's wife. After Michelle's shocking departure, he had struggled to get his life back. Maybe it had grown boring and predictable, but at least it was secure. This sudden, unexpected new rush of feeling was threatening to swamp the boat.

Throat dry, he swallowed. "I think I better go."

Zhenya drew a ragged breath. Her face contorted and he thought she might cry again. *"Po 'zhaluista,"* she said quietly.

It was part of the meager store of Russian words he knew from his childhood. *Please.* She wanted him to stay.

"I have to go," he said again, regretting it deeply before he was even gone.

CHAPTER ELEVEN

The night was still dark, though the western sky was beginning to glow—at least what Jack could see of it, above the surrounding tall buildings. He could smell the fish from blocks away. Very incongruous: here on Fulton Street the only other pedestrians were a few business-suited financial traders, hurrying to the New York Stock Exchange through the narrow, canyonlike streets, seeking an early edge on the competition. Jack continued on toward the Manhattan waterfront. After only five hours of sleep he should have been more tired, but he was still jazzed, with excitement at the memory of Zhenya's kiss, with anger as he pictured the sour face of Semyon Balakutis. In a few hours, he would pay another visit to the thug and warn him off, but Zhenya seemed safe for now—if the man had already given her a warning, he had no reason to repeat it in the middle of the night.

The Fulton Fish Market occupied a big open space next to the South Street Seaport, a tourist trap of nautical-themed restaurants and catalogue stores. By the time those stores opened, the fish market would have already shut down—its business day reached its peak before dawn. On its western edge, a number of open storefronts lined a cobbled street, but the real activity seemed to be taking place on the sidewalk, where stacks of Styrofoam boxes held the catches of the day, identified by the thick New Yawk accents of the sellers: Dover sole, razor clams, red mullet... The smell was intense, and Jack was thankful that the night was relatively cool; he would hate to be here in the middle of a heat wave.

Across the street more rows of boxes covered a brightly lit asphalt lot under the elevated FDR highway, which rocketed overhead along the eastern edge of Manhattan. Jack stepped out into a lane between the boxes, dodging beeping forklifts and busy workers. The vendors wore galoshes, low-slung work pants, and stained T-shirts. They carried big metal hooks, casually slung around their necks or hanging from greasy back pockets. The hook was evidently an all-purpose tool, good for prying open boxes and for lifting out heavy fish. Or burying in someone's head, Jack thought, glancing around warily.

For decades the Italian mob's Genovese family had kept a stranglehold over this wholesale outlet, controlling unloading, parking, and even "security," but the city had finally chased it out. Jack wondered if Russians might be trying to fill the gap.

He asked a vendor where he could find Daniel Lelo's office. As he made his way around scummy puddles toward the other side of the market, he wished he had worn older shoes. (Actually, he wished he had worn shoes he could later throw away.) He found an eddy in the swirl of activity and paused to study the workings of the place before he plunged deeper in. Normally, this was one of the things he loved most about his job: while most people were stuck in one place all day, he got to roam around and plumb the city's hidden worlds.

Throughout the lot, pairs of men stood engaged in fierce but jovial negotiations.

"Whaddaya need?"

"Sea scallops. How much?"

"T'ree dalluhs a pound."

"T'ree dalluhs! Fuck you, ya fuckin' bastid!"

"They're t'ree dalluhs. Don't gimme a song and dance—if you wanna dance, come back Saturday night."

The vendors seemed to come in three sizes. There were huge musclemen who looked as if they could heft a whole swordfish by themselves; a few Hasidic Jews, medium-sized; and a number of small Asian men with tough faces. Dwarfed as he was by the big guys, Jack was glad of the shorter company. There wasn't a woman in sight—it was an all-male preserve, like the NYPD had been a generation or two before. At first Jack wondered why anyone would want to work here—up all night, ankle-deep in fish guts—but as he listened to the men barter and banter, he could see what drew them. The place was not really so different from nearby Wall Street: both were self-enclosed realms, like locker rooms. Everyone knew how he fit into this milling world. Daniel Lelo's world. Daniel had invited Jack to come down, but he had never managed the enthusiasm for such an early, smelly visit. Now that he had seen this brawny place, it was hard to reconcile it with a man who liked to read fancy novels. But then, smart Russians had been forced to take up all sorts of manual labor when they hit these shores—Daniel's quip about brain surgeons and taxi drivers had not been so far off the mark.

Jack dodged another forklift and ventured out. At the open north end of the market he could see the East River. The sun, now rising over the hulking Brooklyn Bridge, filled the puddles here with gold. In a covered section of the market, the shouts of vendors were punctuated by the slap of fish being thrown onto hanging scales. Bright lamps shone from

high in the rafters onto tables piled with ice and gleaming carcasses. The place was a morgue for fish.

Each company had its own lane, and the ethnic origins of
each were often obvious. There was a LaRocca Fish Company,
a Mount Sinai Fish . . . Jack moved along the bright rows until
he came to Daniel's business, Black Sea Imports. Several big
men were hard at work there. One used his hook to snag fish
under the gills and flip them onto a table; another steered a
circular saw through a mighty tuna. Outside, the fish was dull
gray, but its flesh was ruby red.

A short, bald-headed man wearing clean clothes
marched down the lane bearing a clipboard; he stopped now
and then to give orders in Russian. A manager. He had an air
of brisk competence—he needed to, since most of the workers
were twice his size—but he looked haggard; maybe he'd had
to take on a lot of extra responsibility since the death of his
boss. Jack noticed that his left hand was wrapped in a big
white bandage.

Jack moved into step beside him. "That looks like some
top-quality fish."

"I have tuna and swordfish. Also mako." The man kept
glancing at his workers; his harried air did nothing for his
salesmanship.

"If I was buying, I'd definitely shop here."

The manager paused to tell a forklift driver where to un-
load, then looked at Jack. "You are not buying?"

"I'm sorry about your boss."

The man's blue eyes searched Jack's face. "Who are
you?"

"I was a friend of Daniel's. We were in the hospital together a while back."

The man's gaze softened, then grew puzzled. "Why you are here?"

"I'd just like to ask you a few questions. Have you ever heard of a man named Semyon Balakutis?"

The man's face closed up as if a steel shutter had just gone down—but not before Jack noted an unmistakable flicker of fear. The manager moved on quickly. "Excuse me. I am very busy today."

Jack kept pace with him. "I just—"

"Valery!" the man called out. One of his largest employees, a somber giant wearing a bloodstained dress shirt with torn-off sleeves, turned around, then picked up a hook big enough to gaff a whale.

"I'm also a detective," Jack said quietly. "NYPD. We're just going to have a peaceful little talk."

The little man looked pale as a fish yanked out of water. He said something in Russian to his colleague, who set down the hook. "We go upstairs," the manager said, and hurried off down the aisle.

Above the side of the market, a row of picture-windowed offices looked down over the lanes. Jack followed the manager up a drab stairwell into an equally drab fluorescent-lit room. Cheap paneling, plastered with calendars, schedules, health department notices. The man walked over to the big window, which blocked out the cacophony of the market below. His eyes darted to a pull cord for a louvered shade.

Jack shrugged. "You want a little privacy, go ahead."

The man lowered the shade. If he was a target of extortion, Jack mused, he would not want to be seen having a private discussion with a cop. The manager came around behind his desk and sat. He looked as if he was about to cry.

Jack took the other seat, an orange plastic chair. "Don't worry. I'm here to help. What's your name?"

The manager muttered a reply, and Jack had to ask him to repeat it. Andrei Goguniv.

"Was Balakutis trying to extort money from you?"

The manager gripped the edge of the desk, then winced. Jack noted the bandage on his left hand again. A little spot of blood was seeping through the back of it. Fresh. "I don't know this name. Please, I have to meet a customer."

Jack leaned back, doing his best to keep his body language open and unthreatening. "Is he giving you a hard time?"

Goguniv pretended to busy himself with a pile of papers on his desk; it was obvious that he was thinking furiously.

"If this is about extortion," Jack said, "then there's only one way out. If you're paying him, he's not going to let up until your company is sucked dry. You need to come to the police, and we'll put a stop to it."

The manager looked up, a pained expression on his face. "Please, mister, this is a mistake. I don't know nothing about it."

Jack softened his voice; the man seemed likable, and he felt sympathy for him. "What happened to your hand?"

Goguniv looked down, but then his eyes rapidly shifted away. "An accident. There is many accidents in this kind of work."

Jack leaned forward. "We can put a stop to this. We can put this man away, where he won't be able to hurt anyone for a good long time. I promise you'll be safe—you have my word on it. He's just one punk; we have forty thousand cops."

The man squirmed like a fish trying to escape a hook. "You are arresting me?"

"Of course not. Why would I arrest *you?*"

Goguniv stood up. "I think that if I am not under arrest, then I do not have to talk with you." He scurried out of the room.

Jack followed him down the staircase and out into the lane, which was brightening with the morning sun. "I can help you, whatever it is."

The man kept walking. "I do not need help."

Jack grabbed his arm, but Goguniv pulled away.

"*Please*, mister. Go away. I don't want no trouble here."

Jack stood back and watched him flee. He turned to find the huge employee with the bloodstained shirt staring curiously. Daniel's manager was surrounded by such massive friends, yet he was still shivering in fear.

Before he left the fish market, Jack stopped in to the security office to show Balakutis's photo and ask if anyone had seen him around. The officer at the desk took a good look but couldn't recognize him. He showed the picture to a couple of guards who happened to be in the office: no luck. They promised to check with their colleagues.

Jack was not deterred. The panic on the face of Daniel's manager had told him what he needed to know; it was just a matter of time before the evidence backed it up.

He hoped that the proof would not end up being this man's blood-soaked ear.

A COUPLE OF HOURS later, he found Semyon Balakutis alone in his doughnut shop office. The man looked up in surprise. Jack hadn't even said anything to the girl behind the register this time, just headed straight for the back.

He glanced down: Balakutis was counting some money. Jack didn't know much about the doughnut business, but he doubted that it brought in stacks of hundreds.

The man started to say something, but Jack cut him off. "Listen, dirtbag: I'm on to you."

The man started to rise, but Jack held up a warning hand. "I don't know what happened with you and the police in Detroit," he said, "but this is New York. And I'm conducting a homicide investigation. If I hear that anyone I talked to had any kind of an 'accident,' I'm gonna come looking for you. And this time, you'll end up in prison so fast it'll make your head spin. You understand me?"

Balakutis's alarm had turned to outrage, but Jack didn't wait to hear what the man might have to say; he turned on his heel and left him sputtering.

CHAPTER TWELVE

After, though his eyelids were grainy from lack of sleep, he drove straight to Brighton Beach, like a scrap of iron drawn by a powerful magnet.

But he didn't end up at Eugenia Lelo's building. At the last moment, he resisted the attraction and kept going. He took a right several blocks down, pulled over, and parked.

Most of the buildings in Brighton Beach were dull brick towers. This one was different, though—it had a faded Art Deco façade that suggested the set of a Fred Astaire movie, or maybe an ocean liner. When he was a kid, he had imagined it coming unmoored and sliding down the block until it drifted out to sea.

No one answered the intercom for Apartment 3-R. He turned around. A young Hispanic man in a blue jumpsuit was kneeling out on the front walk, prying at the back of an air conditioner.

"Excuse me," Jack said. "Can you tell me if Leon Leightner still lives here?"

The man looked up, squinting against the bright morning sun. "Who's asking?"

"I'm his nephew."

The man shook his head. "He's not here. Try outside the pharmacy on Neptune Avenue." He pointed. "Down there and take a left."

Jack thanked him, then turned back and crossed busy Brighton Beach Avenue, thankful for the moment of shade as he passed under the elevated tracks. He continued on to Neptune. Just as in Coney Island, the avenue in Brighton Beach had little character—it seemed like just a way to get from here to there. He passed Trump Village, a row of monumental apartment buildings that would have looked at home in communist Russia, and then a humble little strip mall with a dry cleaner, cobbler, and Chinese restaurant.

A block down, outside a pharmacy, he spotted a row of old folks lined up on benches and folding chairs, sitting with their heads tucked into their chests like roosting birds. Jack scanned the faces, searching for his uncle. Back in the sixties Leon and Jack's father had had a mysterious falling-out. Leon had attended Jack's wedding but left before the reception. In 1977 Jack's father died. Leon showed up at the funeral, looking like a man with two wild animals wrestling in his guts: anger and remorse. Jack had seen him only a few times since.

He found him near the entrance, talking to a frail woman with blue-tinted hair. Despite the heat, Leon wore a beige windbreaker with epaulets, and a tweed cap. In Jack's memory he had been a hale and hearty middle-aged man; now he was a little old geezer with a head shaped like a peanut.

"Leon?"

The man looked up. "Yes?" It took a moment for recognition to dawn. The old man turned to his companion. "This is my brother Max's boy, who never comes to see me."

Jack frowned. That was hardly a fair way to put it, but he didn't want to get into family business in front of a stranger.

The old man turned to Jack. "This is Yvette, the most beautiful lady in Brighton Beach."

The woman smiled and flapped a liver-spotted hand in protest.

"Can I talk to you?" Jack said. "In private?"

"Sure, *bubbelah*." An old Yiddish term of endearment that Jack hadn't heard since he was a kid. Leon reached under his seat and picked up a cane. That he still had a Russian accent was surprising, considering that he'd been living in New York since the early fifties. He stood up slowly, then bent forward and kissed Yvette's hand. "Arrivederci."

She laughed shyly.

Leon set off, using the cane more as a fashion accessory than a support; he seemed to be in pretty good shape. As soon as they were down the block, Jack turned to him. "What was that business about me not coming to see you? How many times did Louise and I invite you over for the holidays?"

Leon didn't answer. What could he say? "How's your wife?" he asked instead.

"We got divorced fifteen years ago."

Leon shrugged. "I'm sorry. She seemed like a nice girl."

"What about you? Did you ever get married again?" Leon's wife had died when Jack was just a kid.

His uncle cocked his eyebrows back toward his lady friend. "Why bother?"

LEON'S APARTMENT WAS THE same as Jack's childhood memories of it, only dustier and smaller. A hallway lined with plastic plants that somehow managed to look withered. A smell like old egg salad. Jack had always loved a picture of a waterfall over the kitchen door: it had a light inside and the water shimmered. It was still there, though the light wasn't on.

"The place looks good," he said. He would have liked to start asking immediately about Semyon Balakutis, but he didn't want his uncle to think that he had just come for such a selfish reason, after so many years.

Leon led him into a narrow kitchen. The room was walled up to shoulder height in translucent milky orange tiles that reminded Jack of a wax candy he had liked when he was a kid. This was definitely a bachelor's kitchen, but he admired the sense of neatness and order. Leon pulled out a couple of stools from under a small table. Then he went over to the sink, ran a dishcloth across a bar of soap, and washed out two little cut-crystal glasses. He held them up: "From the Old Country." Jack half expected him to pull out a box of saltwater taffy, but instead the old man set out a chipped plate on which he arranged sausage slices, a couple of pickles, and some cubes of rye bread. He pulled a bottle of vodka from the freezer and filled the glasses.

Jack's eyebrows went up. "Not my usual breakfast, but thanks."

Leon's back straightened and he assumed a dignified expression.

"*Odem yesode meofe vesofe leofe—beyno-lveyno iz gut atrink bronfn.*"

"I don't speak Russian," Jack said.

Leon made a face. "What Russian? This is Yiddish. Your father didn't teach you anything?" The bitterness was still there.

"What does it mean?" Jack said, avoiding the old grudges.

Leon let go of his sour expression and grinned. "A man comes from the dust and in the dust he will end—in the meantime, is good to take a sip of vodka."

They clinked glasses and tossed down the liquor, followed by a bite of food.

"You still a cop?" Leon asked.

"Yeah. I'm a detective."

"A big shot, eh? Good for you—you were always a sharp kid."

Jack looked up in surprise. He wanted to say, Are you sure you don't mean Petey? It was his brother who had been sharp. Good in sports, funny, popular . . . "How about you?" he asked. "You must be retired, no?"

Leon shrugged. "Life is wonderful. I sit in front of a drugstore all day with a bunch of old people, like a bunch of goddamn penguins, waiting to see who falls off the iceberg next. I should never have given up my store." He went to the refrigerator and got out some chopped liver, then came back with a bashful look. "I'm thinking about writing my memoirs."

"Your *memoirs?*" Jack tried not to scoff. Who'd want to read a book about a man who'd spent most of his life operating a luggage shop?

"What?" Leon said. "You don't think I have stories? My whole life I wasn't selling suitcases. Let me ask you something: how many men can say that their lives were saved by a giant pig?"

Jack laughed. "A pig?"

"Your father didn't tell you this story?" The disapproving expression was back.

Jack shook his head. "He didn't talk much."

"He didn't say how we escaped from the Nazis?"

"He always said there was no point in digging up the past."

"Maybe if he had talked more, some anger would have gone out of him. Like a balloon."

"Why did you stop speaking to each other?"

Leon frowned. "That's another story. Right now, I'm telling the one about the pig."

"Okay." Jack settled back on his stool. Life held many mysteries, and he was grateful for an answer to any of them.

Leon hunched down on his stool and clasped his hands between his knees. "When the Nazis invaded our town, it was nineteen forty-two. Ten of them came, and they rounded up eight hundred Jews."

"How could so few of them do that?"

"They had help from thugs in our village. People who were happy to do it."

"How old were you?"

"I was twelve. Your father was fifteen. In the middle of one night, they came for our family and put us in a barn with many others. All night we heard shooting, but we didn't know what was happening. Me and Max, we agreed that if we could escape, we would meet up at a farm across the river. In the morning, the Nazis came. Max told me to run into a stall and hide. There was a giant pig in there, very mean, but I was good with animals.

"A Nazi came into the stall with a pitchfork. He was poking down into the hay, but I was hiding behind the pig. The Nazi was frightened, I think—he didn't look too hard. They took the rest of the people, including Max, my mother and father, and my sister—"

"Wait a minute—your *sister*? I had an aunt?"

Leon looked sad. "This also your father didn't tell you?"

Jack shook his head. *Unbelievable.* His father had always been incredibly closed off about his past, but still . . .

"Her name was Yuliya. Julia, you would say here. A beautiful kid, very funny, very kind . . ." He sighed and continued with the story. "The Nazis marched them into the woods. There was deep pits dug there. Everyone could see what was going to happen."

Jack winced.

"There was a young man in our village, a big guy, very strong—he used to challenge everybody to wrestle. He shouted, 'Are we going to just die like sheep?' He ran at the nearest Nazi and pushed him down. There was lots of shooting, but a few of them managed to run into the woods."

"What about your parents? And your sister?"

Leon fell silent and shook his head. A moment later he went on. "I was able to swim across the river. Was nighttime— very cold. I came to the farm, but I heard voices so I ran away to hide. There was bee skeps in a field. I went underneath; it was okay because the bees was sleeping. Soon the voices came closer, and I recognized my brother. Such a reunion we had!

"We went deep into the woods, and there we found a group of partisans. You know what this means? They was citizens who fought the Nazis. For the next year we lived in a shack they had made in the middle of a swamp—"

"My father lived in a swamp for a year?"

Leon nodded, then stood up—evidently he had had enough of these memories, for the time being. He put the dishes in the sink. "This is just one of my stories. So maybe I have a memoir, no?"

Jack felt tired; this was too much to take in at once. He had always thought of his father as a man who inflicted punishment, but he had never imagined the extent of what the Old Man might have suffered. He looked up at his uncle. It seemed incredible that this man and his brother could have lived through such horrors together, yet spent the last decades of their lives apart. "Uncle Leon, I know you don't want to discuss this, but why did you and my father stop talking?"

Leon seemed to shrink. "It was a business disagreement.

Something stupid." He shook his head, misery etched into his face.

Jack stared down at the table. His uncle had managed to talk about the death of most of his family without much visible emotion. Maybe he had come to terms with it somehow or figured out how to distance himself from the memory. But this wound was still fresh. Jack thought of his own brother, dead at just thirteen, and wanted to put an arm around his uncle. Instead, he got up, filled a glass with water, and set it down in front of the old man. As if that would help.

Leon ignored the gesture. After a minute he pushed himself up from his stool. "You want more vodka?"

Jack shook his head.

"Me neither," Leon said. He put the bottle back in the freezer, then sat down again. "So. After all these years, why do you come to see me?"

"I want to ask you about somebody."

"Who?"

Jack reached into his jacket, removed a computer printout, and passed it across the table. A mug shot. "His name is Semyon Balakutis. Have you heard of him?"

Leon made a face. "I have heard things. He likes to call himself a businessman. I think he has something to do with the Cosmopolitan nightclub, on Brighton Beach Avenue."

Jack leaned forward. "What have you heard?"

Leon snorted. "He's a thug."

"Russian mafia?"

The old man frowned. "I don't like this talk. Because of the movies, people think we are all hoodlums here in Brighton Beach. Most of us work very hard; we just want to make a success of our little beauty parlor or tchotchke shop."

"Yeah, but that doesn't mean that there isn't a Russian mob."

Leon shrugged. "In the eighties and nineties, we had some big shots operating here. I don't know about all this mafiya business, though. They were not like the Italians. They came from Russia, and in Russia there's not so much difference between the criminals and the people that are running the place. I went to Moscow on vacation last year. I saw guys like this Balakutis crawling all over the place. *Novye Russkies*—New Russians. They call themselves businessmen, but they're just out for a fast buck. Capitalism has not worked out so good for most people in Russia, but for criminals, *yes.*" He grimaced. "They drive fancy cars, eat in the best restaurants. They have no class." He stood up to put away the rest of the food. "Why are you asking me this?"

Jack told him about his contacts with Balakutis so far. "I think he might be trying to extort Daniel's company."

Leon scratched his chin. "*Extort* might not be the best word. Maybe he's offering them a *krysha.*"

"I don't know what that is."

Again, Leon shook his head at his nephew's ignorance. "It means roof. It's like protection, but different. In Russia or Ukraine, if you want to get a business going, a lot of the time you have to pay off some hoodlum to protect you from other criminals. But he also helps you cut through red tape and get things done. It's like taking on an unofficial partner who grabs a big chunk of the profits. Thousands of businesses over there pay it."

"How about here?"

Leon shrugged again. "Some new immigrants might fall for pressure, thinking that they need it. But others realize that they can say no and get help from the police."

Jack frowned. Daniel, evidently, had said no without the help.

Leon crossed his arms. "Whatever he's up to, this guy is someone who, if you see him coming, it's a good idea to cross the street."

AFTER LEAVING HIS UNCLE, Jack walked toward the beach, thinking about his uncle, the "boring" little shopkeeper with the amazing past. And he thought about his father. About the Nazis. About an aunt he'd never known he had. When he reached the boardwalk, he stood at the railing; the midday sun baked the beach. On the horizon, huge ships plowed out across the sea. Across the world.

Jack wandered along the boardwalk until he came to the sidewalk cafés, where the old women gathered around the gypsy medicine-sellers and the old men played their chess. He wondered how many of them had survived terrible times in World War II. The war had always seemed as if it had happened far in the past, something for history books, yet it had scarred his own father, and he himself had been born just five years later. Five short years.

His cell phone trilled. He pulled it out and leaned against the boardwalk railing, watching a flock of seagulls beating against a stiff shore breeze.

"Detective Leightner? This is Semyon Balakutis."

CHAPTER THIRTEEN

There were stars in the ceiling, thousands of them, twinkling against black velvet. Several hundred people sat in the dark below, eating dinner and watching the floor show. In front of the band, a guy with a strap-on synthesizer and three female singers in gold hot pants were singing some shrill, cheesy pop song.

The maître d' led Jack around the dance floor to an empty half-circle booth. He soon felt conspicuous—he saw no other single diners, and very few couples; people seemed to come to the Cosmopolitan club in groups. The maître d' leaned down and spoke into his ear. "Mister Balakutis will like for you to have dinner and watch the show, with his compliments."

Jack frowned. "Where is he?"

The maître d' pressed his hands together in apology. "He says he will be a little late, but don't worry: he is coming."

Jack almost smiled. Balakutis was no dummy. He was working a game detectives played all the time. He'd left Jack wondering all day what this evening appointment might be about, and now he was keeping him waiting even longer, trying to establish who was in control.

A stone-faced waiter appeared and set down a bottle of vodka in an ice bucket. A couple of others glided up with big trays and started setting down appetizer plates: eggplant caviar, pickled beets, smoked salmon, and whitefish. Jack didn't touch the food. He was hardly going to break bread with a man who might have murdered his friend. It didn't matter what he said, though—the waiters kept appearing, like grim genies.

He sat back and checked out the landscape. Rumors always floated around that some of these clubs were frequented (or owned) by the Russian mafia, but tonight the scene just resembled a salesman's retirement party. Most of the men in the audience looked paunchy and mild, and the women were clearly wives or grandmothers. They were all dressed up. Occasionally they stared at him, and he felt like an uninvited guest at a wedding. There had been a couple of surly-looking bouncers in the gaudy, chandeliered lobby, but that was about it for the potential criminal element. So far, at least—there was a balcony ringing the club, and it was too dark to tell much about the shadowy figures in the booths up there.

Onstage the emcee, a hyper little guy with a spiky rooster haircut, came out and made an announcement in Russian. As a favor to the few noncountrymen present, he translated: "Good evening, ladies and gentleman. We welcome you tonight to Brighton Beach and Cosmopolitan nightclub! Is time for cabaret!" The stage dimmed and a strange blue light came up. The band churned out some sinister spacey music as a group of dancers in spandex tiger costumes strutted out from the wings; their stripes glowed in the dark. They arched their backs and pretended to claw at each other. The music picked up and they launched into a synchronized disco dance. After the tigers crawled away, a man and a woman came out wearing costumes from some prior century: he sported a ruffled shirt and a powdered wig; she was strapped into a corset with a plunging neckline. The guy serenaded her with a maudlin ballad.

Jack noticed a teenager at the next table covering his eyes in embarrassment—evidently the Russians had their own version of a generation gap—but the rest of the customers seemed quite happy with the entertainment. Most of them were middle-aged; they sat staring at the stage, nodding misty-eyed to music that reminded them of younger days, an ocean away.

Jack wanted to rest his elbows, but there was no room: the table was covered with food. He glanced around, noting the exits. A bouncer the size of a large bear had taken up a post nearby; he leaned against a wall, hands folded over his crotch.

The man suddenly straightened up. Jack followed his gaze out across the club: a stocky man was moving toward them from the back of the hall, leaving a ripple of nervous glances in his wake. Balakutis took his time making his way to Jack's booth; he stopped along the way to greet other diners.

Jack watched him, frowning. Linda Vargas had checked out the man's alibi for the night of Daniel's murder; Balakutis's wife had confirmed his story about being home for dinner and after—but so what? How reliable was a confirmation from a suspect's own spouse?

The man sat down without a word. A waiter rushed up to ask if he wanted anything. He said something sharp in Russian, and the man backed away.

Balakutis wore a silvery dress shirt; it reminded Jack of the polyester outfits his patrol buddies had worn when they went nightclubbing back in the eighties. The man's whole bearing seemed stagy and self-important, as if he were starring in some second-rate gangster flick. Such posturing was silly, but Jack had learned long ago not to laugh. The most dangerous people in the world were the ones with the lowest self-esteem, the ones who always felt they had something to prove.

Balakutis took a couple of cigars from his breast pocket and offered one to Jack.

Jack shook his head. He glanced over his shoulder: the bouncer had come around and stationed himself a couple of yards away. He turned and spotted another steroids fancier watching him intently from the edge of the dance floor.

Balakutis reached into his pocket for a lighter and set it on the table. He pulled out a silver cutter and slowly and deliberately clipped the end of his cigar. Jack's chest tightened; he couldn't help picturing the man hacking off a shop owner's ear.

The waiter came back, set a big glass of red wine down carefully in front of Balakutis, then slipped away. Balakutis lit his cigar and inhaled with gusto. "*So*. Thenk you for coming."

Jack frowned. "What's this all about?"

Balakutis shrugged. "Nothing much. Somehow, it seems you have gotten some bad ideas about me. I want to make friends. That's all. Is better to make friends than enemies, no?"

Jack shifted in his seat; he was supposed to be the one asking the questions. "What did you argue about with Daniel Lelo?"

Balakutis shrugged. "I already told you: I knowed him just a little. We are both *biznessmeni*, and the community here is not so large."

"What did you talk about?"

Balakutis shrugged again. "If I remember is correct, he asked to borrow money. If, like me, you are successful businessmen, this happens all the time."

"What did you tell him?"

Balakutis sipped his wine. "I said, for a loan, go to a bank."

"Did you argue about it?"

Balakutis shook his head. "He asked; I said no. No argument. Just business."

Jack frowned. No progress. It was this man's word against Zhenya's.

Sometimes interrogators would purposely rile a suspect, as if throwing peanuts at a tiger in the zoo, just to see what he might let slip. The tactic took on a new dimension when you were both sitting in the same cage. Jack leaned forward. "Word on the street is that you might have been involved with Lelo's murder."

Balakutis didn't rise to the bait; he just made a pained face. "I tell you the same thing I telled the other police. I never kill Daniel Lelo. In my life, I never kill nobody. Why you peoples persecute me?"

Jack frowned. The man's tone reminded him of an interrogation he had once conducted with a child rapist: the big creep, 240 pounds, had claimed that the eleven-year-old victim had seduced *him.*

"You've been very lucky with your court cases here in the United States. Nobody's luck lasts forever. I'm watching you, and if I find out that you had anything to do with this, you're going away for a long, long time."

Balakutis's mask of humility and forbearance dropped away. "I don't know you, mister. I offer you hospitality. I never done nothing to you." His fists clenched and his face grew red. "Now you come to my club and make threats to me? Who the fuck you think you are?" The man had worked himself into a rage. He slammed his hand down on the table, knocking over his wine, which splashed like a bloody red bomb across the white tablecloth.

And that's when Jack realized that it wasn't some old bully this man reminded him of—it was his own father. Sober, the Old Man had been reserved and relatively quiet, but when he got drunk he could be just like this, prone to sudden tempers that blew up out of nowhere, dark tornadoes.

The nearest bouncer stepped closer, but Balakutis waved him away. A bevy of waiters and busboys rushed up. Within literally two minutes, they had whisked the food and broken glass away, yanked off the stained cloth, replaced it with a fresh one, and brought Balakutis a new glass of wine. All of the diners at the neighboring tables seemed careful to avoid expressing the slightest curiosity. Jack blinked; it was almost as if the unpleasant little episode had never happened. That was the way things had been with his father, too; after a sudden blowup, everyone in the family had to pretend that it was forgotten, even though the damage remained, deep inside.

When he glanced back, the rage had completely left Balakutis's face, replaced by a slight, canny smile that revealed his little teeth. The man spread his arms extravagantly along the top of the booth. "You know what I hear? Maybe it was the Russian mafiya who killed this Lelo. Very bad problem around here. Very bad people. Of course, I know nothing about this. I am biznessmen." He shifted forward, crowding Jack. "I never been shot before. It must hurt very much, no?"

Jack resisted the urge to flinch. Evidently, he was not the only one who had done a little research.

The other man sat back, satisfied that his barb had found its mark. He glanced at his watch. "You must excuse me—I go to other appointment." He stood up, brushed at his pants, scooped his lighter and cigar cutter off the table. "I hev nothing to hide, Detective. If you are looking for me, here I am. Anytime you want to come to the club and see the show, just give me a call."

Before Jack could reply, he swaggered off.

CHAPTER FOURTEEN

Jack stepped out of the club into a dense, humid summer night. He felt a wetness on his face and looked up into a very light rain, barely visible below the streetlights. Brighton Beach Avenue had quieted now, due to the hour and the weather; the throngs of shoppers had taken their purchases home, and the place seemed lonely. Neon signs along the storefronts shone brighter in the wet; their bright colors smeared across the windshields and hoods of passing cars.

He took a couple of deep breaths. He shouldn't have felt so stirred up—lord knows, in two decades with the NYPD he had run into no shortage of blustering thugs, and more than a few threats. Thankfully, though, even the dimmest street punk knew that the dumbest thing was to attack a cop; within minutes you'd have thousands of outraged colleagues hunting you down. A cop's little metal badge acted as a real shield—or at least he had always thought so. But there was a fragment of metal inside his chest, and he also carried memories of lying helpless and bleeding on a dank basement floor, all because one thug had failed to play it smart.

He reached his car and put his hand on the door handle,

but he paused for a moment. He put the keys back in his pocket, then turned away, down a side street, toward the ocean. Though his office was not far off, he rarely visited the Brighton Beach boardwalk—yet here he was, returning to it for the second time in one day. He needed to walk. The encounter with Semyon Balakutis had been unpleasant, and he wanted some fresh ocean air, as if to wash away the contamination. When he reached the boardwalk, he turned up the collar of his sports jacket against the wind and the damp. Only a few other hardy souls were out: a lone jogger, an elderly little couple in matching raincoats, determined not to miss their evening promenade. Streetlights radiated misty halos above the walkway; the beach was dark gray, the ocean purple with night.

He walked, and it didn't take him long to figure out that his restlessness was not just due to concerns about Semyon Balakutis. He paused by a railing and stared unseeing toward the water, remembering the feel of Eugenia Lelo's lips. He wondered if she was home right now, just a couple of blocks down this same boardwalk. "Please," she had murmured to him. *Please.*

Daniel's grieving wife. He scowled at himself and shivered, though the night was relatively warm. He felt uncomfortable in his own skin and wondered if this was what it was like to be a junkie, this prickly mix of shame and desire, of desperately wanting something you knew was bad for you.

He groaned. Stupid. He was acting like a goddamn teenager, all hormones and no brain. He had finally gotten his life settled again, so why shake things up? Happiness didn't come from some other person; that was a sucker's game, and he was old enough to have that figured out by now.

He moved toward his car.

He stopped.

And then he turned back toward the boardwalk.

ZHENYA ANSWERED THE DOOR in some old sweatpants and a faded red T-shirt, and he was surprised to find that she wore reading glasses, and he was surprised again that she looked more attractive than ever. He had expected to catch her in another sad mood, maybe half drunk, but tonight she seemed alert, as if she had been interrupted in the middle of some household chore. Not very romantic.

He realized that he had not prepared any good reason to be standing here in her doorway at this hour of night.

She looked up at him quizzically. "Is about my husband?"

He shook his head. "Can I come in?"

She nodded gravely and stepped back a little. "You are wet. May I take your coat?"

He nodded, tempted to smile at her phrasebook English.

She reached into a closet and hung up his sports jacket. Overhead, the chandelier glittered. He glanced at her shelves of knickknacks, his eye stopping on a little shepherd kneeling at the feet of some fair damsel—like the couple who had just sung the corny ballad in the club. A sucker's game . . .

He brushed his palm over his damp hair.

"Wait here," she said. She went off down the hall and came back with a towel.

"Thanks," he said, and took a moment to dry himself.

She looked at him, puzzled. "Something has happened?"

He handed the towel back to her. "Not really." He frowned. "Maybe I better go."

"You just arrive," she said, and her face broke open in a sudden, shy, gap-toothed smile.

It pierced him to the core.

"I just . . . I came by to see how you were doing," he lied. Unbelievable—he actually felt himself shivering.

"You are cold?" she said.

"I'm fine." The last thing he wanted was for her to go away and come back with some of Daniel's clothes. He wondered what he could possibly be doing here. He had never committed adultery in his life—not when he had been married, and not with someone else's spouse. But could you call it adultery if the third party was deceased?

"I was making a snack," Zhenya said. "You are hungry?"

Yes, he wanted to say. I'm hungry for another taste of your mouth. He just nodded.

She led him down the hallway into a small bright kitchen, where she turned with an embarrassed shrug. "I was going to eat some cereal. But I can make you something. An omelet?"

He smiled. "Some cereal would be fantastic."

She lifted a stack of papers off a little dining table set against the wall and laid them down on top of a microwave.

"Bills?" he said.

She shook her head, serious again. "No. I am trying to understand Daniel's business."

She poured two bowls of Cheerios, and they both sat down to eat. It was hardly the romantic scene he had envisioned, back on the boardwalk a few minutes ago, thinking about being with her out on the dark balcony, overlooking the sea. . . .

"How's it going?" he said, nodding toward the papers, though he did not want to talk about her late husband.

She raised her slight shoulders. "It's all Greek to me." Her eyebrows went up. "You say this, yes? American idiom?"

He nodded. "I suppose we do."

She frowned earnestly. "Why 'Greek'? Is difficult language for Americans?"

He smiled, charmed. "I never thought about it before." He did so. "Maybe it's because the Greek alphabet is hard for us to read."

She considered this answer for a moment. "Then I think you can say, also, 'It's all Russian to me.' "

He realized that, despite her serious expression, she was making something of a joke, and he smiled. He watched her lift a spoonful of cereal to her small, perfect mouth. "You didn't eat dinner?"

She shook her head. "These days, my appetite is not so good. And you: no dinner tonight?"

He pictured all of the food piled on his table at the night-club earlier. He pictured Semyon Balakutis's rage-contorted face. He didn't say anything about either, though; just shook his head.

They ate in silence for a minute, until their spoons clinked against empty bowls. She stood, gathered the bowls, and set them in the sink. Turned the tap on and started to wash them.

He jumped to his feet. "Let me do that."

She turned, surprised. "Really?"

He nodded. "Sure. Let me get in there."

She shrugged, handed him the sponge, and moved several feet away, where she leaned back against the counter, giving him a wry look. She shook her head.

"What?"

She crossed her arms across her chest. "In his whole life, my husband never wash a dish."

He almost winced at the mention of Daniel, but managed a smile. "What can I tell you? I'm a modern, progressive type of guy." He finished cleaning the bowls, set them in the drying rack, then started to rub his hands on his pants.

Zhenya pushed herself away from the counter in mock

affront. "What you are doing?" She reached into a drawer and pulled out a dish towel. Moved forward, offering it like a gift.

He didn't reach for it, but for her instead, and pulled her toward him. He thought she might push him away, but instead she stepped inside his embrace, reached her arms around him, and kissed him back. Hungrily.

A shiver ran up his spine, and for a split second he thought of ghosts.

They made their way down the hallway awkwardly because they were still half intertwined, and then she pulled him toward the living room and its couch, which was fine, because he had half feared that they were headed toward the bed she had shared with Daniel. The room was dark, save for what thin light made it in from beyond the balcony. He banged his shin against what he assumed must have been the coffee table, but he didn't even pause to register the pain.

They kissed as if they were devouring each other.

"Wait," he said, breaking away. "Are you sure this is okay?"

She stepped back, mock-pouting. "You would like to have a discussion?"

He grinned. "Not really."

They stumbled over to the couch. He kissed her lips, the side of her mouth, the little hollow at the base of her neck. He inhaled her sweet scent. She grabbed his head and pulled him back to her mouth. He reached out and cupped her firm, lovely breasts through the thin material of her shirt. She trembled and pulled him down on top of her.

There was no turning back.

AFTER, HE LAY THERE in the dark, spooned against her on the narrow couch. He almost didn't trust his luck. He was a realist: he was a relatively attractive person, but no movie star. His wife had been relatively attractive, and so had his last girlfriend, but they had not been movie stars either. Unlike some of his other middle-aged male colleagues, he fetishized neither youth nor beauty. Yet Zhenya was physically stunning. Not in some showy or extravagant way, but with a refined, jewel-like grace. His hand rested against her flat little belly, and he nearly expected to hear her purr.

The sex had been a revelation.

As the sweat dried on his skin, he thought of past loves. He had enjoyed sex with his wife at first, but they had been so young, and neither of them had really known what they were doing. She had seemed to like it well enough, but she had mostly lain back as if sex was something that happened *to* her, rather than something she might participate in. And then, when things had gone sour, it had become a bargaining chip, a trial, their bed a Cold War battleground. With Michelle he'd thought the sex was pretty good, good enough for him to be content with the thought of loving only her for the rest of his life. But Zhenya . . .

All of her shyness, her wariness, her standoffish behavior disappeared in bed. And she certainly didn't just lie back. She was giving, and clear about what she wanted, and direct about pleasure in a way that made him feel as if he had just experienced real sex for the first time. It was more than just sensual pleasure; they were two people who had experienced deep pain, finding profound relief in each other. They had moved together, deeper than he had known possible.

She ran her fingertips over the little round scar on his chest. "This is where the bullet was hitting you?"

He sighed. "Yeah." He had such a heavy whirl of emotional associations with that time, and he didn't want to think about it now. He turned on his side and ran his fingers over her chin, feeling the deep indent beneath her own scar. He wondered if she would turn her head or push his hand away, but she stayed still.

"How did this happen?" he asked.

She shifted into a different position on the sofa cushions. "I am ten years of age, in Ukraine. My father is buying me a bicycle. The first day, I fall off the side of the road. We have no money for plastic surgeon."

He leaned forward and kissed the scar. His fingertips moved, tracing her delicate collarbones, sliding down and circling her nipples.

He heard something and turned to look outside; the rain had picked up again, and it was spattering against the half-open glass door to the balcony.

He turned back to Zhenya. "You want me to shut it?"

She shook her head and nestled into the crook of his body. "I like it. I like the sound. And the smell."

He lay back and nodded in agreement. The ocean air had a lush, briny smell that blended with the aroma of sex in the room. He closed his eyes and listened to the rain. As he drifted between wakefulness and sleep, the sound of the drops hitting the glass led to another memory.

A BATHHOUSE ATTENDANT DIPPED oak leaves into a soapy tub and then slapped them against Daniel Lelo's bare back. This was called a *platza* and was supposedly a sort of massage.

Jack sat across the subterranean room, which was lit only by a single bare bulb. A few feet away, a massive stone furnace gave off enough heat to grill a steak. He felt like his head was about to melt.

"Use the bockits," Daniel counseled.

Above the tiered benches that lined the walls, water dripped from spigots into buckets. Every once in a while a bather would rise from a bench and dump one over his head. Jack put his hand in a bucket and yanked it out; the water was ice-cold. "I'm okay," he said.

Daniel grinned. He lay on his stomach on the upper tier, where the heat was most intense. As part of their informal rehab program after the hospital, he had brought Jack to this old-style *bania* for some rejuvenating steam and relaxation. The man was at home here in this hot, watery realm; he reminded Jack of an old mural on the side of the New York Aquarium, right next to Brighton Beach. The faded painting showed King Neptune raising his trident, guiding a chariot pulled by giant seahorses.

After two more minutes, Jack became concerned that his head might actually catch fire. Wincing, he grabbed a bucket, stood up, and poured it over himself. He sputtered as the liquid ice cascaded over his flushed body. Surprisingly, the shock felt good.

The attendant, also Russian, said something to indicate that the *platza* was finished. Daniel sat up, rubbing his head free of sweat. "Next time, you will try the pool," he told Jack. Outside the radiant heat room, true fanatics took a plunge in a little swimming pool filled with ice water.

"I don't think so."

Daniel smiled. "Don't worry—it may give you a *leetle* heart attack, but it won't *keel* you."

Daniel stood up from his bench, lifted a bucket of ice water, and let it splash down over his head, roaring at the shock.

Jack realized that he was hungry. He and his friend put on robes and went up to the main floor, where there was a little café presided over by an old Russian woman who spoke no English. Jack enjoyed a chicken cutlet, but Daniel didn't eat. Jack had never seen his friend without an appetite before. The man stared up at a TV mounted in the corner but didn't seem to be watching.

"Everything okay?"

Daniel frowned. "Just some problems with my business." He rubbed a broad hand across his eyes. "Let us go to steam room."

There they sat on a bench, enveloped in a white cloud. Jack spread out a towel and lay facedown. Soon he felt the heat penetrating his muscles, loosening him up. He sat up and leaned back gingerly against the hot tiles. "Hey, Daniel. How did you leave the Soviet Union?"

His friend rolled over and sighed. "For many years, I was wanting to go. When I am young, I try two times." Daniel looked down at his burly forearms; sweat was starting to bead there, and he brushed it away. "One time, I try to go into Romania. Is very hard. Fourteen kilometers before border begins control zone. If you are not resident there, police can arrest you. Imagine this: in your country, border is for keeping peoples out; in Soviet Union, was for keeping peoples in. There was towers for police, electric fence. I try to go over, but they catch me. I am twenty-two years old. I am afraid I am going to prison, but they send me to psychiatric hospital. They say, If you want to leave wonderful Soviet Union, you must be crazy." He made a sour face. "I am there for three months; was scary place. After this, KGB makes life very difficult for me. I know I must escape or nothing good can happen in my life." He stretched out his legs. "I wait five years for opportunity. Other countries will send me back if I go there. But Turkey, they don't do this. So: I was on a sheep—"

"A sheep?"

Daniel shook his head. "A *ship*." I get permission to visit a person from my family in Ninotsminda, in Republic of Georgia. On return, I am on the Black Sea, going to Odessa. I wait until middle of night. Then, very quiet, I jump over side. I have bag with some foods, some water. I take—" He pantomimed holding something around his chest.

"A life preserver?"

"Yes. And an umbrella."

Jack chuckled. "An umbrella! Why would you care if you got wet in the ocean?"

"Was for sail."

"Did it work?"

"Too difficult. But I am good swimmer. When I am young, I have training, for sport. *So*—I swim south, on way to Hopa, in Turkey." Daniel turned on a tap and scooped up a drink of water. "I swim all night and next day."

Jack sat in a cloud of steam, imagining this feat, this heavily muscled Neptune stroking out across the sea.

"And then," Daniel continued, "in the next night, I am very close to Turkey, maybe one hour only."

"How could you tell?"

"Lights in Soviet Union are yellow. Here I see lights of many colors: advertising. But I cannot swim no more. I am thinking, please do not let me have failure now, in sight of my freedom. And then, like answer to wish, comes fishing boat. They save me."

"*Jesus.* What a story!" Jack sat marveling at his friend's difficult life—it certainly put his own problems in a different perspective.

Daniel suddenly changed the subject. "In your job, you are good detective?"

Jack looked up. Out of 1,800 detectives in the NYPD, only about a hundred like him had reached First Grade. "Yeah," he said quietly. "I'm pretty good. Why?"

Daniel just stared thoughtfully. Jack sensed that his friend was about to say more, but the man stood up. "Time for shower."

JACK LEIGHTNER HAD WALKED out of the baths that day as relaxed as a rag doll. It had seemed like such a simple, uncomplicated afternoon. In retrospect, though, several things stood out. Daniel's edginess and lack of appetite. His vague reference to business troubles. His question about Jack's abilities.

From this vantage point, a new possibility emerged: maybe his friend had been about to ask for help. . . .

Next to him now, the man's wife shifted her beautiful naked body in her sleep.

CHAPTER FIFTEEN

"You've really never spent any time here?"

Zhenya shrugged. "I have seen it. But Daniel does not like the noise, all the people."

Jack could see the man's point. The previous night's wet weather had been burned away by the bright August sun, leaving a perfect, breezy beach day at Coney Island; as they had for generations, hordes of working-class New Yorkers had flocked to the resort, and they clogged the boardwalk. He didn't have to be at work until four today, an evening tour. For now, he could pretend to be having a normal weekend.

The place was loud as hell: seagulls cawed overhead like shrill party noisemakers, the rides in the two amusement parks clanged and dinged, rap music thumped out from a nearby bumper car emporium. Jack himself didn't come here, except when duty called. He had fond childhood memories of the place, back when Steeplechase Park had provided the setting for a rare family day of fun and relative peace, but Coney had fallen far short of its glory days.

It wasn't so strange that Zhenya and her husband had not spent time here, either, even though they'd lived just a short ways down the boardwalk. Many New Yorkers lived parochial lives, bound to one tight-knit neighborhood. He thought of Mr. Gardner, who had visited neighboring Manhattan only a few times in his entire life. Hell, he had met old Brooklynites who had *never* gone in to the City, never seen the Empire State Building up close, or Central Park. It was a peasant mentality, really, a fear of the unknown.

But Zhenya looked thrilled to be here today. He glanced at her, noting how she had prepared for the occasion. Most of the passersby looked schlubby in their basketball shorts and T-shirts, but she wore skintight designer jeans, another in her collection of silky blouses, and strappy high-heeled shoes, hardly the best footwear for the uneven, roughly weathered boardwalk. She also wore a bit too much makeup, though he figured that she was the last woman on the planet to need it.

As they strolled along the boardwalk, men swiveled to stare at her. Jack imagined that if he weren't here, they might be making crude comments as well. She was a walking contradiction: she liked to dress up, but she was clearly uncomfortable with the attention her looks brought her. There were two Zhenyas: the beauty men were attracted to (including one Jack Leightner), and the woman she felt herself to be, inside. Even though he had known her only a short time, it was clear that these two were worlds apart. He wondered what it would be like to have such a problem; for once, he was grateful that he was a pretty average-looking guy.

In any case, he was touched by her naïveté, dressing up for an afternoon at the beach; he sensed that she had not had a lot of fun in her young life. Funny, he had always assumed that Daniel had been burdened by a glum, severe spouse, but now he wondered who'd held back who.... Either way, he reasoned that the marriage must have been troubled—otherwise, she would never have been at the beach today with him, her somber face opening into occasional heart-stopping smiles, her incredibly fine hair shining in the sun.

She was wide-eyed, like a kid—and there was plenty to gawk at. As they threaded through the crowds, they saw a man with a massive boa constrictor wrapped around his neck; another man with his entire body covered in brilliant tattoos; yet another guy, dressed in a suit made entirely of soda cans, riding along on a tall unicycle. Jack snorted: you didn't need to go to the sideshow to see the farther ranges of human behavior. The beach was thick with sunbathers, dancing to salsa music broadcast by little boom boxes, chugging forbidden beers, or just lying like beached whales as their weekday tensions seeped down into the sand. There was a lot of flesh on display, which was not necessarily a treat for the eyes.

As he and his date strolled along, though, he found his usual cop's cynicism melting away like hot tanning lotion. He glanced around at the incredible mix of passersby—two giggling Japanese girls, a black family sharing a couple of ice-cream cones, a couple of barrel-chested, hairy old Russian men who strutted along like former weightlifting champions—and he was warmed by a love of his native city. New York, New York, it was a hell of a town. These were his people, all of them, the ones he had sworn to protect and to serve.

At first he felt self-conscious about appearing in public with Zhenya, but when she held on to his arm he felt a rush of pride: here he was, out on a date with the most gorgeous woman on the boardwalk.

She turned to him with a very earnest expression on her face. "Zhack, can I ask from you a favor?"

"Sure," he said, wondering what it might be.

She turned north, staring across the gaudy, whirring playground of Deno's Wonder Wheel Amusement Park, past the giant 150-foot aquamarine-and-orange hoop of the Ferris wheel itself. "May we ride the roller coaster?"

He grinned. It had been forever since he had taken such a plunge. When he was a kid, there'd been a number of such rides here: the Thunderbolt, the Tornado, the Cyclone. Now the Cyclone was the only one left.

"I'd love to," he said.

THEY MADE LOVE AGAIN at her place that night, after he got off work.

They lay in the bedroom this time, which was not easy for either of them, trying to love each other with the ghosts of Daniel and Michelle keeping watch at the foot of the bed.

In the midst of it, Jack looked down in the dim light and saw tears streaking Zhenya's lovely face. He considered stopping, asking her what was wrong, but hell—he knew what was wrong: her husband was dead. He decided that the best thing he could do was to keep his trap shut and make love to her as tenderly as possible, and that's what he did.

Later, she fell asleep, but he lay awake, staring up into the dark. After the enjoyable afternoon, her mood had certainly shifted. She obviously had good reason, but he wondered if it wasn't more than that—if it wasn't also some cultural or ethnic predisposition. He thought of his father, a glum man if ever there was one, and his mother, prone to slow, sad days. It was said that the Russians were a sad people—but soulful. Jack felt it in himself sometimes, like a long, low cello chord resonating deep inside.

Lying here now, with the vast moonlit sea outside the window, he thought of a conversation he had had with Daniel Lelo, back in the hospital, after they started to become close. The month had been September, the year 2001, so of course the news had been all about the tragedy in the towers. He and Daniel had lain in their beds, watching the same channel, some local reporter interviewing families of the victims. Jack, of course, had been stunned and horrified, thinking especially of all the cops and firemen who had perished, but Daniel seemed oddly unmoved.

Later, when they turned off their TVs, Jack lay back, struggling to make sense of the event. He shook his head. "I can't believe this happened here in New York—it's like some kind of weird nightmare."

Daniel remained silent.

Jack sighed. "I work with homicides every day, but the scope of this—it's just staggering."

Again, Daniel remained silent. Jack glanced over at him. "I don't know, maybe this doesn't mean as much to you, I mean, being an immigrant and all."

Daniel just shrugged.

Jack started to get a little pissed off. "Doesn't it bother you, what happened?"

Daniel shrugged again. "You know what is difference between people from my country and your country? In your country, people are surprised by bad news. In my country, we never expect life to be good."

Jack had frowned. "A lot of people died here, Daniel. That sounds kind of cold."

Daniel frowned back. "*Cold?* I tell you something cold. I come from a town in Ukraine. Was eight thousand of us there. After the Nazis come through, was seventeen people left. There was *hundreds* of villages where such things happen." He shifted his bulk in his bed. "You know how many Russians was killed in the war? Twenty-seven *million.* You know how many

Russians Stalin was killing, all by himself? With famines, purges, executions—maybe twenty million more."

Jack found his temper rising. "So what are you saying? This isn't important, because less people were involved?"

Finally, sorrow touched Daniel's face, and he raised his hands in a gesture of conciliation. "Please, my friend, I don't mean no offense. The numbers only mean so much. Every death feels like end of the world to somebody."

IN THE MIDDLE OF the night Jack rolled over and put his arm around the dead man's wife, and soon they were making love again. This time, the urgency was not so great, but it was replaced by a deep tenderness and affection. For the first time, it occurred to him that this might be more than just a glorious, temporary fling.

CHAPTER SIXTEEN

"Shit," Jack muttered. He pushed himself up off his knees, wiped moist soil from his hands, and rubbed his tired eyes. The last thing he wanted was to be at the back of this Crown Heights community garden at nine thirty in the morning, squinting in the bright summer sun, looking at another empty, dry condom.

He walked out to the middle of the garden. About twenty little individual plots, spread out across a narrow vacant lot between two brick buildings. Some serious gardeners, evidently; the place was bright with summer vegetables. Cherry tomatoes peeped out of tangled vines; little pumpkins and squash lay bulbous on the ground; tall, radiant sunflowers rose above the last plot in the back. Not tall enough to obscure the sight of a young woman hanging from a branch of a low fruit tree, above a shaded little picnic area. She looked to be about nineteen, and her hair was dreadlocked. She wore a little diamond in the side of her right nostril, and fashionable clothes: a cute, formfitting blouse and a type of silky pants that Jack's ex-girlfriend had once referred to as "parachute pants." Probably not a hooker, this one; a student, maybe, or a counter girl in one of the fashionable little boutiques that were springing up around Fort Greene and Prospect Heights . . .

His stomach felt sour. If he hadn't spent his two days off worrying about Daniel Lelo and making love to the man's widow, if he had just worked a little harder on the first Crown Heights case, maybe he wouldn't have to be here today. Maybe this girl would still be alive. He roused himself; he couldn't let these thoughts interfere with his concentration. There was a killer to be caught.

The usual crew of techs bustled around the vic or made trips back and forth from their vans parked out on the street, careful to keep to the slate stepping-stones that marked the central path. The first officer on the scene, a young patrol cop, had been summoned by the traumatized first gardener of the day, an elderly West Indian woman who had run quaking from the site and found him on a corner just a block away. The uniform had done a good job of securing the scene. That, combined with the dry weather overnight, boded well for the investigation.

As Jack had learned back in his Academy days, in the 1920s a forensic scientist named Edmond Locard had come up with the motto that had governed crime scene investigation ever since: *Every contact leaves a trace.* That meant that the perp would almost inevitably leave some sort of physical matter at the scene of his crime, whether it be DNA, clothing fibers, or his own stray hairs. (Under natural circumstances, three or four hairs fell from the average human head every hour.) He might also leave dust from his workplace: yeast for a baker or brewer, ink droplets or paper fibers from a printer's clothes, bright multicolored dust from an auto paint shop.

The flip side of the motto was that the perp would also probably take something *away* from the scene, whether it be blood from his victim, soil in his shoe treads, or tiny slivers of broken glass. In this instance, there was a chance that he might have taken away something of a more botanical nature: seeds from a tree, burrs from a berry plant, pollen from a flower. Such traces tended to fall off clothing shortly thereafter, but some might have lodged in a seam or pocket—and they might prove crucial later in tying him to the crime scene.

Of course, the forensic evidence might be a little more unusual. At the moment, the Crime Scene techs were keeping a particular lookout for stray animal hairs.

Jack watched a fat bumblebee wander above a bush of bright red flowers like a drunk stumbling home from a bar. The garden had its practical side—it provided some good food for its patient keepers—but there were a lot of flowers too, which people had taken the trouble to cultivate just for the pleasure of looking at them. He thought of his mother, who always kept flowerboxes in the window of their dark little Red Hook apartment when he was growing up. Her husband was a drunk and her life was hard, but she always had some small bright spot in her life, courtesy of a few treasured blooms—

"I got you some coffee," Kyle Driscoll said.

Startled, Jack looked up to find his partner from the Seven-one coming up the center path. He reached out gratefully for the cup, even though iced coffee would have been better on such a hot, humid morning.

The young detective frowned. "What've we got?"

Jack nodded toward the crime scene. "I found another unrolled, dry condom back there, under that wooden bench. And the victim's got double ligatures on her neck—one of them made by what looks to have been an electrical cord."

Kyle grimaced. "You think it's the same guy?"

Jack shrugged. "Crime Scene is looking for any kind of forensic match. I'm gonna ask for a DNA sample from both condoms. They looked pretty empty, but who knows? Maybe he left a little pre-somethin'-somethin' in there."

He glanced at the body, then turned back to his colleague. "You know what bothers me? With that first killing, I was thinking maybe it was a real spur-of-the-moment thing. Like, the guy just got enraged and lost it and did the strangulation with whatever he found lying around."

"And here?"

Jack rubbed his chin. "What are the odds that another electrical cord happened to be lying around in the back of a garden?"

Kyle's eyes narrowed. "You think it was premeditated?"

"Who knows, maybe the first killing *was* just random. But what if he discovered that he liked it."

Kyle made a sour face. "Man, I hope we're not looking at some kind of serial thing."

"It's too early to say, but I doubt it. Serial murder is a pretty rare, specific syndrome. Those guys get this terrible tension that builds up inside them, psychologically, and then they feel some relief when they kill. It takes a while for the pressure to build up again. Here we've got two murders in just a few days. If you ask me, I think this is some macho creep who's experiencing some of that erectile dysfunction they're always yammering about on TV, and he's got major anger management issues. Bad combo."

He picked up a pebble and shook it in his cupped palms. He didn't want to get the young detective all jazzed about the serial killing theory, but if this *was* the beginning of such a run, they usually started somewhere close to the killer's home. The comfort zone . . . Maintaining control over his victims would be very important to the guy, and—at least at the beginning—he'd want to operate someplace where he knew the terrain.

He turned toward the front of the garden. "I'm thinking about how he got the girl to come in here . . . unless she was killed somewhere else. But that seems like a real risk, transporting her body."

Kyle glanced at the back of the garden. "Did, ah, did Crime Scene happen to find any beaver fur?"

"They're still looking."

"Did they say anything about evidence of a struggle?"

"Nope."

"How about the M.E.'s crew? Any indications of sexual assault?"

"There's no sign that she was forced." Jack stared thoughtfully at the garden entrance. "It looks like he was smart enough to get her to walk in here voluntarily. On the other hand, he was dumb enough to stage this fake suicide crap again. Maybe he's not the brightest crayon in the box."

Kyle looked back at the victim, hunched his shoulders, and stuck his hands in his pockets. "Unfortunately, that doesn't mean he's too dumb to pull off something like this again."

"Detective Leightner?"

One of the Crime Scene techs was coming down the path from the back of the garden, holding up a little waxed paper envelope. "We found something," he said. "Some hairs. Probably animal."

"What kind?" Kyle asked.

The tech shrugged. "We'll have to look at these back in the lab."

After the tech walked out to his truck, Jack turned to find his partner staring at him.

"We need to talk to some Hasids," Kyle said.

Jack sighed again. "Maybe so. But let's get the lab results first."

PLACED SMACK-DAB ON THE center of a wall in the Homicide squad room was a bold little sign that read GOYAKOD. It was an acronym and stood for Get Off Your Ass And Knock On Doors, a reminder that the bulk of cases—as Jack had told his young partner on the case—were closed not with TV-style forensic magic, but old-fashioned shoe leather. And so it was that Jack and Kyle Driscoll and a bunch of uniforms spent the rest of their day canvassing the neighborhood around the little community garden.

After the young victim had been taken down from the tree but before the M.E.'s boys had done their carryout, Jack took some Polaroids of the girl, taking care to close her eyes so that she wouldn't look so grim. And then they'd left the garden and fanned out, climbing stoops and ringing doorbells, asking if anyone had seen two or more people enter the dark garden the night before, if anyone knew the girl in the photos.

Kyle was professional but a bit frosty toward his partner from Homicide. Jack bore it in silence. What was he going to do, stir up a whole community on uncertain evidence?

They had hardly been welcomed into the neighborhood, yet it didn't take long for them to get an I.D. Another stylishly dressed young woman, walking down a street two blocks away, recognized the victim as a fellow student in her jewelry design class over at Pratt Institute in Fort Greene. *Shantel Williams.* And then they talked to Shantel's grandmother, with whom she had lived, and who was frantic because Shantel had never come home the night before, and then they tracked down a couple of girlfriends who had spent the early part of the previous evening hanging out with her in a couple of trendy new neighborhood watering holes. As Jack discovered after some tactful prodding, it turned out that Shantel had a drinking problem that could make her become rather unpleasant to be around, so her friends had left her in a bar around midnight. And so it was that Jack and Kyle spent the last couple hours of their tour visiting bars, asking if anyone had seen someone chatting up the girl or maybe escorting her away.

But there the trail went cold, and then the tour ended, and Jack passed his info on to the evening Homicide squad, and he got in his car, glad to be headed back to Brighton Beach and Zhenya Lelo's waiting arms.

CHAPTER SEVENTEEN

Tribes. Though they all lived in the same nation and shared the concrete and asphalt of a single city borough, Brooklynites had come to America from all over the planet, and for every citizen who was happy to shed the past and assimilate, there was another who held fast to some other culture, some other place. There were Poles in Greenpoint and Mexicans in Sunset Park, Italians in Carroll Gardens and Pakistanis in Midwood. Ideally, a cop here should be a walking ethnic encyclopedia and a speaker of several dozen languages.

To make life more complicated for the humble detective, each tribe was divided into smaller camps, some of them fiercely different from one another. A casual visitor might see men in side curls and big black hats and think "Hasidic Jews," yet be ignorant of the fact that Satmar Hasidim lived in Williamsburg and Borough Park and were severely religious and strictly insular, while the Lubavitchers of Crown Heights and Midwood were more relaxed in their religious rules and somewhat more open to New Yorkers of other stripes.

That relative openness did not provide much comfort to Jack Leightner now, sitting in front of two visitors to the Seven-one Precinct House. Business seemed slow in the squad room; other detectives glanced idly over at the pair of Luba-vitchers parked next to Kyle Driscoll's battered gray desk. The men were volunteers; they served as liaisons between their community and the local police.

One of them was a stooped old man. "My name is Mandel," he said. "This is my grandson Oren." Both men wore full beards, side curls, black fedoras, and—amazingly, considering the almost nonexistent air conditioning inside the building—full black suits. The grandson looked to be about twenty; he shared his relative's pinched face and pronounced Adam's apple. His granddad had the twinkling eyes of a department store Santa. (Maybe not the most appropriate comparison, Jack realized, but still . . .)

"Thanks very much for coming," Kyle said. This time, *he* had insisted on doing the talking.

"We're glad to help," the young man said. He wore braces, and his voice sounded as if it had just broken.

"Can I get you anything?" Kyle said. "A soda?"

The visitors shook their heads. The old man had a cane; he rested both hands on top. "What can we do for you?"

Kyle cleared his throat and hunched forward in his seat. "This is, ah, it's a matter of some delicacy. And we're very grateful for your assistance." He spread his palms out on his knees. "It's about a couple of homicides. The body of a young woman was found in the neighborhood yesterday morning. And we found another woman several days ago."

The old man's cheery face grew puzzled. "Members of our community were murdered? We have heard nothing about this."

Kyle looked uncomfortable, but Jack was not inclined to jump in and help. The Hasidim evoked complicated feelings in him. He could admire their stubbornness in maintaining their ideals in such a compromised, crass society, which celebrated

Baywatch babes and celebrity cokeheads, yet—like a number of more secular Jews—he was embarrassed by how he felt embarrassed by them. They seemed trapped in an unhappy circle, the way they showed off their difference and righteousness— and then reacted to prejudice by becoming even more insular.

"Actually," Kyle answered, "the victims were young African-American women."

The younger visitor frowned. "I don't understand. How can we help with this? You think one of us might have witnessed one of these killings?"

Kyle shifted in his chair. "Not exactly. As I said, this is a matter of some delicacy. And I hope you won't be offended if I speak frankly. We, ah, we have some forensic evidence. It's not at all conclusive, mind you, and we're not making any accusations against anyone. We're just looking for some advice."

Both visitors seemed utterly confused.

"Look," Kyle continued. "I know that your people are model citizens. An incredibly low crime rate, fantastic participation in community affairs . . ."

The Hasidim just stared.

Kyle plunged on. "I'm sure that if someone in your community was having a problem, you'd want to identify this person, right?"

The old man's hands tightened on top of his cane. "What kind of a problem? Are you suggesting that one of us might have killed these women?"

Kyle cleared his throat. "As I said, we have some forensic evidence."

"What kind of evidence?"

Kyle lowered his voice. "This is confidential information. We, ah, we found some animal fur at the scenes. *Beaver* fur." He paused to let the implication sink in.

The old man frowned. "And this proves what, exactly?"

Kyle raised his hands in a placating gesture. "It doesn't prove anything. But you have to admit, it's pretty unusual."

The old man looked at his grandson, and then both men suddenly rose to their feet. Mandel shook his cane at Kyle. "I'll tell you what is *not* unusual, Mister Detective: this sort of slander against the Jewish people has been going on for thousands of years. And you should be ashamed of yourself." He turned, grabbed his grandson's arm, and both men marched out of the squad room.

The room went silent for a moment.

"Well," Jack finally said, "*that* went well."

At least Kyle Driscoll had the good grace to laugh.

"Excuse me."

Both detectives looked across the room at a stout fireplug of a man with slicked-back hair. He wore jeans, a sweatshirt, and a significant gold chain. Jack pegged him as an undercover. The guy had been talking to a couple of the squad detectives over in the corner, but now he was headed toward Driscoll's desk. He stuck out a hand. "How ya doin'? I'm Rob Tewks. I used to work with a Street Crimes squad here, before I got transferred to the Eight-four."

Jack and his partner introduced themselves.

"You mind if I ask what that was all about?" the other detective said.

Kyle filled him in.

The man shook his head. "I wish I'd known what you were looking for earlier. I got just the guy for you to talk to."

YOSI SILBERBERG WAS ALSO a Lubavitcher. Unlike some of his stern compatriots, the Hasid was openly cheerful, a roly-poly, red-haired clerk who spent his days perched on a stool behind the counter of an electronics store on Atlantic Avenue, where he sold big automotive sound systems to young African-American men. (As often happened in New York City, commerce had a way of trumping—at least temporarily—all sorts of tribal differences.) The air conditioning inside was pumped up high, and Jack and the Street Crimes detective stood to the side, enjoying it, as Silberberg finished demonstrating a powerful new speaker system to a couple of homeboys wearing gold chains, gold-capped teeth, and incredibly slouchy jeans. He cranked up a volume knob, and the store practically shook with heavy hip-hop bass. Then he reached back, flicked the sound off, and turned back to the potential purchaser.

"Well, my friend? What do you think?"

The customer smiled at his sidekick. "Yo, dawg, that shit is bumpin'!" They knocked fists together in a dap.

The salesman winked at Tewks, then smiled at his customer. "That's right—and I give it to you for fifty dollars off, today only."

The salesman and the detective had met several years earlier, when Tewks caught an assailant of Silberberg's uncle—a mugging attempt gone bad. The young man had been very grateful.

After the clerk rang up his new sale, he turned to the two detectives. (Kyle had reluctantly agreed that it might be best if he waited outside in the car.) "So, Detective, what can I do for you today? Are you in the market for a 'bumping' new sound system for your police car?"

Tewks smiled. "No, thanks. This is Detective Leightner from Brooklyn South Homicide. We're actually here to talk about hats."

Silberberg's bushy eyebrows rose. "Hats? I think you might have the wrong store."

Tewks leaned forward and rested his forearms on the counter. "It's for a case. We're trying to identify someone."

The clerk's cheery face grew grave. "A killing involving one of us? I haven't heard about it yet."

Here we go again, Jack thought. He stepped in before the other detective could explain. "We'd like to know about hats. I know there are different sects of Hasidic people here in Brooklyn. Do you all wear the same kind of hats?"

The clerk shook his head. "Oy—do you have a couple of days to discuss this? First of all, we don't say 'sects.' We say 'courts.' And there are a number of these: the Lubavitchers, like me, the Satmars, the Ger, the Bobov, the Belz . . . All wear different hats. We Lubavitchers prefer the black Borsalino, a fedora. The Bobov like a good bowler; the Satmar, a wide-brimmed, flat-topped—"

Jack cut in again, seeing that he was about to get more information than he could handle. "What about fur hats? Which ones would wear beaver fur?"

The clerk considered the question thoughtfully. "We call this *biber*. Now, do you mean beaver *felt* or beaver *fur*?"

"What's the difference?"

"Felt is made from wool or animal hair, compressed into a dense fabric. We call this material 'smooth.' Like my hat here," he said, lifting a fedora from a shelf behind him.

"And the other kind?"

"There are a couple. Some wear hats with what is called a beaver finish, which is sort of like a thick velvet—but it's usually made from rabbit."

Jack shook his head, impressed. It seemed that the various Hasidic sects—no, *courts*—had a sartorial code as complex as that which separated the Crips and Bloods. And the rivalries were almost as intense. (He had heard stories—possibly apocryphal—of Hasidim from one group kidnapping a young man from another, throwing him into the back of a van, and cutting off his side curls.) "How do you keep track of all this?" he asked.

The Hasid just shrugged. "How do you keep track of what different police wear?"

"That's my full-time job."

The clerk shrugged again. "Being a Hasid? Also full-time."

Jack smiled. "What about those big, round hats, shaped like, um, an angel food cake, made of thick fur?"

"Ah," the clerk said, nodding. "Those are *shtreimel*. We Lubavitchers don't wear them."

"Who does?"

"The Satmars, and some of the others."

Jack frowned; he was starting to go cross-eyed with the complexity of the topic.

Rob Tewks looked at his watch. "You okay here? I gotta run."

Jack nodded and thanked the detective, who seemed relieved to split, like a schoolkid saved by the bell.

"So tell me," the clerk said to Jack. "What did the hat of your victim look like?"

Jack pinched his lower lip, feeling a bit guilty about not explaining the details of the case, but not so guilty that he was prepared to ruin the interview. "We didn't find a hat. Just some beaver hairs."

The clerk stroked his red beard. "The victim—what did he look like?"

Jack shook his head. "We just found the hairs."

The clerk frowned. "So you don't know if there was a Hasid involved at all?"

Jack shook his head, rather sheepish.

Yosi looked pensive. "All is not lost. Tell me something: this incident, which I assume you believe is connected to a homicide—what day of the week did it occur?"

Jack scratched his head. "Let me see . . . there were actually two. One happened on a Saturday or Sunday, the other on a Thursday. Why?"

Yosi smiled, eyes twinkling. "This is good news. I think no Hasid was killed at all."

Jack's eyes widened. "How could you possibly know that?"

The clerk shrugged. "Simple deduction. First of all, the *shtreimel* hat is often actually made of sable or fox fur. And it is worn only on *shabbes*"—Friday nights—"or on holidays or special *simchas*."

"*Simchas?*"

"Formal celebrations, such as weddings." The clerk smiled, proud of his reasoning. "Someone wearing a *shtreimel* on any other day would stand out like a pork chop on a bar mitzvah buffet."

Jack thought about this for a moment. It had been hard to imagine a young West Indian woman and a Hasid in full regalia meeting for a tryst in the dark community garden. But what if the perp had not actually been wearing the hat that night?

Yosi raised a hand. "I know what you're thinking. Maybe the man had these hairs on his clothing, and they fell off at the time of the incident."

Jack's eyes widened further.

Yosi grinned, then glanced at his fellow Hasidic salesmen and lowered his voice. "Once or twice—and this must be our little secret—I may have watched *CSI* on the television. The fact is," he concluded, "that these hairs would not have gotten on the man's regular clothing because the *shtreimel* is only worn with the *kapote*."

"The *who*?"

"It's a long satin robe, also worn on these special occasions. So the hairs from the *shtreimel* would have fallen on the *kapote*, which your man would not have been wearing on a recent Saturday, Sunday, or Thursday. And surely he would have bathed between the Sabbath and those other days, so any hairs on his person would have washed away."

Jack whistled. "Maybe we should start up a Hasidic Homicide auxiliary." He looked off into the distance and mused aloud. "Where else would beaver fur come from, then? Ordinarily, I'd guess a fur coat, but that would be pretty unlikely in the middle of August."

The clerk shrugged. "I'm afraid I don't know the answer to that one. But if you would like to buy a car stereo, I'm your man."

Another salesclerk cranked the volume. Jack thanked his technical adviser and stepped back out into the morning heat. He joined Kyle Driscoll in the front seat of his unmarked Crown Vic.

"How'd it go in there?" the young detective asked.

"It's not looking good for the Hasid theory."

Kyle frowned.

Jack was in the middle of relating Yosi Silberberg's convoluted explanation when his cell phone trilled.

"Detective Leightner?"

"Yeah."

"This is Anthony Rinzella, with security for the Fulton Fish Market. We've had a bit of a situation here."

As soon as he got off the phone, Jack jumped out of Kyle's car, got in his own, slapped a rotating beacon on the dash, and sped off, not toward the fish market, but toward Bellevue Hospital Center.

CHAPTER EIGHTEEN

"Let me get this straight," Linda Vargas said to the manager of Daniel Lelo's fish company. "A while back you had an accident where one of these big metal hooks went into the back of your hand. And now you're saying that the same thing happened again, another accident in the exact same spot, and this time the hook just happened to dig around in there a bit?" The homicide task force detective stood next to the man's hospital bed, arms crossed, frowning, and Jack was glad that he was not the subject of her interrogation.

Andrei Goguniv lay back, hooked up to I.V.s, and he nodded miserably. The man's bald head gleamed under the fluorescent lights like a sickly white cue ball.

Jack sat in a plastic chair on the other side of the bed. He was keeping silent for the moment.

"That's incredible!" Vargas said dryly. "What are the odds?" She looked up at Jack, as if sharing amazement at the coincidence.

"Not only that," his colleague continued, "but this 'accident' just happened to take place in your *office*. Do a lot of fish processing up there, do you?"

The manager squirmed.

"As if all that wasn't enough," Vargas continued, "this happened after the market was closed for the morning. Interesting time for a work-related injury."

The fish market security man had reported that the manager of one of the Seaport's clothing boutiques was opening her store when she heard muffled screams coming through a wall that adjoined the market offices. By the time she alerted mall security and they discovered the source of the noise, Goguniv was sitting slumped over the desk in his office, soaked in blood, passed out, alone.

Jack stared at the manager. He thought of his own hospital stay, after he had gotten shot. He knew how belittling it felt to be lying there in an open-backed hospital gown, at the mercy of the doctors. His heart opened to the man, even though the poor bastard was still refusing to cooperate.

Vargas took out her notebook and slapped it impatiently against her palm. "Well? Are you planning on sharing how this miracle might have occurred?"

Goguniv looked as if he was about to pass out all over again. Weakly, he flapped his uninjured hand in protest. "*Please.* I don't feel so good. I need to sleep."

Vargas's cell phone trilled. She answered, then stepped out into the hall to talk.

As soon as she left, Jack sat down, pulling his chair closer to the manager's bed. He spoke softly and earnestly.

"Andrei, listen: I'm here to help you. Really. You're not gonna get in any more trouble by talking to me. The way things have been going, this can only get worse for you—unless you help me put a stop to it. All you have to do is tell me who did this to you."

Goguniv remained silent.

"Was it Semyon Balakutis? Just nod your head if it was."

The manager turned his face toward the wall.

Jack groaned and sank back into his chair. The task force detectives hated mob-related cases for this same reason: nobody ever saw anything, heard anything, or knew anything, and the investigations tended to drag on forever.

He leaned forward again, preparing to come at the fish company manager from a new angle, but the man's head had sunk down on his chest. Zonked out on painkillers? Jack was tempted to scratch the bare sole of his foot with a pen, to see if he might be faking, but a nurse chose that moment to bustle in.

He got up—reluctantly—to leave.

THE FISH COMPANY MANAGER'S second "accident" sure seemed like a bogus miracle, but Jack still had a real one in his life. Standing in Zhenya Lelo's brightly lit little foyer, he drew her into his arms, kissed her sweet lips, and all his troubles melted away.

"Are you hungry?" she asked.

"I'm hungry for you," he replied, and he led her down the hallway to the bedroom. He lay back on her comfortable bed and decided that this was his favorite moment in all the world, watching her stand there and gracefully pull her blouse over her head, revealing her lovely rose-tipped breasts. A few minutes later, he changed his mind; *this* was his favorite moment, when he first moved inside her, and she wrapped her arms around him, drawing him deeper, and they both gasped with the utter rightness of it: *home.*

He realized, lying next to her after, that he usually just thought of his body as a hollow shell, a vehicle for moving his mind from one place to another as he worked. He fed it, he slept, he felt himself slowly age, yet his flesh was of little importance to him. But this woman had the power to return him to himself, to help him feel a richness of sensation again, a powerful connection to the living world. He almost shivered with a realization: it was more than that—he was not just passionate about the sex. Something seemed to be happening that he had given up hope of ever experiencing again.

CHAPTER NINETEEN

The next day, Jack left Linda Vargas to her pursuit of the Lelo case, while he spent another fruitless morning pursuing his Crown Heights murder. (The thought of Semyon Balakutis messing with the fish company manager riled him up, but the possibility of another dead girl turning up seemed more urgent.)

The average murder was committed within a social network. There were dis murders (homeboys who shot each other over some stupid slight); turf murders (drug dealers fighting over corner sales spots); and the increasingly popular "I loved her so much I had to kill her" crimes. In most of these cases, the victims knew the perps, and the vics often had criminal records themselves, and there was often someone involved with a powerful motivation to snitch. There were witnesses, or the killers were dumb enough to brag about their deeds. The problem in this case was that no one would go around bragging that he had killed due to his own sexual inadequacy. The Crown Heights killer had chosen private crime scenes, and his victims might be totally outside his normal circles.

Jack's discussions with Kyle kept popping into his mind, and he couldn't help wondering if the Crown Heights assailant was Jewish, and how the answer would play out on the streets and in the press. He shook his head: this was a pointless line of thought—he just needed to follow the evidence and make sure he nailed the right guy.

A great deal of work had already been expended. All of the neighbors near the crack house and the community garden had been canvassed, without a single witness coming forward. No common thread had been found in the lives of the two victims. Jack had even had someone at the DMV look up recent traffic-enforcement activity near the crime scenes. (He was thinking about how, back in 1977, the Son of Sam had been caught due to a traffic ticket.)

He thought about Shantel Williams's last minutes, that night in the garden. The girl had been seriously intoxicated; he hoped, for her sake, that she had not known that anything bad was going to happen until the last possible minute. It had been a moonlit night. He imagined her stumbling down the garden path, past plants shining in the silvery light, with someone at her side. Someone who didn't inspire fear or a wish to flee ... Someone she knew? Someone she felt comfortable with? There had been no eyewitness reports about her entry into the garden; he needed another angle.

The beaver fur still seemed like it might provide the answer. He could have easily imagined the perp wearing a fur coat or jacket if it had been winter, but the temperature had been in the seventies or eighties every night for the past couple of weeks, and such attire would have stood out to even the most casual passersby. The fur seemed to suggest a sort of bravado; it made sense, maybe, as a symptom of the man's overcompensation for his sexual inadequacies. What could it have come off of, though? Jack smiled, sitting at his desk and thinking of seventies exploitation flicks, pimps strutting around wearing crazy outfits, fur-trimmed capes or fur hatbands or big hats trailing fur tassels. . . . Such attire wouldn't play too well in today's Crown Heights, though, especially in the solidly respectable neighborhood near the community garden.

He ran "uses for beaver fur" through an Internet search engine and found some interesting commercial Web sites. One advertised beaver fur bedspreads and throws—again, not likely for summer use. Another offered a variety of other products made from the fur: a belt buckle, a saddle blanket, a fur-covered pen, car seat covers . . . He sat for a moment examining the accompanying photos. It was hard to imagine someone using the car-related product in hot weather—unless the car was always air-conditioned. He thought about vinyl car seats and how they could be brutally hot to the touch after sitting in direct summer sun. Would a fur cover make them feel hotter or cooler? He smiled again: Hell, *beavers* still wore the damn stuff during the summertime. He sat thinking about it for a few more minutes, and then he circulated a computer memo to patrol officers and traffic-enforcement agents working in the area, briefing them on the case and asking them to keep an eye out for anything unusual.

BY THE TIME HE ended up in Zhenya's apartment again, in the early evening, he was doubly grateful to be off duty.

It didn't matter if he was coming off an afternoon shift or an evening one; they were already settling into a routine. First, a kiss in the foyer, which usually led them straight back to the bedroom, followed by a cocktail out on the balcony, savoring the view of beach and sea, and then dinner, either prepared in her small kitchen or ordered in. (Normally, he would have enjoyed taking her out, but both had their reasons not to be seen together in Brighton Beach, and by the time he got to her place, he didn't feel like driving elsewhere.) It didn't matter; there was something magical about this bubble they had created together, and neither wanted to leave it. He had not invited her to his place yet; it was still haunted by his memories of Michelle. He supposed her place felt odd to her too, with Daniel's clothes still in the closet and his shaving things in the bathroom cabinet, but she didn't comment on it.

Tonight she had convinced him to try sushi for the first time. She had ordered in, not from a Japanese restaurant, but a Russian place on Brighton Beach Avenue. (It made sense: these Russians were used to living in seaside towns, and they had always had a taste for fish, whether pickled, smoked, or fresh. Jack couldn't help thinking of Daniel's company in the Fulton Market, but the adventure and ritual of the meal—the pink scraps of ginger, the blast of green wasabi—distracted him.

"Would you like another drink?" Zhenya asked, on the balcony, after. She sat with her bare feet up, arms around her knees.

Jack set his glass on the little side table. "I'm good. In fact, I'm great. Thank you."

The beach and boardwalk were crowded below. Zhenya was staring at something way off and up. He followed her gaze out and found a kite hovering in the late day sky, its beribboned tail whipping in a stiff shore breeze.

He watched Zhenya watch the kite. She didn't say anything. She didn't say much in general. In fact, he had never met a less talkative woman. It wasn't just the language barrier. She didn't seem to feel any need to tell him about the events of her day or ask him when his next day off was or anything. She was self-sufficient, like a cat that did as it pleased, that didn't bother to try to ingratiate or assert itself. Sometimes he wished she would talk. The sex was great, but it occurred to him that it could also act as a substitute for conversation. He didn't really want to discuss Daniel, but the topic was always there, lurking beneath the surface, and eventually they'd have to bring it up.

Zhenya tucked a strand of fine blond hair behind her ear and licked her lips, dry from the sun and wind. What did he know about her? She was from a small town near Kiev—not far from where his own grandparents had been born, actually; she had shown him on a map. When he had asked about her parents, her voice became quiet and small. Her father, she said, had been sent away when she was a little girl.

"For what?" he had asked.

She shrugged. "He was a Jew. And he was not afraid to talk."

"He was a political prisoner?"

She nodded, her face etched with pain. "When I am small, I am only allow to see him three or four times. The place where he is staying: *very bad.*"

"What happened to him?"

"He died in prison. Nineteen eighty-eight. He never was coming home, and he never saw end of Soviet Union. When my mother dies, five years ago, I have no reason to stay there."

She and Daniel had met just after she arrived in the States, when she was working as a waitress in one of the boardwalk restaurants in Brighton Beach. Now she was thinking about taking courses at Brooklyn College, studying business, perhaps, or communications. She had even confided once, shyly, that she had thought of being a weather reporter on TV. She was young enough to see life as a field in front of her, open with possibility.

He wondered how much she cared for him. It was funny: he had been skittish at first, *once burned, twice shy* and all. He had expected that he would soon feel a need to back away from his emotions, but the fact that she demanded so little of him left him continually intrigued, as if he was always leaning toward her.

The kite traveled across the sky, and she followed it with her intense green eyes. He heard a shout down on the beach, and when he looked up again he saw that the kite's string had snapped, and it was plunging around in wild circles over the beach. He followed it until the wind sent it careering around the corner of the condo development.

They sat for a while in easy silence. Jack sighed with contentment as the day's problems drained from his mind.

Off to the west, the glowing orange orb of the sun seemed trapped in the spokes of Coney Island's Wonder Wheel, and then it sank lower and disappeared below the horizon. The air grew cool as a soft mauve light settled over the beach and deepened in hue.

He turned back to find that he had become the subject of *her* inquiring gaze.

"May I ask a question?"

He nodded. "Of course."

She reached down and grasped her toes. "Semyon Balakutis—you will stop him?"

He refrained from wincing. Talk about a mood spoiler . . . He nodded. "He's smart—but not smart enough. I promise you: I'll stop him." He tensed. "Why? Has he bothered you?"

She shook her head, but he was not entirely convinced. He stared at her, wondering if she had received any threats. "You'll tell me if he calls or anything, right?"

She nodded slightly but didn't speak.

LATER, HE LAY IN bed next to her, listening to her even breathing. Sleep eluded him—too many thoughts buzzing around inside his head again. He thought of Semyon Balakutis's angry face—and Andrei Goguniv's frightened one. He turned to Zhenya; she lay with her back to him, one bare, fragile shoulder exposed in the dim light. *Don't worry*, he thought. *I'll take care of you.* He was realizing what he had really missed: it wasn't having someone to love him—it was having someone to love.

He moved closer and slipped his arms around her. He held her for a moment, his hand resting against her belly. But then he started thinking about the smooth rise of her breast, and his hand moved north, as if by its own volition, and he was cupping the firm liquid weight of it, and he felt her nipple hardening into his palm.

His heart started beating faster. Good grief, he had been prepared to slide into a sexually subdued middle age, but here he was, like a teenager again. Even so, he would have resisted the urge to wake her, but she arched back against him subtly, like a cat stretching, and he was emboldened to slip his hand down between her thighs, and he heard her breath catch and then its rhythm grew quick and eager.

They stayed awake for hours.

LATER, HE WAS HALF awakened by the sound of a cell phone, but it wasn't his ringtone. The faint light in the room said early morning. He felt Zhenya slip out of bed and heard her pad across the floor. She picked up her phone and went out into the hall. He thought he detected some sort of surprise or unease in her voice as she answered, but she was speaking in Russian. She softly closed the bedroom door, and he was so tired that he dropped back into sleep. Soon he was deep into a dream.

He was sitting in a little cabin of the Wonder Wheel, and

Zhenya—excited—sat next to him. At ground level the noise of the amusement park was deafening, but as the wheel turned it lifted them above the chattering hordes, high above Coney Island. The beach expanded out to his left, dotted with thousands of half-naked sun worshipers, and the sea spread out to the curve of the horizon. He looked straight down. From above, the park resolved into a bright, orderly grid. As their car rose toward the top, 150 feet in the air, the din of the rides disappeared, giving way to the gentle whisper of a shoreline breeze. Twisting in his seat, he could look back at the Cyclone, cars full of tiny screaming patrons plunging down its slopes. Farther back, he could see the apartment towers of Brighton Beach. And then he turned back toward Zhenya, but somehow she had disappeared—and he was sitting in a huge underground cave with Daniel, and the man was rubbing his bald head, and warm water was pouring down from somewhere up above, and Daniel was trying to tell him something, but the sound of the rushing water was too loud—

He woke to an empty bed.

Groggy, he got up, wearing only his boxer shorts, and he looked for Zhenya in the other rooms of her apartment. He found a note on the kitchen counter. "Sory. I hav many erends today. Will call U later. xoxo, Z."

He remembered something about an early morning phone call but wondered if he had dreamt it. As he made himself a cup of coffee, he noticed that dirty dishes were piling up in the sink. Then he saw some Cheerios spilled on the little kitchen table, and a few on the floor. He was starting to realize something about Zhenya. She would slip out of her clothes by the side of the bed, and he was always happy to witness that, but then she might leave them puddled there for several days. Or she would finish painting her toenails and leave the polish bottle and dirty cotton swabs sitting by the side of the couch. Hell, it was her place, and Michelle had always teased him about his neatness, but still—he didn't think it was neurotic to not want to see food left on the kitchen floor. And he had exaggerated her beauty. She was attractive, there was no doubt about that, but she wasn't the perfect vision he had made her out to be in his first throes of desire. She had her physical flaws, just like everybody else, and a closet full of tacky clothing.

He shook his head; he was just grumpy this morning. Seeing Zhenya's little messes made him feel as if he were her father or something. Christ, he wasn't *that* much older. . . . He refilled his coffee cup and slumped down at her table. What was he doing here? Was this some sort of midlife crisis? Next thing he knew, he'd be wearing designer jeans and dyeing his hair. He frowned. The girl was lovely, but what did they really have in common? Where did he think this could ultimately go? He scoffed at himself. He had been starting to think he was falling in love. *Pah*—it was just infatuation, pure and simple. He wanted some company, someone to eat dinner with, to watch a little TV with. He hoped to get laid now and then. And it was the same old stupid middle-aged-guy story: he wanted to be with someone young, with fresh skin and no wrinkles, someone who could help him ignore his own aging body.

Over the years, he had seen so many people who had died suddenly, been shot, stabbed, strangled, electrocuted with radios thrown into their baths. But it wasn't a gruesome death he was afraid of, no—it was growing old. Getting sick, becoming infirm, becoming helpless, being alone.

Oh well, at least there was one bright side: he hadn't abandoned some perfectly good wife in order to play out this little fantasy.

He took a shower, briskly washing his body, as if scrubbing himself free from foolish notions.

After, as he dressed, he picked up his cell phone from her bedside table and slipped it into his pants pocket—and felt a crinkly piece of paper that he didn't remember putting there. He took it out and unfolded it. A note: *I will mis you all day. Luv, Z.*

Big dope that he was, it made his heart light up all over again.

CHAPTER TWENTY

"Sex crimes," Jack said.

"Huh?" Kyle Driscoll looked up from his desk, where he was busy eating a steak-and-cheese sub.

"Our Crown Heights killer," Jack said. "This guy didn't go from having a little problem getting it up to suddenly going around murdering multiple victims. That's like zooming from zero to sixty in two seconds. You gotta go through some gears first, and I would guess he's got a record for more minor offenses. I'm betting sex crimes."

Kyle set down his sub. "I already went through all the convictions in this area in the last five years. And I cross-referenced for the ones that included attempted strangulation."

"You've been doing an excellent job," Jack said, and he meant it. Despite their occasional touchy moments, he had grown to like the young detective and was proud of the way the man was handling his first homicide. But you could always dig deeper. "The thing is," he said. "We've been looking for *convictions*. Maybe our guy was involved in a case that never got that far." He was thinking about Semyon Balakutis and his trail of dropped charges.

The other detective frowned. "I hope you don't mind my saying so, but this case is turning into a real pain in the ass."

"C'mon," Jack said, manufacturing enthusiasm. "Patience and perseverance made a bishop of His Reverence."

Kyle raised his eyebrows. "Kind of a strange motto for a guy with a name like Leightner." But he raised his hands in surrender. "I know, I know: it's all about the legwork."

"Tell you what," Jack said. "You start calling cops in the neighboring precincts, and I'll call everybody I know in the D.A.'s office."

FIVE HOURS LATER, THEY stood in a hallway of the Seventy-first Precinct House. Both men were excited, though Jack was too much the veteran to show it.

"You ready?" he asked gravely. A lot might be riding on this interview; it didn't happen every day that detectives could talk to one suspect about two different homicides. He straightened the knot of his tie, a pre-game tic. "Remember: let's start things off nice and easy."

The other detective followed him into an airless little interview room, where they found one Joseph Joral, a resident of Crown Heights. The man sat on the left side of the table there, digging a pinkie into his ear as if he had not a care in the world. A couple of uniforms had just picked him up at work, on the outdoor lot of a car rental office. He was a big Caucasian, midthirties, with a Caesar haircut and a finely trimmed little line of beard that ran from his sideburns down along the edge of his chin. Along with his blue polo work shirt, the man wore oversize athletic shorts, big basketball shoes, a hoop earring, and a gold chain—generic Brooklyn street style. Jack was curious about the guy's ethnic background; the name was unusual, and he couldn't place it. Joral looked like the kind of mook who might spend his days off hanging out on a corner outside a deli, scratching his balls and boasting about his sexual conquests. The kind of guy who would have a Playboy air freshener hanging from the rearview mirror in his car, along with a couple of fuzzy dice.

If the man's looks just suggested a certain lifestyle, his record was more specific: he'd been charged with soliciting prostitutes and with battery (on a date from a classified ad). The latter charge had gone through to a conviction six years earlier, and Joral had done a brief bid upstate.

Jack matter-of-factly dropped a manila folder on the table and sat down across from the man. Kyle remained standing, leaning back against the only door. The room was tiny and absolutely bare except for the table and three chairs. (Jack supposed there might be police interview rooms somewhere that featured potted plants and other homely touches, but he had never seen one. The idea was always to strip things down to the barest essence: two or three people in a little cage, dancing around the truth.)

"How ya doin' . . ." He pretended to consult his file folder for the name, as if this was just one of many routine interviews. "*Joseph*. What do your friends call you? Joe? JJ?"

"Whatever" was all their suspect had to say. He sat back with his legs splayed wide, like a guy who was used to taking up two seats on crowded subway trains.

"Must be hard work, being Superman's father and all," Jack said.

Their suspect didn't even crack a smile. "That's Jor-*El*."

"Right. You want something to eat? My partner here can run down and get something from the snack machines."

"I'm good."

The man didn't ask why the uniforms had brought him here or complain about missing time from work. He just sat back with his meaty arms folded across his bull chest. Jack thought of the killer's evident belief that he was fooling the cops with his staged suicides.

The fact was that Joral didn't have to be here at all. He had not been charged with any crime, and technically he could have just said no to the request that he come in. Thankfully, though, television cop shows set a powerful example for the average guy on the street. On TV, the suspects always came in. (There was no story if they didn't.) In real life, even if a suspect was arrested and *had* to come in, he could simply lawyer up and refuse to be interviewed. The fact of the matter was that the Fifth Amendment protected all citizens against self-incrimination, which meant that they didn't have to talk to a cop. *Ever.*

Jack asked a number of innocuous questions about where Joral worked, what the job was like, how long he'd lived in Brooklyn. The man gave relaxed, ungrudging answers. Then Jack started getting a little more specific, asking what he did for fun in his spare time.

Finally, the man started to tighten up. "What's goin' on?" he said. "Is there some kind of problem?"

"No problem," Jack said. "We're just checking out a little situation."

Joral frowned. "What kind of situation?"

Jack ignored the question. He reached into the manila folder and pulled out a blank monthly calendar. He pointed to the probable date of the first Crown Heights murder. "Do you remember what you did on August twenty-one?"

Joral shrugged. "I went to work, man. It was a Thursday."

"Okay . . . what about after work? Where'd you have dinner?"

Joral threw his hands up. "How the hell should I know? I don't remember what I ate every day!"

"All right, how about after dinnertime. Did you go out?"

Joral shook his head. "Naw, man. That was a weeknight. I stayed home. I save my money."

"You sure?"

Joral nodded. "Yeah. I was at home. Watching TV. Then sleeping."

Jack picked up the calendar and pointed to the date of the second murder.

The answers were equally unhelpful.

Jack picked up the manila folder and opened it, holding it just below the man's line of sight. "All right. Now let's talk about LaTanya Davidson."

Joral shrugged. "Don't know nobody by that name."

There were two kinds of punks out on the street, the mutts and the mopes. The latter tried to act accommodating in interviews, even if they were lying through their teeth. The mutts were harder: they were cocky and wouldn't voluntarily give an inch.

Jack's eyebrows went up. "Really? She's the young woman who had you picked up last December for sexual assault." The young *African-American* woman.

Joral's relaxed demeanor disappeared. "Nobody charged me with nuthin'."

This was true: the woman had ultimately decided that she didn't want to risk the additional trauma and publicity of a court case. She'd declined to press charges, and the case had never gone to trial, which was why it had not shown up in the databases Kyle had checked.

"She said you tried to strangle her."

Joral rolled his eyes. "Man, that bitch was crazy. All into

some kinky shit. She invites me over to her apartment, and we're havin' sex, right, and she *asks* me to choke her. I was like, 'Hey—*whatever.*'"

Jack stared at the man. This was the same line the so-called Preppy Killer had used to justify his strangulation homicide in Central Park back in the eighties.

Joral didn't stop there; he shook his head scornfully. "She said I was *trying* to strangle her? That's bullshit. You think if I was trying to strangle somebody, I wouldn't just do it?"

Jack's pulse picked up at this oddly cocky comment, but he remained calm and nodded. "It's funny you should mention that." He reached for the manila folder, pulled out a couple of photos of the two Crown Heights strangulation victims, and spread them out on the table. The pix showed the women's faces after their bodies had been laid out on the ground. "It doesn't look like somebody had any problem strangling these two women at all."

Joral stared down at the pictures and grew flushed. "You trying to pin this shit on me? Those were *suicides.*"

The air in the interview room went electric. Jack's eyes and his colleague's widened involuntarily, and they exchanged a stunned look.

Joral clearly realized what a stupid thing he had just said. "I want a lawyer" were the next words out of his mouth.

THE SUSPECT'S ATTORNEY WAS a heavyset man with a yellowing white beard and a food-stained tie. *Nice*, Jack thought—he'd seen his share of incompetent public defenders. But even if the guy was a complete schlub, he'd have had to be criminally negligent to miss the weakness of the detectives' position.

The P.D. clasped his hands in front of him, sitting next

to his client in the little interview room. "The fact that these victims were found hanging was published in several city newspapers, gentlemen. My client read about them. So what?"

Kyle frowned. "There were no pictures of the victims in the papers. How would he know these were the same women?"

The lawyer shrugged. "It's a pretty logical guess."

Kyle shook his head. "The photos just show the faces of the women. How could he connect them to the stories in the paper?"

The lawyer pointed down at the table. "The photos clearly show the necks of the victims, Detective. It's obvious they suffered some kind of trauma."

Inwardly, Jack groaned. It was true. He wished they had cropped the photos. "Why would your client say these were suicides, when the papers clearly labeled them homicides?"

The lawyer shrugged again. "Mr. Joral was merely offering a speculation."

Jack's hands clenched. The lawyer was sharper than he looked.

Kyle leaned down and placed his palms on the table. "Would your client be willing to take a lie detector test to prove that he had nothing to do with these cases?"

The P.D. shook his head, as if disappointed by this gambit. "Everybody knows how unreliable those are."

Joseph Joral nodded smugly. "That's *incontrusive* evidence."

"All right," Jack said. "How about a DNA test? If your client is innocent, I'm sure he'll have no objection." The NYPD farmed out its DNA testing to an independent lab, and he was still waiting to hear if they could recover any useful DNA from the two crime scene condoms. If they could, and Joral's sample matched, he'd have a much stronger case—certainly grounds to arrest and charge the suspect.

The P.D. scoffed. "Show me your court order, and my client will be glad to submit a sample."

Jack did his best to remain calm. "Would your client have any objection to our taking a look at his apartment?"

The lawyer rolled his eyes. "*Please*, Detective. You're just fishing. Now, do you have any evidence at all against my client? If not, I'm going to have to demand that he be released. *Immediately.*"

OUTSIDE IN THE HALL, Jack and Kyle held a quick pow-wow with the sergeant in charge of the precinct's detective squad.

"What do you think?" the man asked.

Jack spoke up first. "This could be our guy. I know we've gotta let him go, but I think we should put him under surveillance, in case he tries to go off and destroy any evidence. Or kill another girl."

Kyle added his agreement.

The sergeant crossed his arms. "I don't know. The guy certainly seems hinky, but he could just be some kind of nutjob, offering his opinion to make himself seem like a big shot." The detectives started to mutter in disagreement, but he held up a hand. "I'll tell you what: I'll assign a couple of people to tail him for a day or two, and we'll see if we can get anything more definite."

IT PAINED JACK DEEPLY to watch Joral skate out of the precinct house, but there was nothing he could do about it. It was one of the worst parts of the job: every once in a while you had to let a guilty person walk.

Temporarily, anyhow.

The two precinct detectives assigned to the surveillance

gave the man a few seconds' lead, then followed. Jack would have given his eyeteeth to be part of their team, but he'd already spent too much time face-to-face with the suspect in the interview room.

Instead, he reviewed Joral's file. Then he drove over to the suspect's residence, hoping that—warrantless—he might at least be able to peer in a window. As it turned out, though, Joral lived on the third floor of a brick row house. Next, Jack and a couple of local uniforms spent an hour driving around the nearby blocks, looking for Joral's car—maybe, he thought, they'd catch a break and find that it had fur seat covers. The DMV had the guy in a late-model Acura, but they couldn't find the plate out on the streets.

Jack sighed: he'd already put in a couple of hours of O.T. Frustrated and tired, he called Zhenya to see what she wanted to do about dinner.

"I am sorry," she said. "Tonight . . . I have made plans. We can have dinner tomorrow?"

He noted the hesitation in her voice but didn't feel that he had a right to question or press her. They weren't in a committed relationship yet—at least, they hadn't talked about it. "No problem" was all he said, but he hung up feeling vaguely uneasy.

Had she gotten another call from Balakutis? No, she hadn't sounded scared, and anyhow, she would have told him if she was. She had done so before. It occurred to him that maybe she had a date. They had known each other only a short time; he supposed she still had a right.

He shook his head. He was just chasing his own tail, getting paranoid over nothing. He pulled the morning's crumpled note from his pocket and read it again. *I will mis you all day.*

He wanted to kiss her something fierce.

He went over to Monsalvo's and had a beer. He didn't join in with the old-timers' banter, though; he felt too restless. He sat by himself at the end of the bar. His lower back ached and his shoulders felt very tight. Ah well, it had been a long day. A long *week*. It wasn't that he had too many investigations to deal with; he often had four or five open cases on his plate at one time. But there was something about these two. . . . He pictured Semyon Balakutis's menacing face and Joseph Joral's loutish one. Why was he letting them get under his skin?

It took him half an hour and two beers to remember the insight he'd gotten a couple of days ago, back there in the Cosmopolitan club: as a child, he had felt this same tightness in his back and his shoulders often—it was the tension his family had lived with every payday, waiting for his father to come home from the bars. He wondered what kind of parents Balakutis and Joral had grown up with—and he pondered why he had not turned out like them. Such angry and unhappy men . . .

Down on his hip, his cell phone buzzed. He flipped it open without checking the caller I.D.

"Hello?"

"Dad? Where are you? I've been waiting for twenty-five minutes!"

His son Ben's peevish voice.

Jack smacked himself on the forehead, remembering their dinner plan. He had stood the kid up—too busy thinking about work, as usual.

"I'm sorry," he said. "Are you still there? I swear, I'll be over in just a few minutes."

CHAPTER TWENTY-ONE

They met, as always, in a Greek coffee shop in Boerum Hill, a few blocks from Ben's apartment. Their meals together were infrequent and were often rather tense affairs, but the twenty-four—no, *twenty-five*-year-old—was Jack's only child.

He rushed in, breathless, and found Ben glowering in a back booth, with no food in front of him. "I'm sorry," he repeated. "I had to park four blocks away."

Ben was a gangly kid, taller than his old man, usually rather reserved and shy (he suffered from a case of acne). "You *forgot*," he accused, sounding like he had as a child, back when his parents had first divorced.

Not that Jack could blame him; it seemed that no matter how old you got, when you thought about your parents, you always felt like just a kid. . . . He held up his hands in apology and slid into the booth. "I told you: I'm really sorry. I'm in the middle of a couple of really tough cases right now. I'll make it up to you," he said. "Order anything you want: a steak, some lobster, whatever. We'll get a bottle of their finest champagne."

His son started to say something, something angry, but Jack quickly held up a hand. "Hold on—don't get pissed off. I remember: you don't eat meat. So order all the vegetables you want."

The waitress, a portly, kind-faced Polish woman who had been working there forever, glided over to take their order.

"I'll have a cheeseburger deluxe," Ben muttered, to his father's great surprise.

After the waitress walked away, Jack bit his lip. *Whatever*, as the kids were so fond of saying these days.

Ben looked sheepish. "I guess I fell off the wagon."

Jack smiled. The air between them felt a little less thick. He looked around: the coffee shop had not changed an iota in all the years they'd been coming here. The décor had a nautical theme: a deep-sea diver's helmet, a plastic lobster and crab trapped in a fishnet, a giant swordfish shellacked and mounted on a board. That reminded Jack of Daniel's fish company, but he blinked the thought away—he was going to forget about work for the next few minutes and concentrate all of his attention on his kid.

Ben was looking at him. "You jonesing for a cigarette?"

"Huh?"

His son nodded at Jack's hands, and he realized that he'd been drumming his fingers on the tabletop. He shook his head. "I haven't smoked since I left the hospital. Cold turkey."

"Really?"

"Really. Michelle helped me quit." As soon as the words were out of his mouth, he wished he could take them back. At first, his son had resented the new woman in Jack's life, who had suddenly appeared there in the hospital, after the shooting, but the two had bonded in the visitors' lounge, over watery coffee and sugary snacks.

Ben was silent for a moment. He picked up his fork and held it between fingers, as if testing its tensile strength. "Have you, ah . . . have you heard from her?"

"Nope," Jack said. At first, he avoided his son's eyes, but then he looked up. "Have you?"

"Why would she call *me*? After what happened between you two." The edge was back in Ben's voice. Jack loved the kid and wanted the boy to love him back, but it was often like trying to hug a cactus.

He thought for a moment. All he'd told his son at the time of the breakup was that he and Michelle had decided to part ways. He hadn't gone into any details—there was no reason to disappoint the kid any further.

"She was really nice," Ben added, with a mix of wistfulness and implication. *You screwed it up, just like you screwed things up with Mom.*

Jack frowned. "She was having an affair, if you want to know the truth."

His son made a pained face. "What did you do?"

Jack shrugged. "I didn't do anything. I watched her go."

Ben sighed, exasperated. "That's not what I meant. What did you *do* to make her leave?"

Jack stared at his son. He wanted to slap the self-righteous look clean off the kid's face. That's certainly what *his* father would have done.

He clasped his hands together tightly on the tabletop and looked away for a minute. He stared at the nearest wall, at the plastic lobster and the crab, locked in mortal combat. As the seconds ticked by, he began to feel ashamed about his anger. Christ, what was the point of being a father if you couldn't try to do things better than your own father had done?

He cleared his throat. "I, ah, I guess I never really told you much about my old man."

"You're changing the subject."

"Actually I'm not." Jack stared down at his own hands.

"My father was not a bad guy, really. He was very hardworking, down on the docks. He always supported us, even when times got bad—and they did get bad, back there in Red Hook. I know he loved us, in . . . in his own way. But he, ah, he had this drinking problem."

Ben stopped scowling and listened.

"Like, I said," Jack continued. "He was a decent enough guy, most of the time. But he had a lot of pressure on him, financial pressure, and when he drank, I guess he needed to blow off some steam." *Financial pressure,* he'd said, but it was certainly more than that. Who knew why the Old Man was so angry? Images rose in Jack's mind: his father hurling a full plate of food at the wall because it wasn't hot enough; his father's face, contorted with rage, as he pulled off his belt to give his sons a whipping. As no doubt his *own* father had once whipped him. And so it moved, on down through the generations, a poison in the blood.

He winced. "I'm kind of rambling here. What I want to say . . . what I want to say is that I know that I've never really talked to you enough. I know I've kind of held back a bit, as a father. I guess . . . I guess I was kind of afraid that I'd turn out like my old man." *And,* he didn't say, *I hope you'll turn out happier and less uptight than me.*

He fell silent. Ben didn't look at him; he just stared down at the table. Jack didn't know what his son had made of this rare personal speech, but then he saw Ben swallow several times, and he realized that the kid was fighting not to cry.

FORTY-FIVE MINUTES LATER, BACK in his car, Jack sat quietly for a minute, thinking about this latest get-together. After his big speech about the Old Man, he'd changed the subject and told the story of Uncle Leon. Ben had been amazed to hear about these dramatic family adventures, to learn that he'd had a long-dead great aunt. Then the conversation had finally turned to lighter things, to small talk that—for once—didn't feel too small. They had sat together, almost like friends, and then, when Ben stood up to leave, he had actually given his father a quick hug.

Jack started his engine and drove away from his son's neighborhood, with no destination in mind. He was feeling pretty good about his parental ability, for once.

Soon, though, he started thinking of Joseph Joral again, and the man's arrogant certainty that he had put one over on the NYPD, and then—on his own time—he drove back to the suspect's neighborhood and circled around again, searching for the car.

After another hour, he decided to drive to the bar where Shantel Williams had last been seen alive. Kyle had already gone out there in the afternoon to show Joral's mug shot to the bartender, who said he'd been too busy the night of the killing to remember individual faces, but the bar had been nearly empty during that daytime interview. Now Jack would show the picture to the nighttime clientele to see if anybody could put Joral and the murdered girl together.

CHAPTER TWENTY-TWO

Joseph Joral crouched on the roof of his Brooklyn house, brushed some sticky tar from his hands, and edged forward toward the street. The moon was only a quarter full, which was helpful, and big, dense sycamore trees rose up over the lip of the roof, also good: he was able to lie down, peer over the edge, and see the unmarked cop car parked about twenty yards down the block without worrying about getting spotted. Two men sat in the front seat, waiting for him to make a move.

He crouched low again and made his way past a series of chimneys and trapdoors, like the one he had climbed out of. Thank God these were connected row houses, 'cause he wasn't up for any movie-stuntman-jumping-roof-to-roof shit. At the end of the row, he eased down a rusty fire escape—praying that the damned thing wouldn't wrench away from the brick wall—and soon he was able to drop down into the last back garden, shinny over a low chain-link fence, and stroll unconcernedly out a back alley onto the other side of the block.

He walked a couple of streets away, leaving the dumb fucking cops sitting back there, and then he stopped under a streetlamp to inventory his clothes. He had to look sharp if he was gonna meet any bitches tonight. He frowned at a small tar smudge on the left knee of his pants, and he licked his fingertips and tried to wipe it away. The stain on his clothes made him think about another kind of stain, how his stepmother used to whip him with an electrical cord when she'd find evidence of his dreams on his bedsheet. He grimaced. Some drunk girl was not gonna be worried about some little smudge on his pants, right? He was a big guy, handsome, and his clothes were obviously expensive, and that's all she'd need to know.

He checked his pocket again to make sure that he hadn't forgotten the condoms. He hated the damn things; to have to fumble one on, right in the middle of a good groove. No wonder he'd had problems. But he couldn't do without them, not if he didn't want to get the goddamn crabs again—or worse.

He looked around for cops, then strutted off down the dark sidewalk. This time he wouldn't have any problems getting off; he could feel it.

He wished he had his car, but he'd lent it to a work buddy that morning; the guy needed to move all his shit out of his ex-girlfriend's apartment. Joseph felt naked without his ride. Yeah, it was just an Acura, but girls loved what he had done with it: the chrome rims, the purple light around the back license plate . . .

He needed to find some girl who liked to party. He wasn't gonna pay for it tonight. That had been a terrible idea, that other time. No wonder he couldn't get it up, with some street skank . . . Hell, women should pay *me*, he thought, that's how things *should* go. . . . A memory of laughter rose up in his head, and his fists clenched. *What's the matter, hotshot?*

He made a face. He needed a drink. A couple of drinks. He'd stop at the next bodega, buy a couple tall boys, get primed. Who needed to pay fancy bar prices for a goddamn beer?

He thought of the girl from the other night. He'd offered to buy her a drink, but she'd given him a cool brush-off. It wasn't as if he'd been the only white guy in the bar or anything, but there'd been something about the people in there, the upscale, trendy crowd, mixed black and white—they looked like young lawyers from some prime-time TV show. What was going on? This was *Brooklyn,* for chrissakes. *Fuck them.* The music had been loud, seventies funk mostly, and people were dancing in the back of the room and buzzing around the bar, and soon the joint had totally filled up. He'd sat on the end of a big sofa in a corner, scoping the place out—it had been so crowded that nobody had really paid him any mind, except some women giving him snobby goddamn looks. He'd watched the young chick at the bar, watched her drink nonstop, saw the friends she'd come with eventually split. By the time she finally left, she'd been all by her little lonesome, unsteady on her feet, and he watched her stumble out the door. He waited thirty seconds, then slipped out after her.

He caught up with her easily, a block away, because she had stopped; she was leaning against an iron fence.

"You all right?" he said.

"'m fine," she said, voice thick with alcohol.

"You look like you might need a little help getting home."

She shook her head emphatically. "What I *need* is another goddamn drink."

He recognized the type: no Off switch when it came to booze. He thought quickly: there was no chance of scoring any hard stuff at this late hour unless they went to another bar, but then maybe the bartender would see how drunk she was, offer to call a cab, which would screw up everything.

"How about a nice cold beer?" he said.

"Who *are* you?" she said, pushing herself, with effort, away from the fence. Her voice had a kind of a white Valley Girl thing going on, which Joseph found discordant. He wanted to sound more hip, but this girl wanted just the opposite. . . .

"I'm just another thirsty person," he replied. "Like you." He hoped she wouldn't pass out.

She shrugged. *"Whatever."*

"C'mon," he said. "I'm parked just around the corner, and we can go get us a six-pack."

He practically had to carry her to his car and pour her into the passenger seat, and then he drove them to the nearest deli, where he bought a six-pack of Coors.

"Ewww," she said, *"nasty,"* but he knew she'd drink it. He tried to think where he could take her, somewhere private, where he could get a bit more friendly. A block on, they came to a little community garden. He stopped the car and peered through the iron fence; saw the dense vegetation shining faintly silver in the moonlight. He could barely see the back, dark and shady as it was. Without really thinking about it, he reached into his right pants pocket and was reassured when his fingers closed on a short length of electrical cord. Just in case . . .

"Why don't we go sit down?" he said. "Make ourselves comfortable while we have a little drinkee . . ."

CHAPTER TWENTY-THREE

The Sandalwood Lounge was the name of the bar where Shantel Williams had bought her final cocktail.

Despite its rows of ornate brownstones, Jack had long known the neighborhood as a rather rough place, site of quite a few heroin spots and abandoned buildings. Now it was coming back, part of the general gentrification that seemed to be sweeping Brooklyn. The bar had red velvet drapes, fancy candles on the little tables, polished wood, plush sofas, and expensive specialty martinis. Back in the day, a "lounge" had meant something else, a place where tough street folk could smoke up a storm and drink cheap rail drinks and slowdance to Barry White. Now it seemed to be a place where sleek young people in expensive clothes could mingle and "network." Interestingly, the clientele was about half black, half white, and they seemed to be getting along with a minimum of tension.

Jack was a bit self-conscious in his work attire, and he wondered what Joseph Joral might have felt like in here. The man didn't exactly ooze sophistication.

Keeping things low-key, he caught the attention of the bartender, a tall, handsome young man with dreadlocks. First, he ordered a glass of seltzer; the heat outside had been powerful, even in the evening. Then he showed his badge and laid a photocopy of Joral's mug shot on the bar. "I'm investigating the homicide of a young woman who was in here the other night. You recognize this guy?"

The bartender looked down, then shook his head. "I've been off for the last week. I had an acting gig."

Jack showed the photo to the patrons along the bar. They seemed surprised to find a police detective in their midst, but they were relatively cooperative. Unfortunately, they didn't recognize the photo. Jack kept going, circling the room, showing it around, getting nowhere. The place was crowded, especially toward the back, where a knot of people were dancing to a seventies soul song. He moved along methodically, completing his canvass. A young couple thought they recognized Joral, "some white dude that was sitting on a sofa over there the other night," but they weren't sure enough to make a definite I.D.

Jack was making his way toward the farthest corner of the room, dodging dancers and cocktail waitresses, when he glanced toward the bar and saw a big white guy with a Caesar haircut. He blinked; it was impossible. If Joral was out and about, the surveillance team had been instructed to page him. The lighting was low, and the crowd was dense—maybe he was just imagining things. He threaded his way back across the little dance floor, frustrated by his slow progress.

Joseph Joral glanced over and spotted him, and then he was gone.

CHAPTER TWENTY-FOUR

"*Unbelievable,*" Jack said. "Un-freaking-believable." He scowled at the two detectives from the Seven-one, who were sitting in their squad room. "If I hadn't happened to be in that bar last night, we might have another murder on our hands."

The detectives remained silent. There was nothing they could say.

Their boss sighed. "Well, we're damned lucky the bastard showed up this morning."

That was something they could all agree on. Joseph Joral could have fled for good, and who knew if they would ever have found him again? But no, the cocky bastard had strolled in to work at 8 A.M. And what could they do? They couldn't arrest the man for sneaking outside of his own home the night before. They couldn't arrest him for visiting a neighborhood bar.

They made arrangements to double up on the surveillance and ensure that he wouldn't evade them again.

Then Jack and Kyle went back to recanvass the areas where the two women had been found, this time showing Joral's photo.

No hits.

The day went by. Joseph Joral spent his morning parking

and cleaning rental cars for his employer. At noon, he went to a local Kentucky Fried Chicken and had lunch by himself. He returned to work at 12:32, and he stayed there until 5:01 P.M. He took a bus home, stopping at a local deli for a six-pack and some toilet paper before he entered his residence. He stayed inside for forty-seven minutes. He did not leave the apartment through the roof or enter the back alley—this time the surveillance team made sure of that. At 6:12 he went out and ordered some food to go from a local McDonald's restaurant.

And that's what the latest report had to say by the time Jack got to Zhenya's apartment.

"I AM JUST GETTING home," she said, after he kissed her in her foyer, under the chandelier. "Is no food here. Can we go to market?"

He shrugged. "Sure. Why not?" They didn't go out to eat at local restaurants, but surely a little shopping expedition would look innocent enough.

She gathered her purse and her keys and they set out. An old woman, back twisted with scoliosis, was in the elevator when they got on, so Jack and Zhenya just stood in silence, not too close to each other. As they walked out through the lobby, he glanced at their reflection in a big wall-length mirror. They didn't look like much of a couple. When they walked out into the evening heat and turned down a narrow side street toward Brighton Beach Avenue, he wondered how she would react if he stopped and kissed her. They walked beside a huge block-long brick apartment building.

"How was your day?" Jack asked, when what he really wanted to know was what she'd been doing the previous night. But he wasn't going to play detective now that he was off duty, talking to someone he cared about.

"Busy," she replied.

"That's good, I guess. . . ."

They walked on, making only small talk as they turned onto the busy avenue, with its subway trains shuttling overhead on the elevated line, its colorful street stalls and sidewalks thronged with shoppers. It was the kind of old-fashioned neighborhood where people shopped each day for the dinner they would cook that night.

As Jack walked along, next to Zhenya but not touching her, he couldn't help thinking how strange relationships were: you had to open up and put your trust in someone else, and that started to feel like something solid and substantial, but then some wind moved the curtains and you saw behind them: you realized that what you were counting on was just a fragile, tenuous, utterly voluntary agreement floating in the air between two people. At any moment, either one of them could snatch it back.

Zhenya took him to a local food market. Jack had heard about the shortages of the U.S.S.R., the endless lines and empty shelves. This place was a hungry Soviet's wet dream. To the left stood display cases full of raw, smoked, and grilled fish. To the right, steaks, roasts, salamis, sausages . . . Deeper into the market, which turned out to be big and mazelike, more counters offered freshly baked bread, dumplings, potato pancakes, pickled salads, cheeses, stuffed chicken breasts. Even the aisles were jammed with mounds of canned goods. While Zhenya was ordering something from the bakery, Jack picked up a can: the label was covered in Cyrillic writing and bore a picture of a strange artichoke-like vegetable he couldn't even recognize. Shoppers called out orders in Russian to the hairnetted women behind the counters, who wore white outfits like lab coats. Jack felt overwhelmed by the foreign language, the hubbub, his sense of being an interloper. He imagined that these people felt the same way when they ventured out into the rest of America—that must be why they clustered together so.

He was staring at another unfamiliar canned product when he felt a tug on his shoulder.

"Jackie?"

He turned to find a little old man staring up at him.

"How are you, Uncle Leon?"

The old man shrugged. "I can't complain. Well, I *can* complain, but it doesn't do any good."

"What are you buying there?"

Leon lifted a couple of dark brown bottles. "Russian beer. Tastes like goat piss. But not worse than your American 'light beer.' The Germans make good beer, but will I buy it?" He made a face. "Never!"

Zhenya turned away from the bakery counter and rejoined Jack.

The old man's bushy eyebrows went up.

"Uncle Leon, this is Zhenya," Jack said. "She's . . . a friend."

Leon took off his sporty cap, bowed, and kissed Zhenya's hand. *Here we go*, Jack thought.

"What a beautiful girl you are," Leon said, turning up the charm to full wattage. "You remind me of the springtimes of my youth."

Jack had to break down and grin at that one.

"Are you in a rush?" Leon said. "Can I buy you young people a nice cup tea?"

Jack stood there, uncertain, but Zhenya smiled, clearly taken by the old man. "Of course," she said. "It is a pleasure."

A stairway rose up to a second level, where Leon led them through a showroom piled with deluxe candies and chocolate assortments, on to the café. He bought them tea.

They began to chat, and soon Zhenya and Leon slipped into Russian. They had an animated little conversation while Jack looked on, feeling like a fifth wheel. He was almost jealous of the old man.

Zhenya excused herself to go to the bathroom.

Leon leaned forward. "*So*—who is this lovely girl?"

Jack snorted. "She's a woman, Leon. We don't say 'girl' anymore."

Leon rolled his eyes. "Please. You get to my age, and a girl is any female below sixty. You know her how?"

Jack restrained a wince. "We met through a friend."

Leon nodded. "Very nice. You going to marry this one?"

Jack laughed. "For chrissakes—I just met her!"

His uncle shrugged. "Let me tell you, my friend: you could do a lot worse. . . . This one's a keeper."

Despite himself, Jack was pleased. He had probably had enough of marriage, but still . . . pleased.

Zhenya returned, they finished their tea, they bid Leon farewell. The old man insisted on kissing Zhenya's hand again— his signature move.

DINNER WAS TOUGH FOR Jack. Zhenya heated up some prepared food from the market, some salmon and very gar- licky roasted potatoes and broccoli, and they took their plates out on the balcony and watched the sun set. Every few min- utes Jack took out his cell phone, checking to see if the Joral surveillance team might have called, but his mind wasn't re- ally on the case.

He thought of how uncomfortable he had felt the first couple of times he had been in Zhenya's apartment, and then how suddenly things had changed, opened up, grown intimate. For a few evenings he had felt profoundly comfortable here, but now things seemed to have somehow regressed a little, and that hurt. Love was a fishhook: the more you struggled, the deeper it set.

Zhenya went into the kitchen to prepare some dessert. When she returned, Jack announced that he had to leave shortly, to go deal with a work situation.

She looked surprised and a little hurt.

He didn't go back to work, though—he just turned toward home. As he drove there, he felt like a fool. He had been jealous and wanted to teach her a little lesson, to show her that he still had his independence, but he had succeeded only in robbing both of them of another shared night.

BEFORE HE HIT THE sack, he called one of the detectives on the surveillance team. A slow evening: their suspect had gone to a local video store, rented a couple of movies, and returned to his apartment.

Lying in bed, Jack tried to watch *The Tonight Show,* but he couldn't stop thinking about Joseph Joral and about Zhenya Lelo. After a while, he turned off the lights. Surprisingly, he was asleep within minutes.

He was in some kind of dark warehouse, with narrow, constricting hallways. He was looking for something, or someone, but he didn't know what. He climbed a couple of flights of stairs, then walked down another hall, stopping to peer into empty rooms that looked like abandoned classrooms. He opened several doors— offices—and then he opened another one: a janitor's closet. He gasped—a young woman was hanging by her neck over the big metal sink, twisting slowly, and as her body swung around he saw that it was Zhenya.

He shot upright, breathing heavily. Over the years, he had

learned not to bring the job home, even in his dreams, but every once in a while . . . He lay back and tried to calm his heart rate, but he was thinking of Joseph Joral again, hoping the creep was still in his apartment, far from any potential victims.

JACK WOKE LATE, SORE and cranky from another bad night's sleep. He didn't have time to make himself breakfast; he stopped off at a deli on the way to work and picked up a cup of coffee and a fried egg on a bagel. He settled back into his car and was trying to eat the sandwich without dripping egg yolk on his tie when his cell phone trilled. A few seconds later he hung up, stuck his rotating beacon on the dash, and zoomed off toward Eastern Parkway.

Nine minutes later, after running several red lights, he careered onto Eastern Parkway and raced past the giant old classical façade of the Brooklyn Museum. At the next corner, he veered right. A block and a half down, on a side street outside the Brooklyn Botanic Garden, he spotted a Traffic Enforcement vehicle double-parked in the street. He pulled up behind it, got out, and jogged up to the driver's window. The agent, a plump little woman with marcelled hair, nodded toward a silver car parked across the street.

"There you go," she said matter-of-factly.

Jack wanted to kiss her. "You're gonna get a gold medal for this," he said.

She rolled her eyes. "I'd settle for a vacation day."

Jack approached Joseph Joral's car slowly. He didn't have any legal authority to search the trunk or to get the doors opened, but that didn't mean he couldn't peer in the goddamn windows. From the outside, from thirty feet away, there was nothing suspicious about the car, but after he walked just a few feet closer, his face opened up in a big smile and he sang himself a little song: *Boom, boom, boom, another one bites the dust.* . . .

A Playboy air freshener hung from the rearview mirror.

And the steering wheel was wrapped in luxurious brown fur.

CHAPTER TWENTY-FIVE

It took the rest of the day to get a search warrant, open the car, run the steering wheel cover down to the lab, and get the results, but Joseph Joral was back at the Seven-one Precinct House by 6 P.M.

Jack, Kyle, and the sergeant held another powwow out in the squad room. They'd have to wait several days for DNA testing of the fur but were confident that the results would tie Joral to both crime scenes. The problem was that this was all the new evidence might accomplish—it wouldn't prove that he had actually committed either murder.

To accomplish that goal, the detectives had two different tools. The first was simply their skill at drawing out a confession. The second was more technical: they would provide Joseph Joral with a beverage at the start of the interview, whether he asked for one or not. At the end of the interview, after he abandoned the container, they'd have it tested for DNA. (The courts had ruled that such "surreptitiously sampled" material—discarded coffee cups, cigarette butts, even spit—was legally up for grabs, with no need for a court order.) The problem was that the results on the two condoms had still not come in. If they didn't provide any analyzable DNA, this whole line of inquiry would be shot.

Before Joral's lawyer showed up, Jack and Kyle joined their suspect in the little interview room while the sergeant and some other precinct detectives looked on via closed-circuit TV. The two lead detectives came in sipping from cans of Coke. They "casually" set a fresh can down before their suspect and did their best to distract him with small talk. Joral wouldn't answer any questions. "I want my goddamn lawyer" is all he'd say. The detectives shrugged, left the room, and then watched on the monitor, waiting to see if their suspect would open the soda.

After a minute or two, Joral started looking very bored. He got up and paced around, but the room was so small that he soon gave up and sat again. After another minute, he picked up his Coke can.

Next door, the detectives made pumping motions with their fists. "Yessss!" Kyle said.

But Joral just rolled the can between his palms for a few seconds. Then he set it down. He got up and paced again, waiting for his lawyer.

The detectives groaned. It was like watching a baseball game. Two outs, bottom of the ninth . . .

Finally, Joral picked up the can again, cracked it open, and took a couple of sips.

Five minutes later, his lawyer arrived. "What the hell is going on?" he said to the detectives as they followed him into the interview room. "What grounds do you have for bothering my client again?"

Jack and Kyle just sat calmly on the other side of the table, their chairs squeaking on the old linoleum as they moved as close as possible to their prime suspect.

"We'll get to that in a minute," Jack said. "First we have

a few questions for Mr. Joral here. We'd like to know where you were on the evenings of August sixteen, seventeen, and twenty-one."

The lawyer shook his head. "My client has already answered those questions, Detective."

Jack stared at Joral. "You're sticking by your story?"

"You're damn right he is," the lawyer replied.

"Is that what you say, Joseph?"

Joral nodded. "Damn straight."

Jack opened a manila folder. "Were you at the Sandalwood Lounge at any point on the evening of August twenty-one?"

The lawyer started to say something, but Jack held up a hand. "Joseph?"

Joral stared at him, wary.

Things were starting to get interesting. If the man stuck by his original alibi, then he could be caught out in a lie here. If he said that he *had* been at the bar, he'd be placing himself at the scene of Shantel Williams's last known public appearance.

Joral opted for the lie. "I was home, man. Watching *Law and Order.*"

The lawyer sat up in his seat. "Now, are you going to—"

Jack held up a hand again. "One minute. Now, Joseph: was your car, a 2000 Acura with license plate number GFC-237, in your possession on the evenings of August sixteen, seventeen, and twenty-one?"

Joral frowned. "What do you mean?"

"I mean, did you lend it to anyone? Or maybe it was in the shop?"

He watched Joral mull over this new question; another opportunity to get trapped in a lie. He could practically see the gears turning in the perp's head. If he said that it was in his possession, it might somehow tie him to the murders. If he said that it wasn't, he'd be stuck trying to back up another lie.

Jack pressed him. "Which was it?"

Joral scowled. "I don't know what you mean by 'possession.' I park my car on the damn street. Anybody could'a got hold of it."

"Are you saying it might have been stolen?"

Joral was looking sickly now. If he lied and said it was, the next question would be why he hadn't reported the theft. Jack looked on with satisfaction: it was like watching a checkers champion suddenly forced to figure out future moves in chess.

"Nobody said nuthin' about it bein' stolen."

"All right." Jack nodded. "So your car was in your possession all three of those nights."

The lawyer drew himself up. "You know what, Detective? It sounds to me like you're just on another fishing expedition here. Once again, if you don't have any evidence against my client, I'm going to have to demand that he be released immediately."

Jack sat back and smiled. "But that's the thing, Counselor. We *do* have evidence." He reached into the manila envelope and pulled out a Polaroid of Joral's fur-wrapped steering wheel. "We found a certain type of animal fur at both crime scenes, and it matches what we found today in your client's car. DNA doesn't lie."

The lawyer crossed his arms. "There's no way you would have had time to conduct a DNA test."

"You're right," Jack admitted. "But a preliminary forensic exam indicates that the fur is the same, and we'll get the DNA results soon. What would you like to bet that we don't get a match?"

"You can't do a DNA test on no goddamn animal," Joral muttered.

Jack smiled. "Why not? Animals have DNA, just like we do. And it's just as traceable. Interesting fact, huh? Maybe you should've been watching some nature TV."

After all this talk of DNA the lawyer's eyes alighted on his client's soda can. He turned to his client. "Say, Joseph, are you finished with your soda?"

Joral nodded.

"Would you mind if I have the can?"

Joral looked puzzled. "Why?"

"I collect them," his lawyer answered, smirking to let the detectives know that he was on to their ruse.

"Help yourself," his client said. The P.D. picked up the can and tucked it into his briefcase—now *he* was in legal possession of it.

Jack nodded at the man. "*Your point*, Counselor."

The lawyer grinned.

Joral looked on, mystified.

Jack shrugged. "The match on the fur will do. It's over, Joey." He knew that he needed to regain the power in the interview, not to mention distract the lawyer. It would only take a minute for the man and his client to realize that the fur was not evidence of murder. Jack leaned toward his suspect. "Why don't you just tell us why you did it? It'll make things easier for you if you cooperate."

The public defender held up a hand. "Not so fast, Detective. All this evidence might establish is that my client could have been at these scenes. You haven't presented anything that directly implicates him in any crimes."

Kyle spoke up angrily. "We know he did them, and I'm sure a jury will agree."

The public defender kept his cool. He stood up. "If you think you have what you need to prosecute my client, then go right ahead and arrest him. Otherwise, let's put an end to all this dancing around."

He nodded at Joral, who started to stand up.

Jack saw his case walking out the door again. He spoke up quickly. "Tell me something, Joey: do you consider yourself good in bed?"

The lawyer's eyes went wide. "What the hell do you think you're doing?"

Joral scowled. "Why you asking, cop? You some kinda fag?"

Jack tapped his manila folder. "I was rereading LaTanya Davidson's complaint. She said that when she wanted to have sex with you, you couldn't perform. Is that right, Joey?" He didn't feel good about teasing anybody about their sexual difficulties, but given the circumstances . . .

The precinct was air-conditioned, but not much of that cool air made it into the little interview room. Of course, Joseph Joral might have had other reasons for starting to sweat.

"This interview is over," the lawyer said, but his client wasn't done.

"That's a goddamn lie! I didn't *wanna* have sex with her. She was too skanky."

The man's hatred of women was practically pouring out of him, and Jack ached to take him down.

"Is that so?" he tapped the folder again. "Here's an interesting little fact from our crime scenes: at both of them, we found dry, empty condoms lying on the ground." He turned to Kyle. "What does that suggest to you, partner?"

Kyle picked up on the last-ditch strategy. He leaned forward and sneered. "We know why you killed those girls, Joey. You were ashamed 'cause you can't get it up."

Joral jumped to his feet. His lawyer put a hand on his client's arm, but it was too late.

"That's a lie, motherfucker! I banged *both* those stupid bitches. And they only got what they had comin'."

The lawyer slumped back and put a hand over his eyes.

BACK OUT IN THE squad room, Kyle traded high fives with the other cops. "Beautiful!" said one. "Schweet!" crowed another.

Jack just shrugged. "Like shooting ducks in a barrel." He was pleased, though. Talk about job satisfaction: this was what it was all about. They had caught the killer of two young women and likely saved others from a similar fate.

Sometimes it was just this simple: the Good Guys won.

ON A NORMAL NIGHT, Smith Street made Jack Leightner feel severely out of place. He couldn't believe how this humble little thoroughfare from his childhood was now swarming with twentysomething hipsters who thought nothing of dropping nine bucks on a trendy mojito or saketini.

Tonight he was feeling a bit old and square, but those feelings were balanced by the situation: he was out for a celebratory dinner with a beautiful young woman. It was funny: Zhenya didn't really fit in here either. Jack didn't know anything about fashion, but he knew that his date didn't blend in with the casually chic women roving these crowded sidewalks. She had dressed as if she were going to some expensive but rather garish 1940s Manhattan nightclub: she tottered along on impossibly high-heeled shoes, wore fishnet stockings, and sported a skintight evening dress. She looked—Jack was ashamed of the thought—kind of like a high-priced escort. Even so, she was so sincere in her excitement about this rare night out that she somehow pulled it off. Young hipsters dressed all in black swiveled around as she walked by; she was like a brightly plumed bird passing through a flock of crows.

The setting was so foreign to both of them that they didn't have to worry about bumping into Russian friends who might disapprove of the young widow, or cop friends who might wonder what he was doing socializing with a victim's widow. The restaurant choices were dazzling: French bistros, Japanese sushi, tapas bars, Peruvian, Jamaican, Korean . . . They settled on a candlelit Argentinean restaurant with tables out on the sidewalk and a live salsa band inside. After a couple of cocktails, they took to the crowded dance floor; neither of them really knew how to do Latin dancing, but they had a great time pretending.

For most of the evening Jack was able to stay in the moment and enjoy himself, but by the time they had finished their dinner—a steak for him, some sea bass for her—his mind had wandered back to the other evening, when Zhenya had suddenly declared herself too busy to see him. He sat pensive, stirring his coffee, a powerful, muddy brew.

Zhenya watched him for a minute. "What you are thinking, Mr. Thinker?"

He tried to smile but failed. Ah, what the hell, why not just bring it out in the open and be done with it?

"Listen," he said, "I know it's really none of my business, but the, ah, the other evening, when you said you had 'plans' . . . I was just wondering what you meant by that?"

She stared at him and said nothing for a moment. Jack sank into a horrible flashback, the moment when, in another New York restaurant, he had proposed to his last girlfriend, and she had stared at him just like this, then burst into tears and announced that she was having an affair.

But Zhenya just shrugged. "I had dinner with an old friend who visits New York."

Jack winced. "I just . . . I thought maybe you had a date or something."

Her eyes widened, and he was afraid she was going to get angry, but she shook her head calmly. "I promise you, on my mother's grave: I did not have a date." She reached out, laid a hand on his, and grinned. "You were zhealous? You know what?"

He smiled, hesitantly but more genuinely this time. "What?"

"When you are jealous, Zhack Leightner, you are looking very cute."

CHAPTER TWENTY-SIX

Jack snorted when he saw the tabloid headline the next morning: NYPD K.O.S RACIST KILLER.

The story was fundamentally wrong: Joseph Joral actually had a thing for black women, and he was clearly into hip-hop style. (It was *women* he had a problem with.) Jack couldn't blame the paper, though—they were just running with the Deputy Commissioner of Public Information's official spin on the story. The Department was trying to score a few points with the black community. Jack shrugged: the brass and the press could do whatever they wanted with Joral's story; he was just glad that he had gotten another killer off the city's streets. *And*, he reflected, still feeling a good buzz from the previous day's events, if he and his colleagues could take down one arrogant creep, surely they could take down another. It was Semyon Balakutis's turn.

He found Linda Vargas in the task force's file room, pouring herself a cup of coffee.

She grinned. "I heard about your win yesterday. Nice job."

He waved the compliment away. "The guy basically hung himself. If you'll excuse the expression." He poured himself a cup, then put a new filter in the machine. "Hey, what's going on with the Lelo case? Anything new?"

Vargas frowned. "Still no witnesses. No forensic evidence. I would kill for a little something exotic here. Maybe a little beaver fur . . ." She shook her head. "If Balakutis is our man, he sure pulled off a slick little murder."

Back out in the squad room, Jack reclined in his desk chair, rotating slowly from side to side. All over the room, his team-mates were doing phone interviews, reading files, scanning computer screens. He scratched his cheek. The Lelo case wasn't his, officially, but that didn't mean he couldn't continue to help out. . . . After a minute, he sat up straight and picked up the phone. For lack of a better move, he figured he'd take another run at Andrei Goguniv, Daniel's fish company manager.

Someone picked up, but it wasn't Goguniv.

"Andrei?" The voice continued in rapid Russian, sounding worried.

"No," Jack said. "I want to *speak* to Andrei. Is he there?"

"Not here." The other person hung up.

Jack called his contact in the fish market security office.

"No prob—I'll go over there and check on it."

A few minutes later, the man called back. "I just went up to the Black Sea office. Goguniv wasn't there. I had a hard time finding anyone who could speak any English, but it seems that the guy didn't show up for work today."

"Is he married or anything?"

"I got his wife's name," the security officer said. "I just called: it turns out he didn't come home last night either."

"And she didn't tell anybody?"

"You know how it is with these people: they think we're all KGB or somethin'."

As soon as he got off the phone, Jack called across the room to Linda Vargas. "You busy?"

She set down a file folder she'd been reading. "Why?"

"I think we should take a little ride."

ANDREI GOGUNIV'S BENSONHURST DOMICILE was a modest brick home, with a white wrought-iron fence surrounding a tiny concrete front yard. An aluminum awning provided a little shade over the front door, and a small American flag, extended on a pole from a second-story window, drooped in the summer heat.

Goguniv's wife, Galina, was a plump little blonde. She looked as if she hadn't slept at all in the past twenty-four hours. She kept jumping up to pace around her small living room, with its big old TV and plastic-upholstered furniture. "He goes to work yesterday, as usual," she said in a thick Russian accent. "Every day, he comes home at eleven A.M.—you know, he works in the night at the market. But yesterday, he doesn't come. One o'clock, two o'clock, he doesn't come."

Linda Vargas sat perched on the edge of an armchair, a sympathetic expression on her face. "Did he call you?"

The wife shook her head. "No. Is not like him. If he is only an half hour late, he will call me. He is good husband."

"Has he ever stayed out all night like this?" Vargas asked. Jack knew where she was heading—maybe the man had a girlfriend stashed away somewhere.

Galina shook her head. "Never. For twenty years we is married, and we is together every night."

"Do you have any idea where he might have gone?"

The woman sank down into the sofa and put a hand over her eyes. "I don't know. I don't know." She began to cry.

Vargas pressed on. "I'm sorry, Mrs. Goguniv, but we need

more information. The, uh, things that happened to his hand . . . what did he tell you about that?"

Galina wiped her eyes. "He says was 'accidents,' but I don't believe. One time, okay—is dangerous job, with saws and hooks . . . But two times?"

"Was he acting differently than usual, around the time of these incidents?"

Galina chewed her lower lip. "He was very . . . how you say? Not paying attention."

"Preoccupied?" Jack said. "Nervous?" He felt sorry for the poor woman.

She nodded. "Yes. *Nervous.* Something is not good at work, but he is not telling me. And now I am afraid."

Linda Vargas reached into her purse and pulled out a photo: Semyon Balakutis. "Do you recognize this man?"

Galina looked at it without any sign of recognition. "Who is he?"

Vargas tucked the picture away. "Don't worry about it. And don't worry: we'll find your husband."

Jack turned away. He guessed that they would indeed find Andrei Goguniv, but he wouldn't be willing to bet that the man would be alive.

He and his colleague headed over to the Fulton Fish Market in the company of an NYPD Russian translator. They interviewed Goguniv's coworkers at the fish market and showed Balakutis's picture around. Several of the big men frowned at the picture, but they wouldn't admit that they recognized Balakutis. Someone at a different company one aisle over finally made a positive I.D., but he couldn't place the man at the scene the previous day—he said only that he was sure that he'd seen him on a couple of occasions in the past month.

The two detectives spent the rest of the day tracking

down friends and business contacts of Andrei Goguniv, without making any progress as to his current whereabouts, and then they headed back to the task force office.

Jack would have liked to go deep into overtime with the case; as usual, though, his boss was tight with the squad budget. Jack shrugged: he knew that the search for Goguniv had spread out over the NYPD's various networks, and he would have to put some trust in the efforts of his colleagues. He punched out and headed down to the outdoor parking lot.

His car was sweltering. He cranked the air con, then called Zhenya; she lived just a mile and a half away. The call went straight to voice mail. He thought of dropping by Monsalvo's for a quick beer or of paying a visit to Mr. Gardner, but both options seemed too flat—they reminded him of how barren his social life had been before he met Zhenya.

He sat there for a moment, tapping his fingers on the steering wheel, and then he threw the car into Drive.

A few minutes later, he stood in the entranceway of Zhenya's building, pressing the buzzer for her apartment, but there was no response. He waited a few seconds, staring in at the chrome and potted-plant-filled lobby, and then he buzzed again. Nothing.

He walked back out to his car. He could see a blue strip of ocean framed by buildings down at the end of the block, and he smelled the thick, salty sea air. He considered going for a stroll on the boardwalk, but even in the late afternoon the temperature was still too high, the sun too bright.

He got back in his car, and then he consulted a folder he had stuffed into the glove compartment.

THE OLD-SCHOOL ITALIAN MAFIOSI took pains to live invisibly. You might never know that the potbellied geezer hosing down his old Cadillac in the driveway of a Bay Ridge bungalow was the capo of one of New York's foremost crime families. They hid their money from the IRS and carried on quietly in the hearts of their old neighborhoods, like tumors.

Semyon Balakutis had chosen a much less subtle home base. A couple of miles from Brighton Beach, along the coast past Sheepshead Bay and Marine Park, Mill Basin had once been an unassuming little Brooklyn neighborhood, but recent sources of New Money—stock market booms? less licit inflows of cash?—had hit it like an overdose of steroids. The fancy cars along the streets spoke of the recent infusion of wealth, but the homes shouted it. Like lottery winners who couldn't quite give up their day jobs, the residents had kept their small houses, only they'd tried to transform them into mansions. As Jack drove slowly along, he had to dodge contractors' vans parked along the narrow streets; they were jamming white columns and *Gone with the Wind*–style staircases onto the front of little brick homes, planting torchlights and statues of lions beside the short driveways, replacing tiny lawns with marble patios.

As he neared Balakutis's house, he started to have doubts about his plans for a subtle recon. The neighborhood was almost entirely residential, a small circular piece of land almost surrounded by an ocean inlet; if you weren't a resident or a contractor, there was little reason to be here.

Balakutis, as it turned out, lived on the far rim of the circle. Jacked glanced at the man's residence as he drove by; it was more modern than most of the others. The place was made of gray marble and brown-tinted glass; all the shades were drawn, and it looked more like a bunker than a house. Jack drove around the block and then coasted to the curb about twenty yards away. He knew Balakutis was home because he had called the number on the way over, then hung up when he heard the man's voice.

He turned off the engine. No more air conditioning—a blast of hot air rushed in as he rolled down the window and sat back to watch. He pictured Semyon Balakutis offering him and Linda Vargas a doughnut, smashing a glass of red wine, burying a hook in poor Andrei Goguniv's shaking hand.

Soon he regretted the impulsive nature of today's surveillance. Normally, he would have set himself up with plenty of water, not to mention a Tupperware container to pee into. (He had learned very early in his career that peeing into a narrow-necked bottle was not the easiest thing to do.)

After forty-five minutes, he was starting to question what he hoped to get out of this visit. He wanted to reconnect with his suspect, to get a better feeling for the man's life, but he wasn't learning much now, just staring at the blank picture window of the man's house.

After an hour, the heat was getting to him—he felt parched.

After an hour and fifteen minutes, the front door to Semyon Balakutis's house slowly opened.

Out came a small boy, carrying something on a tray. Moving slowly, with great concentration, the kid—towheaded, maybe six or seven years old—marched slowly along the sidewalk until he was standing right outside Jack's window. Holding up a glass of ice water.

"My father says that maybe the detective"—he squinted, as if struggling to remember a line in a school play—"maybe the detective would like a nice cold drink."

Jack scowled at the opaque window in front of Balakutis's house, then turned back to the boy. "No thanks." He turned on his engine and drove away.

He wondered how smug Semyon Balakutis would look when he was being transported to a prison upstate.

AT A RED LIGHT on Avenue U, he pulled over and gave Zhenya's number another try. Straight to voice mail. Jack cursed under his breath, then headed back into the traffic.

Instead of making a right on Coney Island Avenue and heading home, though, he continued on to Brighton Beach. He didn't drive to Zhenya's building again—lord knows, he didn't want to become some sort of stalker—but he pulled up in front of his uncle Leon's building. Five minutes later they were sitting at a restaurant on the Brighton boardwalk.

The place had a big outdoor seating area, with green carpeting and lavender tablecloths. (Daniel Lelo had brought Jack here during their first joint visit to the neighborhood.) At the next table over sat two women in bright velour sweat suits; one wore orange lipstick to match her outfit. They spoke in Russian, as did most of the other patrons.

The waiter wore a short tux and a long mustache and carried himself like a retired cavalry officer. He took Jack and Leon's order: big goblets of ice-cold beer, some pickles, a heap of sautéed mushrooms, and a plate of *pelmeni*, served with fried onions and sour cream. Jack recognized the little dumplings— they were what Zhenya had brought her husband, back in the hospital. He frowned, remembering.

"You all right?" said Leon. "Hey, you want I should tell you a good joke?"

Jack nodded; he could use the distraction.

Leon took a sip of his beer. The goblet was almost the size of his head. "Okay," he said. "A chicken and an egg are lying in bed together. The chicken is smoking. '*Well*,' says the egg. 'I guess that answers *that* question." He grinned. "You like?"

Jack laughed; it felt good after such a tense and busy week. He watched the passersby strolling along the boardwalk. It was a cultural thing: the residents of Brighton Beach turned out in droves for an early evening ocean promenade. He nodded toward the scene. "Are these people mostly from Russia, or the other republics?"

Leon frowned. "How is it that you work so close to here but know so little about them?"

Jack threw his hands wide. "Come on—this is Brooklyn. We've got Dominicans, Senegalese, Lithuanians. . . . Nobody can know everybody."

Leon snorted. "These are not 'everybody'—they're your own people."

Jack sighed. *Your own people*—it sounded like such a burden. "I don't know . . . they just seem *rude*."

Leon looked out at the boardwalk parade. "You need to understand something: Brighton Beach is a time machine. Many of these people came here in the late seventies, in the time of Brezhnev, before *glasnost*. They're still stuck there. In the Old Country they had to push and shove to get the last loaf of bread, and they always had to worry about who might be spying on them. Don't expect an older Russian to smile at you on the street—many of them are still afraid to look up."

Jack ran a finger through the condensation that had gathered on his beer goblet. "My father," he said gingerly, since this was always a sore topic with his uncle, "just wanted us to be Americans."

Leon looked out to sea. "I can't blame him. We came to this country when he was young. He wanted to fit in with the people over here."

Jack looked down at the table. "Why do you think he turned out so angry?"

"If you try to forget too much, it goes sour inside." Leon shrugged. "But who knows? There is history, and there is what we are. Maybe it was just his nature."

"When I was a kid, I used to ask him about where we came from, but he would never talk about it."

Leon's eyes lit up. "Do you know the one about the woman from Brighton Beach who moves to Connecticut?"

Jack shook his head.

"She's Jewish, but her big dream is to join the country club. So she changes her last name, loses the Brooklyn accent, buys fancy new clothes. One day she finds herself sitting at a fine luncheon with a hundred Waspy ladies. All of a sudden, a waiter spills some hot soup in her lap. She jumps up and shouts 'Oy vey!' Then she looks around and says, 'Whatever that means . . . '"

A COUPLE OF HOURS later, Jack was sitting on his sofa at home, bored out of his mind with the usual round of "reality" TV shows. He clicked off the set and sat there in the gathering dark, wondering what might have happened to Andrei Goguniv.

CHAPTER TWENTY-SEVEN

"I tried calling you yesterday afternoon," Jack said.

They were out on Zhenya's balcony. She was bent over the little glass side table; she was gluing a handle back on a broken teacup. She didn't look up. "Perheps I was leaving my phone in my bag. When the TV is on, at times I do not hear it."

Jack frowned. "You were home yesterday afternoon?"

She nodded but didn't look up. She worked on her teacup.

Jack squinted toward the beach below. He didn't mention that he had stopped by and buzzed her apartment. He knew how loud the buzzer was, from when their takeout food deliveries came, and he knew that it was audible with the TV on. . . .

He noticed that she looked tired, with circles under her eyes—maybe he wasn't the only one who'd had trouble sleeping recently. And she seemed jittery today; one of her bare feet tapped up and down on the concrete floor of the balcony.

He thought of Andrei Goguniv. *Nervous.*

He frowned. "You haven't heard from Semyon Balakutis, have you?"

She didn't look at him, just squinted down at her teacup.

"I mean," he continued, "you'd tell me if he was bothering me, right?"

She nodded but didn't look up.

He felt a quick stab of irritation. *These goddamn Russians, playing it so close to the vest...* He shook his head, thought of what his uncle would say to him. *Your people.*

"I was thinking," he said. "Maybe we could have dinner in Manhattan tomorrow night." He wanted to be with her during every free moment. It wasn't just that he enjoyed her company—he wanted to be around in case Semyon Balakutis made any more of his threats. He thought of Goguniv again; maybe they weren't just threats.

Zhenya chewed her bottom lip, then looked up. "I must see my girlfriend Mika tomorrow night. But we can have dinner the next night, okay?"

He couldn't help noticing that her eyes had slipped to the left just before her answer, and he cursed Linda Vargas and her scientific interview techniques.

He felt a sudden chill. Maybe this wasn't about Balakutis at all. He remembered how stupidly and happily he'd spent his time with Michelle—right up to the moment when she'd announced she was having an affair. He scowled. Christ, Daniel had been dead only a short time. It was weird enough that Zhenya was dating Jack now; was it possible she was seeing someone else too?

She blew on the teacup to help the glue dry. Then she set it down, scooted out of her chair, and came around and put her arms around him. She gave him a delicious warm kiss on the cheek.

He winced. He didn't know whether he was coming or going.

"IT'S NOT JUST THE Lelo murder," he told Detective Sergeant Stephen Tanney. "We're also trying to find out what the hell happened to Andrei Goguniv."

His boss was young, in his thirties, with a full head of curly hair and a carefully trimmed mustache. His trademark was playing it safe and not upsetting the brass down at One Police Plaza. "You know how much manpower it takes to conduct a good surveillance. I'm just not seeing any real evidence here. What have we got on this guy? You have one witness, who didn't see anything directly related to the homicide. Did she even claim that Balakutis did it?"

Jack frowned. Zhenya had done everything but spell it out.

Tanney picked up a pen from his cluttered desk and twirled it between his fingers. "All she said was that this character had an argument with her husband, well before the murder. And the fish company manager: did he ever mention the guy's name?"

The door of Tanney's office was open; Jack heard the bustle of the Homicide squad room behind him. He kept his own voice pitched low; he knew that open confrontation with his supervisor wouldn't do him any good. "When I mentioned Balakutis to Goguniv, the guy freaked out. And we have another witness who places him at the Fulton market. *And* he's got a past history of extortion and violence. Both Vargas and I are convinced that he's involved with both of these cases." He felt a little guilty about dragging Linda into the matter, but he let that ride.

Tanney crossed his arms, looking more defensive than in charge. As usual. "Well, *I'm* not convinced. I'd like to help out, but I can't justify committing these resources to what basically amounts to just a hunch."

You little bean counter, thought Jack. *You oughta be rejecting claims for a health insurance company*. He pressed his fingers to the bridge of his nose, suppressed his usual urge to throttle the man, and then stood up and left the office. He veered into the storage room around the corner, closed the door behind him, and took a minute to think. He poured himself a cup of coffee and stood there stirring in the sugar. He considered taking his case one step higher, to Lieutenant Cardulli, the head of Brooklyn South Homicide, but that kind of chain-of-command jump was always a risky move—and he was afraid that Cardulli would demand more evidence too.

But then, half an hour later, a call came in to the Homicide squad room from the New Jersey State Police. A park ranger had contacted the staties from the northern end of Lebanon State Forest, about sixty miles south of New York City. A couple of hikers had gotten lost in the park, and their dog had trotted off into the underbrush and found an interesting smell under a patch of freshly turned forest mulch. The animal had started to scrabble down into the rocky soil.

It soon uncovered a human arm. Attached to the battered body of Andrei Goguniv.

CHAPTER TWENTY-EIGHT

Jack thought of Semyon Balakutis sending that drink out to his car in Mill Basin. He thought of the man's creepy little teeth, of the way he had asked what it felt like to get shot, of his asking Jack and Linda Vargas if they wanted a free doughnut.

And he thought of Joseph Joral, of the man's brutal streak and his cockiness and his evident belief that he could outwit the NYPD.

The one was gonna go down just like the other. "Maybe you two can share a cell up at Attica or Auburn," he muttered to himself as he pored over his computer screen in the task force squad room.

Linda Vargas and another detective from the squad had tracked down Balakutis this morning—and learned that he had a rock-solid alibi for every day since Goguniv's disappearance. His wife and neighbors testified that he'd come home to Mill Basin every evening, and no one had witnessed any late-night departures.

Jack had a backlog of other cases, but now he was doubly determined to find the chink in Balakutis's armor. He didn't have to find the connection to Daniel Lelo's murder right away, nor that of Goguniv; often the careers of the worst criminals could be unraveled starting with a tax violation or a drug possession charge, or by busting some associate and getting him to snitch.

He placed calls to contacts at the Bureau of Criminal Information, the Organized Crime Control Bureau, the Department of Taxation and Finance, the DMV, and even—though he was no fan of federal agencies—the DEA and FBI. He worked at it all day; at least his boss wouldn't give him a hard time, not with two unsolved murders on their plate.

What did he come up with? Nada. Zip. Nothing.

At four thirty, after his tour left, he stayed on, working a spare computer, on his own dime.

Finally, when his eyes were starting to get bleary, he went out and got in his car. For lack of anything better to do, he drove by the Cosmopolitan club. He thought of going in, but what was the point? Visiting a nightclub during the day was always depressing, like seeing a crack whore without her makeup. When the spotlights went off and the houselights came up, even the swankest places looked soiled. You saw the drink stains and the chewing gum on the carpets, the duct-tape patches on the stage, the cigarette burns in the upholstery. . . . He wasn't likely to see anything illegal anyway; if there *was* something, it probably went on behind locked doors.

He thought of driving over to Mill Basin to scope out Semyon Balakutis's bunker, but he didn't want to get in the way of the surveillance team that Sergeant Tanney had finally authorized. So far, they'd come up with absolutely nothing. The man had spent the day visiting his doughnut franchises, going to the bank, eating lunch. A model citizen.

Jack found a parking spot on busy Brighton Beach Avenue and pulled over to think. Why had Balakutis's violence escalated? He already owned a modest but relatively lucrative franchise—and was in on the nightclub take too. Why kill Daniel Lelo, and now the fish company manager? Just to put the squeeze on their business? It wasn't taking in all that much profit—Linda Vargas had looked over the books.

Frustrated, he started his engine and drove to nearby Sheepshead Bay, where he had dinner at a fast-food joint with a view of the water and a spectacular, angry-looking sunset. On top of everything else he had to ponder this evening, he couldn't help wondering where Zhenya was and what she was doing with her friend.

THE NEXT MORNING, AFTER another night of bad sleep, he stopped by the task force office to see if any of his fishing calls and e-mails might have paid off, but there was still nothing new. He sat at his desk, frowning and spinning his chair slowly from side to side. And then he picked up his phone and dialed Semyon Balakutis's doughnut shop.

A girl answered.

"Can I speak to Semyon?" he said, making his voice gruff.

"He won't be in till three," she said.

"*Spaciba*," he mumbled, thanking her in Russian just in case the girl told Balakutis about the call.

He hung up. Then he went out and got in his car.

There was a different girl behind the counter this time, a plump teenager wearing too much black eye shadow, like a raccoon, and a big stud in her lower lip. The place was still crowded with the morning rush. Jack ordered a cup of coffee and a cruller, and then he found a little table in the corner with a newspaper lying on it. He pretended to read it as he scoped out the store and his fellow customers.

The business still didn't quite make sense. It was easy to see why Semyon Balakutis would get involved in a nightclub:

he'd get to play the big shot and feel all glamorous, like some movie gangster. Though plenty of criminals moved into legitimate businesses once they'd built up enough ill-gained cash, there was something so mundane about doughnut shops, so silly, almost, that he couldn't see it appealing to the thug's oversize ego. The man might go for a sports car dealership or a partnership in some entertainment management venture. . . .

"I tole you to shut up!" someone said loudly behind Jack, and he turned to see a mountain of a woman threaten to give her cute little daughter a wallop. Across the way, a bleary-eyed old man in wrinkled clothes sat pinching an old-fashioned doughnut into dozens of tiny pieces. Why? Who knew? Maybe he was gonna go out and feed some pigeons.

Jack took a bite of his cruller. The shop did a brisk business, that seemed evident. He glanced down at the paper. The tabloid headlines for the past several days had focused on a Long Island story involving an electrician who had married a multimillionaire's widow just three months after the husband was slain. Over the top of Jack's paper, he saw the line moving forward, people on their way to work, trying to jump-start their sleepy engines with a blast of sugar and caffeine. He overheard little snippets of conversation. "I ain't been there since the last time I was there," he heard a guy in painter's overalls tell his buddy. A minute later, a woman in a pink sweat suit, talking to *her* friend: "I told him, you want some sugar tonight, you better lay off the sauce."

Jack sipped his coffee, trying to make it last. He wasn't going to be able to sit here forever. He hoped the manager wouldn't come out of the back office and recognize him. The room was full of light—a harsh morning sun outside, glinting off parked cars; the totally unnecessary glow of the fluorescents above—but it illuminated nothing. Soon he'd have to call in to

Sergeant Tanney; the boss liked regular reports on what the members of the squad were up to, and what was he gonna say? *I'm reading the paper and eating doughnuts?*

He watched the girl behind the register. Unlike the glut of zombielike youngsters who populated the service industry these days, she seemed quick and efficient. She turned and grabbed doughnuts out of the glass display case behind her, bagged them, and rang up the purchases; the line moved forward quickly. A little old couple who looked as if they had just come off a Caribbean cruise, in matching Hawaiian shirts. A tall, gaunt black man who stepped forward on long legs, like a patient stork. A couple of elderly women who looked like famous Russian dictators in drag. The door opened and a lean, sharp-featured young man in black jeans and a black T-shirt entered. He waited his turn in line, but when he got to the counter, he didn't seem to make any order. The girl behind the register reached down, came up with a small doughnut bag, handed it to him, and then took the next customer's order. The young man didn't hand her any money—he just turned and slipped out of the shop, and the line moved forward, and the girl turned to pour a couple of cups of coffee. Jack shook his head: a couple of free doughnuts for the boyfriend. Semyon Balakutis would never notice the loss.

He sat there for another twenty minutes, stretching out his coffee and cruller—and then the same lean young man came back in, slipped around the line, and left with another little doughnut bag.

Jack sat up and blinked; the odd little transaction would have been very easy to miss if he hadn't been looking for something out of the ordinary, and if he hadn't just seen it repeated.

Doughnuts, he thought—*what a homely little thing to sell.*

(Even if you owned five or more stores.) But then, so was pizza. And back in the mid-1980s, one of the biggest criminal cases in U.S. history had centered around an Italian mafia scheme of distributing heroin and laundering money through a string of midwestern pizza parlors.

He set down the paper and stood up. He needed to get out of the shop immediately, before he was spotted. Whatever was going on here, he didn't want to interrupt it. Not yet.

Out in his car, he gripped the wheel. *Calm down,* he told himself. *Think this through.* Maybe it was just a small-time operation, putting product into the hands of local dealers. . . . Or maybe it wasn't drugs at all—maybe it was something more mundane, like numbers running. But would Balakutis kill two men over something so humdrum?

Five doughnut shops, a fish market. Doughnuts, fish. What was the connection? He considered his drugs theory again. Any such operation would be shaped like a pyramid. The broad base would be made of lots of little transactions, street-level customers buying small amounts of drugs. The street sellers would get their stash from a smaller number of middlemen, who would get theirs from bigger suppliers. The price of the drugs would increase at every step down the pyramid, as each participant marked them up. The most profitable way to run an operation was to control as many steps in the chain as possible, from production to distribution to sales.

Jack started up his car and drove off down the avenue, barely paying any attention to the traffic or the pedestrians moving along in the bright summer heat.

Ultimately, the drugs would have to come from somewhere, usually in large quantities. Crystal meth or marijuana might come from in-state or cross-country. Heroin or coke would have to come from overseas.

Soon he found himself on the Belt Parkway, and then he was cruising along the Shore Parkway, with New York Harbor sparkling on his left and the Verrazano Bridge arcing off to Staten Island high overhead. He passed the old army terminal docks in Sunset Park, then zipped by his childhood neighborhood of Red Hook. He veered onto the Brooklyn-Queens Expressway, then exited in downtown Brooklyn, not far from the Supreme Court and the restaurant where he had interviewed Annette O'Dea.

He left his car near Cadman Plaza and walked across the narrow little park there. Soon the bright sun and heat were getting to him; he took off his tie, folded it, and stuck it in his shirt pocket. At the end of the park, he found a staircase that brought him up onto the Brooklyn Bridge. A hurtling Rollerblader almost clipped him as he moved out onto the pedestrian walkway. Ahead loomed the old stone towers of the bridge, with their harpstring cables. A stream of tourists moved along the wooden walkway; little knots of them stepped aside along the way to take photos. Joggers and bicyclists did their best to weave in and out of the clotted traffic.

By the time he had almost reached the center of the bridge, Jack's shirt was damp with sweat, and he took out a handkerchief to wipe his forehead. He kept an eye out for anyone selling bottles of water. Looking down to his left, he could see the Verrazano way off in the distance, and the piers of Red Hook, and—in the middle of the harbor—low, wooded Governors Island, a site that had figured heavily in one of his recent cases.

The walkway rose until it reached the center of the bridge, and then it began a slow, steady decline toward the office towers of downtown Manhattan. The bicyclists could coast downhill now, and the Rollerbladers picked up steam. Three-quarters of the way across the river, Jack moved out of the stream of pedestrians and stepped over to the railing. The sun was bright in his eyes, and he shaded them so he could look down. A Circle Line tourist boat was gliding down the East River, moving past nearby Pier 17, topped by the big red layer cake of the South Street Seaport mall. Just to its north lay the low, flat gray building that housed the offices of the Fulton Fish Market. Under the shadow of the FDR Drive, Jack could see the big asphalt lot where—in the predawn hours—the fish would have been laid out for sale.

Daniel Lelo's fish company was down there. Big shipments of huge fish arrived there on a regular basis, from many exotic ports of call. Jack thought of how—back in the hospital—Daniel had boasted about how his industry had become so international. *Cod caught off the U.S. West Coast might end up in Tokyo. Pollack served as fish-and-chips might come from the Bering Sea. . . .*

And yes, the fish were valuable, but Daniel's company was small. It cost a lot of money to run. And it didn't provide the sort of profits that would likely attract a shark like Semyon Balakutis. On the other hand, Jack mused now, it might provide an amazing opportunity. If drugs were indeed Balakutis's central enterprise, then the company offered a fantastic way to move large quantities into the U.S., in Styrofoam boxes marked CHILEAN SEA BASS or DOVER SOLE, or maybe even hidden inside the carcasses of the biggest fish.

No, the business might not be about fish or doughnuts at all. It might be about using the former as a cover for bringing drugs into the country, and the latter as a cover for spreading them out into the city's streets.

Jack took out his cell phone and called Linda Vargas about what he'd seen that morning, and then he placed another call to ask his boss about setting up surveillance at the doughnut shop and the fish company. For once—excited, no doubt, about the possibility of a career-boosting case—Sergeant Tanney got right on board.

FIVE HOURS LATER JACK was driving down Coney Island Avenue, freshly showered, attired in his best sport coat, in the best mood he'd been in for a long time. His work was going well, and he was on his way to pick up a beautiful woman and take her out for a fine meal at a seafood place out on Long Island that was not frequented by cops or—as far as he knew—Russian gangsters. He was going to order an expensive bottle of bubbly and some kind of fancy lobster dish for himself and Zhenya, and they were gonna have a hell of a night.

He glanced at his watch. He was early, but he looked forward to surprising her. The summer sky was still bright; they could enjoy a nice cocktail out on the balcony and still make it out to the restaurant in time to watch the sun set over the Long Island Sound. While he was stopped at a red light, his cell phone trilled. He would have ignored it, but he looked down and saw that it was Zhenya.

"I gotta warn you," he told her, "I just showered and shaved, and I'm smelling pretty damn good."

There was silence on the other end.

"Zhenya?" he said. "Are you there?"

"I'm here. But I hev some bad news."

The driver behind Jack honked, and he stepped on the gas again. "What's up?"

"It is, eh, it is my friend Mika. Her, eh, her husband just . . . they have fight, and I must to go to her to the hospital. We can take dinner tomorrow, no?"

Jack frowned. He noticed that her English was even more garbled than usual—and that her explanation didn't feel right.

"Uh, okay," he said slowly. "I hope your friend is all right. I'll call you later."

He hung up, disappointed and more than a little suspicious. *Let it go*, he told himself. *So you'll have dinner tomorrow . . .*

Spider sense. Tingling.

He drove on toward her Coney Island apartment.

A block away, he pulled over and picked up his cell phone again. He dialed her home number. Her landline.

"Yes?" she said.

"Sorry," he said. "I was trying to call my uncle. I pressed the wrong speed dial." He hung up again. At least he was sure that she was really at home.

He sat in his car thinking for a minute. Then he got out and walked over toward her apartment building. He didn't get close, though. He found a building entrance a good eighty yards away and sat down on the stairs.

ZHENYA EMERGED FROM HER building just five minutes later.

She glanced right and left, then moved off down the sidewalk, away from Jack, toward Brighton Beach Avenue.

He felt a bit ashamed of himself, but he gave her a few seconds and then slipped off after her.

She turned east on the avenue, which—lucky for him—was thronged with evening shoppers. She passed under the shadow of the elevated subway tracks and moved off down the crowded sidewalk. Jack quickstepped on behind.

Several blocks down, she turned in to the supermarket they'd visited just a few days before. That was a little odd—if her friend had just been taken to the hospital, why wasn't she hurrying over there? He sighed; maybe he was just being paranoid. Maybe she was buying a box of chocolates for the hospital visit.

He waited ten minutes, though. Surely, even with long lines, it wouldn't take ten minutes to buy a box of chocolates?

Out she came—there was her blond hair, her green summer dress. She carried a large shopping bag, her right shoulder dipping a bit with the weight. Not just chocolates . . .

He gave her a few seconds to get ahead of him, and off he went, figuring that she was headed for Coney Island Hospital, just a few blocks away.

But she turned in to another shop. A liquor store. Jack frowned again: she was definitely not going to be bringing liquor into a hospital. . . .

She came out with another bag and stopped on a corner of the busy avenue, next to a stairway leading up to the elevated trains. She set down her purchases, then took out a compact and applied some lipstick.

Jack's face tightened as he watched.

He thought she might head up the subway stairs, but she set off briskly down the avenue instead. A block down, she turned in to another storefront. Jack risked getting a little closer to see what it might be. A car service dispatch office. With a couple of shiny black Lincoln Town Cars parked out front.

Shit. He glanced behind him. There was no way he'd ever get back to his own car in time.

Zhenya came out of the office with a man who opened the back door of one of the cars for her, then moved around to the driver's seat.

Jack looked around frantically. He saw a yellow cab

double-parked next to a newsstand a few yards away. He ran over and jumped in the back.

The driver, a little butterball of a man, sat calmly eating a sandwich. He took another bite, then set it down. "Where to, mister?"

Jack pointed at the black sedan. "Follow that car."

The driver looked up at the rearview mirror. "Are you kidding?"

Jack groaned. "Come on—it's getting away."

The driver shook his head. "We don't chase people, mister. That crap is strictly for the movies."

Jack thought of flashing his badge but realized what might get better results—he yanked out his wallet, pulled out a wad of bills, and shoved them over the seat.

The driver picked up the money, crumpled the wax paper from his sandwich, and put the cab in Drive. "Which car did you say we're after?"

THE TOWN CAR LEFT Brighton Beach, caught the Shore Parkway, and swooped around the southwest end of Brooklyn, under the soaring Verrazano Bridge, retracing the route Jack had taken just hours earlier. But this time it left Brooklyn altogether, veering up onto the Brooklyn Bridge, cruising toward the office towers of Manhattan. Across Chambers Street, past City Hall, onto the West Side Highway.

Eventually it pulled onto a side street in midtown, in front of a narrow, soot-grimed five-story hotel, one of the few remnants of a once-seedy Times Square. The old red-and-beige sign running down the façade said THE RYAN, but it might just as well have said NO-TELL HOTEL.

"Keep going," Jack told his driver. At the next corner, he

opened his door and looked back to see Zhenya stepping into the hotel.

His driver called out to him, "What, no tip?" but Jack just rolled his eyes; he'd already given double the normal fare. He jogged back down the block and stopped outside the hotel to give Zhenya a brief lead. While he waited, he examined his wallet and discovered that he had sixty bucks left. He took out a twenty, folded it into a neat square, and tucked it into his jacket pocket.

He took a deep breath and entered the tiny lobby, which featured an incredibly dusty plastic plant and a couple of beat-up old armchairs with greasy upholstery. The desk clerk sat reading a paperback. He was a lanky guy in his early fifties, his gray hair pulled back into a ponytail. He wore a faded black T-shirt emblazoned with the words THE CRAMPS, and he hadn't shaved in about three days.

Perfect, Jack thought, *someone who could definitely use a little extra cash.* He glanced over at a narrow staircase leading up into the guts of the old hotel.

The clerk put down his book. "You need a room?"

"No. That woman who just came in here, the blonde . . . I'm wondering if you could help me."

A wary look. "Help you *how?*"

"Is she visiting somebody registered here?"

The clerk frowned. "What are you, some kind of cop?"

Jack pulled out his badge.

The clerk shrugged. "You have a warrant?"

Jack reached into his pocket, palmed the twenty, and pushed it across the counter. The magic substance that greased the city's many wheels . . .

The man looked at the bill as if it were a dead cockroach. "I don't want your money, man. Let me show you something."

He pulled aside some of his hair on the left side of his head, revealing a scar. "See that? It's 1988 and I'm walkin' through Tompkins Square Park, coming back from visiting my mother, who's in St. Vincent's Hospital getting a fucking angioplasty, okay? Suddenly, all hell breaks loose and these fucking cops jump out of this van and throw me down on the ground. . . ."

Jack glanced wistfully at the staircase. He reached into his pocket and pulled out another twenty.

The desk clerk just scowled. "What's your problem? You think I'm gonna violate one of our guests' civil rights for some lousy bribe? Typical corrupt police bullshit." He crossed his arms over his skinny rib cage. "I know the law, man. This is private property. You wanna snoop around, you need a warrant."

Jack winced. After one more glance at the staircase, he retreated out into the street. Across the way stood a dingy deli; he entered and found a couple of café tables near the front. The windows were half-plastered with beer posters and Lotto ads, which suited him fine; he had a good view of the front of the hotel, but he'd be tough to spot.

AN HOUR AND TWO watery cups of coffee later, Zhenya emerged. She patted her hair, then stood out on the sidewalk for a moment, looking both ways. She gestured back at the front door of the hotel.

A slim young man stepped out. He had a blond crew cut and wore a dark blue, high-collared tracksuit. He joined Zhenya on the sidewalk, reached out his arms, and gave her a hug. A long, heartfelt hug.

And then he kissed her.

Jack stared through the grimy deli window; he felt as if he had just been sucker punched in the back of the head. He almost trembled with shock and anger. And misery.

Zhenya and her *friend* parted ways, she heading east, he going the other direction. Jack hesitated for a moment, stunned, and then he hurried out of the deli and turned west.

The blond man strolled down to the next corner, where he stopped in at a Rite Aid drugstore. He emerged a minute later, peeling the plastic wrap off a pack of cigarettes. He tapped one out, lit up, and inhaled deeply.

Jack thought about his uncle Leon's joke about the chicken and the egg and felt sick to his stomach.

The man turned around and headed back. Jack ducked into a doorway, waited until he passed, then set out after him again, moving on the other side of the street.

When Zhenya's lover reached the hotel, he didn't go in right away; he paused out on the sidewalk, enjoying his smoke. Jack ducked back into his deli hideaway and watched the man through the window. He couldn't believe it—what was he, cursed? Two cheating women in a row... Christ, maybe he oughta become a monk....

The lover was handsome, though rather sharp-faced. He was clearly a lot younger than Jack. A stud in bed, no doubt. Jack's hands clenched; he was tempted to step out and kick the guy in the balls.

Lover Boy leaned against the side of the hotel, idly puffing away and watching the passing traffic. After a minute, he stuck the cigarette in the corner of his mouth and pulled off his jacket; even though evening was setting in, the temperature was still oppressive.

Jack moved closer to the window and stared. The young man had a tattoo on the side of his neck.

It took several seconds for Jack to recognize its significance, and then he felt as if he had been punched again. He remembered Tyrese Vincent, back at the Coney Island McDonald's, talking about a blond, sharp-faced young Russian with a tattoo on his neck. Who had shot Daniel Lelo two years ago.

Looking as if he didn't have a care in the world, the man flipped his cigarette butt out into the street, turned around, and sauntered back inside the hotel.

Jack scrambled to pull out his cell phone.

CHAPTER TWENTY-NINE

The hallway smelled of strawberry air freshener and Lysol and cat piss (rather strange, considering that this was supposed to be a hotel).

Emergency Service Unit officers took up positions on both sides of the door to room 312. Under other circumstances, they might have brought up a battering ram, but that had not proved necessary this time. (The desk clerk had lost his will to argue when he saw a truck full of flak-jacketed ESU guys come pouring into his lobby.)

Jack stood a few paces down the hallway, sweating in a borrowed Kevlar vest. His mind was racing, thinking about his conversation twenty minutes ago with the sergeant in charge of Brooklyn South Homicide's evening tour. (Thankfully, Tanney had been off duty.) The other supervisor had wondered what Jack was doing in midtown Manhattan, miles outside his normal jurisdiction, but Jack had cut him off. "This might close two cases: an attempted murder in Coney Island two years back, and a recent homicide. We need to move on this immediately; I don't know how long the guy is gonna be inside the hotel."

The sergeant had called Lieutenant Cardulli, who then called in the ESU. Soon Jack was going to have some tricky explaining to do, but for now he needed to focus on not getting his head shot off.

He watched as the lieutenant in charge rapped on the door; everyone held their breath.

No answer. The LT signaled silently to his officers, and then he held out the room key and slipped it into the lock. A quick turn of the knob, a good shove on the door, and they went in, flowing through the door like a tidal wave.

But the room was empty. Clothes gone. Cleared out.

Jack's heart sank. He peered out the wide-open window: a fire escape, a back alley. He thought of the desk clerk and he growled.

Downstairs, the clerk looked like a guilty dog who had chewed up someone's shoes. He sputtered at first, making angry comments about storm troopers and fascist pigs, but his tone damped down when Jack explained that their suspect had shot several people, including a truly innocent bystander.

Jack sighed. "You told him I was here, didn't you? When he came back in, after the woman left . . ."

"You didn't have a warrant," the clerk muttered halfheartedly.

Jack looked away for a moment. There was no percentage in getting angry now. He turned back. "Did you tell him I was looking for him?"

The clerk shook his head. "How would I know that? I just thought you were looking for the broad. Besides, the guy barely even spoke English."

"What name did he give when he signed in?"

The clerk shook his head. "He didn't. It was the woman."

"Did you get his name at all?"

"Nope. All we care about is making sure the room is paid for."

Jack stood there for another moment, marinating in the frustration and embarrassment of it all, as the ESU squad tromped out of the lobby behind him.

He turned back to the clerk. "What day did she book the room?"

The clerk consulted his paperwork and gave the date. Jack thought for a minute. Zhenya had taken the room on the same day she had received the early morning phone call—and he had just rolled over and gone back to sleep.

He sank into one of the lobby's greasy old armchairs. *What a day.* The whole world seemed to have turned upside down.

Linda Vargas came hurrying in.

"What's going on?" she said, breathless. "My husband and I were out on a date. I got here as soon as I could."

As Jack filled her in, his mind was working double-time. How much should he tell? He decided to go with a bare minimum—he'd try not to lie, but he wasn't going to volunteer details of his affair with Zhenya. Not until he was sure that the blond guy was really their suspect. "I've been putting in a little overtime on this case," he admitted. "Because I knew the vic."

Vargas frowned. "And you didn't tell me?"

He tried not to squirm. "I just wanted to follow up a few loose ends. Like the doughnut shop thing." He started to tell more about his morning visit, hoping that might distract her from other questions.

But Vargas was sharp as ever. "How did you find out about this guy with the tattoo?"

"The kid at the McDonald's told me. Tyrese Vincent."

She brushed this away. "I know that. I mean, how did you know he was here today?"

"I just found out," Jack said. "And I called you right away."

Vargas frowned. "Come on, Jack. Tell me *how* you found out."

Miserable inside, he kept up a poker face. He was known for being a very honest cop, a real straight shooter, and it pained him to behave otherwise. "When I interviewed Lelo's wife, I got a kind of weird vibe. I didn't say anything at the time 'cause it was just a hunch. But I was thinking about that today, after I got off work, and I decided to follow her." He loosened his collar; he'd sweated right through his shirt, under the Kevlar.

Linda Vargas considered him gravely. He sensed that she had more questions, but she turned away instead. Giving him the benefit of the doubt, perhaps—for which he was deeply grateful.

"Let's go scoop this guy up" was all she said.

THE NEXT MORNING, SERGEANT Tanney said that he wanted to bring in Eugenia Lelo right away.

Jack let Vargas do the talking, to explain the game plan they'd worked out the night before.

"If we bring her in now and she doesn't talk, then she'll just alert this guy that we're after him."

Tanney crossed his arms. "He already knows."

"Not necessarily. He knows that someone was asking about Eugenia Lelo at the hotel. But that's all."

Tanney scoffed. "The guy bolted."

Vargas shrugged. "Okay, so he was nervous. But he might still be close by. If we get him seriously spooked, he's liable to leave the state. Or even the country. With surveillance on her, maybe we can find him the easy way."

Tanney tapped a pen against his desk blotter and turned

to Jack. "Now what about the fish company manager? Do you think the wife and her lover might have offed him too?"

Jack rubbed his chin. He had lost considerable sleep last night, wondering about that very question. For once, he didn't have some clear argument to make to his boss. He could only shrug. "I doubt it, but at this point I have to say that I don't know."

Tanney frowned—probably seeing his visions of a head-line drug bust go up in smoke. He leaned forward. "So what do you suggest?"

Jack sat up straight. "First of all, I think we should tell Narcotics to go ahead with checking out the doughnut shop and the fish company. And second, we've got to make sure that this blond guy is the one who did the McDonald's shooting. I went to a sketch artist last night, right after we left the hotel." He produced the drawing. Inwardly, he was still cursing him-self: he should have snapped a cell phone photo, but he'd been too stunned by the sudden proof of Zhenya's infidelity.

"We're going over to the McDonald's now," Vargas said. "We'll see if our witness there can confirm the I.D."

"Where do you think the suspect might have gone?" Tanney asked.

"To Brighton Beach," Jack answered. "Or one of the other Russian communities around. Bensonhurst, maybe. Or Rego Park or Forest Hills. These people tend to stick together, and I think he'll go somewhere where people speak his language."

"We should get ahold of the wife's phone records."

Jack tried not to wince. "I'll get right on that," he volun-teered. Christ, his own numbers would be all over those records.

His stomach clenched. This whole business was just get-ting worse and worse. What were his options? He could be totally honest and up-front. For the fiftieth time in the past few hours, he considered spilling the beans about his affair with Zhenya. But what if it turned out that the blond man wasn't actually the perp? He would have jeopardized his career for nothing. . . . For a second, he wondered if he should have just kept his mouth shut.

And let Daniel's killer go? No, that was out of the question . . .

He frowned. He was going to have to walk this tightrope for a while longer, but the ground seemed to be getting farther and farther away.

CHAPTER THIRTY

Steam rose up inside the car as Linda Vargas bit into a pineapple knish. "Well, I gotta admit that I'm totally out of ideas. What do you wanna do?"

The two detectives sat double-parked on Brighton Beach Avenue next to Mrs. Stahl's Knishes, one of the few local businesses that dated back to Jack's childhood. The store had become dumpy, but the knishes were still great. Jack took a bite of his traditional potato version, a small pleasure in the middle of such a wretched time. He watched out the window as a beautiful, unhappy-looking blond woman pushed a baby stroller across the intersection.

The past forty-eight hours had been damned busy ones.

Acting on Jack's tips, Narcotics squads had set up surveillance on Semyon Balakutis's doughnut shop and Daniel's fish company.

Tyrese Vincent had called the sketch of the blond man a definite match, as did another McDonald's employee who had witnessed the original shooting.

Jack had gotten hold of Zhenya's phone records (and managed to keep them to himself); he'd found that several calls had come in from pay phones in Brighton Beach. The times matched his memory of when Zhenya had suddenly canceled their dinner plans.

Other memories assaulted him: their happy times out on the balcony; the occasions when she had asked him how the investigation was going; nights when they had hardly slept at all, for the very best of reasons. Times when he had watched her staring off into the distance, and wondered what she might be brooding about.

Well, now he knew. She had just been using him.

All that remained was to find out how directly she had been involved in her husband's murder. Whose idea had it been? Had she been there on that dark, lonely night out on Neptune Avenue? Had she pulled the trigger herself?

The detectives had roamed all over the neighborhood. They'd showed the sketch to countermen in delis and coffee shops. They buttonholed passersby on the streets. They tried the old ladies on the benches and the old men playing chess. They asked local patrol cops to question their snitches.

Nada.

Jack turned to his partner. "The word is out that we're searching for the guy here, so I don't think he's gonna stick around. I think we oughta look a little farther afield."

Vargas frowned. "New York is a big place."

"Not for him. He won't hide far from where people can speak Russian. Why don't we poke around Coney a bit?"

His cell phone trilled. He looked down and saw Zhenya's name in the little window. Thankfully, Vargas wasn't paying much attention; she was wiping crumbs off her lap.

She looked up casually. "Aren't you gonna get that?"

Jack picked up his phone, pretended to look at the caller I.D., then set it down again, facedown. "Nah. It's not important."

He had phoned Zhenya from a pay phone the morning

after the hotel incident. It had been a hell of a call to make. He hadn't said anything about what he'd seen; he'd just told her that he wouldn't be able to get together for a few days, that he was working on a very big case. He had neglected to mention that she seemed to be at the center of it. He had also neglected to mention that she was now under twenty-four-hour surveillance. One small mercy for both of them: Sergeant Tanney had applied for a tap on her phones, but a federal judge had turned it down due to lack of evidence.

He wrapped up the remains of his knish; he just wasn't hungry. He felt as if he was getting an ulcer. It was too much to contend with all at once: his worries over his own involvement in the case and how he could possibly emerge unscathed; the struggle to find their suspect; his bitter disappointment over Zhenya's betrayal.

For the past two days, his mouth had been full of a sour taste, and he wanted to smash his fist through a wall.

HE DIDN'T HAVE ANY snitches in Brighton Beach, but Coney Island was a different story. First they paid a visit to a hooker who hung out in front of a fast-food joint on Stillwell Avenue. (He admired the owner's gall: the place was called Kantacky Fried Chicken.)

No luck.

They talked to the owner of a liquor store on Mermaid Avenue.

Zip.

They drove on. Scraps of trash blew along Surf Avenue, swirling outside storefronts selling crappy fried seafood. The new baseball stadium (on the site of the old Steeplechase Park) was supposed to help revive the neighborhood, and maybe it would, but Coney seemed especially desolate that afternoon.

They dropped in on an employee of Astroland Amusement Park, a bandy-legged old ticket taker. Instead of the cheery carnival music from Jack's childhood, this ride now blasted rap music, and homeboys with gold-capped teeth held on to their shrieking girlfriends as the little cars whipped around. Jack stood twenty yards away and gave his informant the nod.

Five minutes later the man joined the detectives in an alley behind Nathan's. A hard life with too much sun had given him a reddish hide like shriveled leather.

"You recognize this guy?" Jack asked, holding up the sketch.

The old-timer frowned. "I think I might'a saw him. About a week ago. Over on the boardwalk where they got that salsa dance thing goin'."

"You know where he hangs out?"

The man shook his head. "Nope. You talk to Little Danny?"

Jack patted the man on his shoulder. "That's our next stop."

Across from the Cyclone roller coaster, Surf Avenue was home to a strange blocklong flea market, a row of run-down stalls filled to overflowing with an incredible assortment of junk: broken eight-track players, belted nylon slacks in various pastel colors, scratched LPs by no-hit wonders. Little Danny Vletko had managed to keep his business going for years, though he rarely displayed anything any sane person might want to buy. It was rumored that his true business was fencing stolen goods, but Jack didn't look too hard—the man's information had proved valuable more than once.

Danny was small in stature but not in weight; his potbelly alone must have weighed a hundred pounds. He looked—and smelled—as if he bathed maybe twice a season. "Not here," he muttered when Jack and Vargas approached him. "In the back."

Jack sighed. This was one of the hazards of getting information from the man. You had to squeeze down a narrow aisle, risking avalanche from the ceiling-high heaps of old clothes and bric-a-brac. In the tiny back room Danny's body odor became almost intolerable. That afternoon, though, the visit proved worth the trouble.

ACTING ON LITTLE DANNY'S tip, the two detectives took up positions on the Coney boardwalk, just downwind of a scruffy, open-fronted bar that sold cans of Coors Light for a buck. Toothless women in bleached jeans paraded in and out with scraggly men sporting biker vests and wallet chains.

"I'm going to the ladies' room again," Linda Vargas said.

Jack shook his head. "I told you ya shouldn't have eaten those clams. Hey, can you buy me a ginger—" He stopped. A blond man was skulking along the edge of the boardwalk. He wore track pants and an oversize red and black jersey. He stopped under the bar's awning, took off his backpack, lodged it between his feet, and pulled out a CD player. He inserted the earphones and stood scanning the beach through blue wraparound sunglasses.

"That's our guy," Jack murmured. "Don't spook him. Why don't you call in some troops?"

Vargas took out her cell phone and made the call. Jack sat watching the Russian over the top of a newspaper. He was tempted to hurl himself forward and start throttling the bastard, but he waited instead, muttering, "Come on, come on," afraid their quarry would slip away.

Finally, a hundred yards to the east, a patrol car drove up and blocked off the boardwalk. A few seconds later, from the west, a dark blue Crown Vic came cruising up the boardwalk itself. The car stopped a good ways off, but seeing as how most vehicles were prohibited from driving there, it was hardly inconspicuous. As the doors opened, the suspect's head snapped up. He turned the other way and saw the patrol car blocking his escape. He bent down to pick up his backpack and then he took off, sprinting across the boardwalk toward the beach. He cleared the railing with a flying leap. Down on the beach, he picked himself up and ran as best he could. Speeding across loose sand was hard enough, but he staggered, trailing one leg. Jack came to the railing and looked down: a bunch of broken bottles littered the sand.

He ran along the boardwalk, shoes thumping on the wood, watching to see which way the guy would go. To his right the Wonder Wheel, Astroland tower, and Parachute Jump rose up like giant children's toys. The shooter ran toward the water's edge, where the sand was hard-packed. Jack found a stairway down to the beach and hightailed it after him. The Russian veered toward the east. Lines of low clouds ranged above him to the horizon. Out across the water, on a spit of land called Breezy Point, a row of beach houses glowed bone white in the late afternoon sun.

A patrol car zoomed out onto the beach about a hundred yards ahead. The suspect spun around, almost falling in his haste, and ran west. A group of seagulls stood on the sand, all facing into the wind—as he plowed through them, they sprayed up into the air. The man limped on, a lone figure silhouetted against the blue-gray water, making his way toward the sun. And two more uniforms. By this time, Jack thought, he must be cursing his instinct to take off toward the ocean; it left nowhere to hide. Except, of course, the water itself. In one last hopeless move he floundered out into the waves.

Zhenya's lover splashed around—he was a terrible swimmer. Jack jogged up to the uniforms at the edge of the beach, where they were cracking wise and making bets on how long the guy could keep his head up. Jack looked on; some fierce, angry part of him was tempted to let the man drown.

He spit on the sand. There was no way he could let a murder suspect just sink beneath the waves. He kicked off his shoes, waded out into the chilly water, and hauled the punk's sodden ass back to shore.

CHAPTER THIRTY-ONE

While Alec Shvidkoy sat shivering in the interview room at the Sixty-first Precinct house with a blanket wrapped around his shoulders, a thoughtful group stood watching him through a two-way mirror next door. Jack's bosses had traveled from their Coney Island headquarters for this, and they were joined by Linda Vargas and Scott DeHaven, the local detective assigned to the Lelo case. And Jack, who had borrowed a towel and some dry gym clothes from another local detective.

At first, their suspect had refused to talk—he was playing the tough guy, the junior gangster—but a driver's license in his soggy backpack had given away his name. Linda Vargas looked it over, then handed it to Jack and pointed to the category. It was a Class M license. For *motorcycles.*

Shvidkoy, it turned out, was only twenty-eight. Evidently, Jack thought with a shiver of repugnance, Zhenya Lelo liked lovers of different ages.

He wondered if Shvidkoy knew he was being watched, but their suspect seemed oblivious; every few seconds, he tilted his head and smacked it with his hand, trying to drain it of ocean water. Or he lifted his foot to examine the bandage there, where the beach glass had cut him. Jack hated to admit it, but the guy was strikingly handsome, with a lean, chiseled face.

"Look at that punk," muttered Sergeant Tanney. "I think we should drop heavy on him, let him know we can nail him for the McDonald's shooting."

"I don't know," Jack said. "If we push too hard he might lawyer up, and then we'll have to run the risk of a bad I.D." Lineups were notoriously unreliable. If Tyrese Vincent and the other McDonald's witnesses failed to identify him, the detectives would be screwed. Better to try for a confession first.

"Let Vargas do her thing," Lieutenant Cardulli said calmly. "We're not in any rush."

Jack and his colleague went into the interview room and sat down; they were joined by a Russian interpreter from the Six-oh, a brisk white-haired woman with the anonymous professionalism of a court stenographer. Jack leaned back in his chair; he had to struggle to keep his distaste for Zhenya's lover from showing.

"Where are you from?" Vargas asked.

The interpreter translated.

Shvidkoy just crossed his arms.

Vargas shrugged. "Okay, Alec. You can remain silent and get a lawyer in here, and then we'll have to officially charge you, and then you can take your chances with the courts. Or you can cooperate a bit. This way, we're just having a little informal talk."

Shvidkoy considered his options. "I'm from Ukraine," he finally said, in Russian, grudgingly.

The translator did her thing.

Vargas nodded. "Okay. That's good. You work with us,

we'll make this easier for you. Now tell me, why did you run this afternoon?"

Through his translator, Shvidkoy replied, "I thought you had mistaken me for someone else. Some bad person."

Jack rolled his eyes.

"*Right*," Vargas said. "Now tell me how you met Eugenia Lelo."

The man tried to play it cool, but instinctively he drew his arms in close to his sides. "I do not know this name."

"You never met her?"

"I don't know anything about this."

"You're sure?"

Shvidkoy nodded, wary.

Jack pictured him kissing Zhenya in front of the hotel, holding her close, and he wanted to ask for five minutes alone with the suspect in the little interview room. Someone would have to clean the place up with a mop after. . . .

Vargas changed gears. "How well do you know Andrei Goguniv?"

Shvidkoy looked completely blank. "I never heard this name."

The answer seemed convincing, but by this point Jack was not too big on trusting his own intuition.

"Let me ask you this," Linda Vargas continued. "Were you in Coney Island in August of 2001?"

Shvidkoy shrugged. "I don't remember."

Vargas eyed him coolly. She asked a number of other questions, but the young man had little of significance to say.

Despite his anger and distaste, Jack regarded their captive thoughtfully. He knew that they were going to have to take this slow. Interrogations were like fly-fishing: you had to play your suspect carefully. First, you let him run out some line. Every now and then you gave a gentle tug, sank the hook a little deeper.

Yank too hard? *Snap.*

AFTER HALF AN HOUR, Vargas had pulled out every trick she knew, but their suspect remained uncommunicative. The detectives regrouped outside the interview room.

"Let me have a go," said Scott DeHaven. "Maybe I can play the pal."

The detective was compact and well muscled. Young, but with rough, chapped-looking skin; he looked as if he might spend a lot of time in sports bars.

Cardulli thought it over, then shrugged.

DeHaven and the interpreter went into the interview room. "How ya doin'?" he said. He extended his hand. "My name's Scott. The other detective's gonna be right back. I'm just here to fill in for a minute." He took out a toothpick, set it in the corner of his mouth, and sat back as if he had all the time in the world.

Shvidkoy didn't know what to make of this new presence.

DeHaven gave his outfit the once-over. "You like rap music? Hip-hop?"

Shvidkoy made a sour face.

"No?" DeHaven rested an arm on the table's edge and leaned forward. "Whaddaya like? Techno? Rock?"

"Techno," the suspect said, relaxing just a tad. No one could arrest him for his taste in music.

"You like Basement Jaxx? How about DJ Keoki?"

Shvidkoy looked shocked. "How do you know these names?"

DeHaven shrugged. "I like to go out after work. You

know, places in Manhattan: the Roxy, the Sound Factory . . . You ever been there?"

Shvidkoy nodded. "I'm going to be a DJ."

"Is that right? Well, good luck to you." DeHaven leaned back again.

In the dark room next door, Jack loosened his collar. He was accustomed to long interrogations, but the small talk was suffocating him. He wanted to reach through the two-way mirror with both hands and force Shvidkoy to finally tell the fucking truth.

Scott DeHaven looked considerably more patient. "You been cooperating with the detective that was in here?"

Shvidkoy crossed his arms.

"You know what? I don't know if you know about cops over here in the United States, but things'll go better if you just tell the truth. I mean, it sounds like they already have a lot of information about you. They know you've been hanging around this woman Eugenia Lelo. And they know you were involved in that shooting at the McDonald's."

At this first mention of that crime, the young man looked stunned, but he didn't respond.

DeHaven leaned closer, in a friendly way. "If you want, I can help you, make sure they take it easy on you. . . ."

Shvidkoy scowled, but he seemed far less cocky. "I have nothing else to say," he told the interpreter.

DeHaven tried to resume the friendly music talk, but at the mention of the McDonald's shooting, the suspect had totally withdrawn, like a turtle into his shell.

Jack, watching, said, "I think we oughta give him some time to worry how much we've really got on him."

Tanney nodded and stepped out to retrieve Scott De-Haven.

"Good job," Cardulli told the young detective when he rejoined the group.

Tanney nodded, impressed. "You're really into this new music, huh?"

DeHaven scoffed. "I did some undercover in a tag-team thing with Narcotics—somebody out here was running Ecstasy into a club in Chelsea. Personally, I think this techno shit is about as exciting as a StairMaster."

THE DETECTIVES WATCHED SHVIDKOY fidget in his chair. They decided to keep him waiting, let him get good and nervous.

"You guys wanna order in some dinner?" Scott DeHaven said. "How about Chinese food?"

Tanney shook his head. "I had Chinese for lunch."

"How about Indian?"

Lieutenant Cardulli shook his head. "I don't like spicy food."

"You can get Indian that's not spicy. There's this creamy sauce called korma. . . ."

Jack couldn't focus on the conversation. He remembered what he had told Kyle Driscoll about not taking the job personally. That wasn't strictly true, of course: any detective worth his or her salt had cases—a child murder or a particularly brutal attack—that became an obsession. For the other detectives in the room, though, this wasn't one of them. Some Russian guy had gotten popped on Neptune Avenue; catching his killer would improve the yearly crime stats. That was about it.

But the case was twisting Jack's guts. He kept trying to think a step ahead. If Shvidkoy finally talked, the next move would be to arrest Eugenia Lelo. It was only a matter of time . . . and then what?

"I been eating a lot of Indian," Scott DeHaven continued. "There's this great cheap place on Church Street where all the cabbies go." He explained to his colleagues: "I was on assignment near Ground Zero for a couple of weeks."

So much for banal conversation. For the next few minutes everybody started trading 9/11 where-were-you-when-you-first-heard-about-the-attack? stories. Even two years later, New Yorkers still felt a compulsion to position themselves in exact relation to the event. Jack didn't join in; on 9/11 he had been lying in a hospital bed next to a living, breathing Daniel Lelo.

Lieutenant Cardulli glanced at his watch. "We've given this creep enough time to consider his sins. Linda, you wanna talk to him again? Let's see what happens if you offer him the Out."

The Out was an opportunity to confess while claiming some sort of special justification for the crime. *It was self-defense. I was just obeying orders. It wasn't my idea....* Many perps welcomed it.

Vargas went back into the interview room. "All right, Alec. Let's talk about that night over on Neptune Avenue. You know, when Daniel Lelo got shot."

Shvidkoy listened wide-eyed to the translation.

"So tell me," Vargas continued, "was Eugenia Lelo there? Did she tell you what to do?"

Their suspect shrank down into his chair.

"If this was her idea," Vargas continued, "there's no reason why you should have to take the blame. If you were just doing what she told you . . ."

Shvidkoy's gaze darted to the interpreter, to the door, down at the floor. Anywhere but Vargas.

"Come on, Alec. You can spare yourself a lot of trouble here."

Shvidkoy muttered something, but the interpreter looked reluctant to pass it on.

"What'd he say?" Vargas asked.

The interpreter shrugged. "Something not very nice about your mother."

Vargas leaned in. "We want to help you, Alec. If you lie, you'll end up in prison. And you know what? You might have heard that American prisons are soft, but it's not true. There are a lot of really bad people in there. And they don't like for-eigners."

Watching from the other side of the mirror, Jack frowned: his colleague might be pressing too hard.

Sure enough, Shvidkoy's next words were "I want a lawyer."

And that was it.

"Well, gang," Cardulli said when they all got together next door, "that was a good effort, but it looks like we're gonna have to take our chances with some lineups."

"Don't worry," Scott DeHaven said to Linda Vargas. "We're gonna nail this bastard. By the time he gets out of prison, techno's gonna sound as old as doo-wop."

EARLY THE NEXT MORNING, Alec Shvidkoy had his lawyer. He had also been charged with attempted homicide. Now he stood in front of some very bright lights along with four other young men.

Behind another two-way mirror, Jack and his colleagues stood in the dark with Shawnique Emory, a young McDonald's employee who had been busing tables outside on the afternoon of the shooting. She was a thin girl with lustrous ebony skin, a solemn face, and—luckily—perfect vision.

"I want you to take your time," said the A.D.A. who'd

been called in to run the lineup. "Don't point to anyone unless you're absolutely sure."

Shawnique nodded gravely, the light from the window glinting on her gold hoop earrings.

Jack stood in the corner, chewing his lip. The criminal justice system often came down to this: the quite fallible perception of one inexpert human being.

The girl clutched her purse to her chest. "Can I see them step forward again?"

"Sure," the A.D.A. said. He got on the intercom.

Jack frowned as each young white male in the lineup stepped toward the mirror.

"That's him," the girl said. She pointed a finger in the dim light. "Number three. The one with the red and black shirt."

Jack exhaled.

Ten minutes later, Tyrese Vincent had his turn.

With equal certainty, he picked the same man.

AFTER CONSULTATION WITH THE D.A.'s office, they offered Shvidkoy special consideration if he would give up the details.

And Shvidkoy began to talk. He explained how the shooting at the McDonald's had gone wrong. He had tailed Daniel for hours and finally seen him sitting still, out in the open. But how could he have predicted that, just as he was about to make the hit, this black guy three tables over—a total stranger— would rise up with a pistol of his own? This was a crazy country, full of guns.

Vargas tried another switchup, asking about Andrei Goguniv again, but Shvidkoy just looked blank.

"That's okay," Vargas said. "You're doing great. Now tell me: did Eugenia ask you to shoot Lelo?"

A pained expression flickered across Shvidkoy's face. "I don't know this person."

Vargas frowned. "Come on, Alec—we have two eyewitnesses who saw you with her at the hotel in Manhattan." She leaned forward and stared directly into his eyes. "How about the second shooting, on Neptune Avenue? When Lelo got killed. Did you pull the trigger, or did Eugenia?"

His lawyer started to interject—his client had only been identified in the first shooting—but Alec looked up, the fluorescent lights reflecting in his anguished eyes. "*I* killed him," he said. "Only me."

In the next room, in the dark, Tanney and Cardulli and Scott DeHaven started congratulating each other. The charge had just gone from attempted homicide to murder.

Jack stared at the twocway mirror. The guy was lying to protect his lover. You had to give him some little credit for that.

He sighed. Maybe Zhenya had not actually pulled the trigger, but she was romantically involved with this perp. And that relationship gave her a clear motive for wanting her husband out of the way.

There were no two ways about it: it was time to bring her in.

CHAPTER THIRTY-TWO

He hung back in the minty-green hallway and let Linda Vargas ring the doorbell. The last thing he needed was to have Zhenya pull him into the foyer and give him a great big (fake) kiss, and then have Vargas and the patrol cop behind her witness the whole damned scene.

He patted the pocket of his sports jacket and pulled out a roll of antacids. Chewed three. This was the last place on the planet he wanted to be right now. He supposed he might have taken some satisfaction at seeing Zhenya brought low for her lies, but he didn't. He just felt awful. He sighed; there was nothing to be done. Nobody had forced to him to have an affair with this woman. It had been his own lousy judgment, and now he was going to have to pay the piper.

The door opened. Over Vargas's shoulder, he saw Zhenya standing in the foyer. She wore one of her pairs of cute designer jeans and one of her silky blouses, and a sudden look of total comprehension. The jig was up.

"Would you like to come in?" she said. Still working the phrasebook.

Vargas entered, followed by Jack. Their patrol backup, a

gangly young cop from the Six-oh house, stood guard out in the hall.

"We'd like you to come down to the precinct for a little talk," Vargas said. "Do you understand?"

Zhenya nodded solemnly. She avoided Jack's eyes. She swallowed. "May I ask, what is this about?"

Vargas nodded. She knew that, legally speaking, Zhenya didn't have to come in unless they were arresting her. And so far they didn't have any actual evidence to support a charge. So the team had come up with a strategy, and Vargas was about to play it out. "We've got your boyfriend," she said. "It's all over."

Zhenya's eyes widened. "My boyfriend?" For the first time, she looked directly at Jack.

"Let's not play any games here," Vargas said firmly. "Alec has already told us all we need to know."

To the detectives' surprise, Zhenya sputtered a short, sharp laugh. "Alec? You think he is my boyfriend?"

Jack's jaw tightened. "I saw you," he said. "I saw you kiss him. Outside the hotel, in Manhattan."

Zhenya stared at him. She blinked, registering his barely suppressed look of hurt and rage.

She sighed and her shoulders slumped. "Oh, Detective," she said, and he thought he detected pity in her eyes. Pity for him. Why? Zhenya shook her head sadly. "I kiss my *brother*."

This time, Jack couldn't keep his surprise off his face.

Vargas tried to regain control of the situation. "What are you talking about?"

Zhenya sighed. "When I marry Daniel, I am taking his surname. But my—how do you call it?—my *maiden name* is Shvidkoy."

Vargas looked at Jack, clearly taken aback by this new

development. She squared her shoulders, though, and regained her composure. This didn't change the game plan. "We
talked to Alec," she said. "He talked to us. And he told us how
you killed your husband." It was a bald lie, but Vargas told it
smoothly. If you had two suspects, you played them against
each other—it was the oldest trick in the interrogator's book.

Zhenya pondered this information gravely. To the further
surprise of Jack and his colleague, she didn't argue or clam up or
demand a lawyer. She just nodded.

"Yes. Is true. I kill Daniel. My brother is nothing to do
with this. I take his motorcycle. I follow my husband to Neptune Avenue. And I shoot."

Linda Vargas snuck another confused look at Jack. She
turned back to Zhenya. "What about Andrei Goguniv?"

Zhenya looked confused. "He is manager of my husband's
company. Very nice man."

Vargas frowned. Maybe they'd only wrap up one homicide
here. . . .

"Eugenia Lelo," she said, "you have the right to remain
silent. Anything you say can and will be used against you in a
court of law. You have the right to have an attorney present
during questioning. If you cannot afford an attorney, one will
be provided for you. Do you understand what I'm telling you?"

Zhenya nodded.

Vargas shook her head. "Please answer yes or no." She
wasn't taking any chances—she didn't want Zhenya's lawyer
arguing later that his client had not understood the English.

"I understand," Zhenya said.

"We're placing you under arrest," Vargas said. "You're
going to need to come with us."

"Okay," Zhenya said.

Jack's heart sank. He had been hoping that she was just

covering for her brother, but she seemed oddly resigned. He'd seen this before, any number of times. Sometimes an arrest could come as a big relief to the guilty party—no more dissembling was required, no more waiting, no more worrying. It was over. Zhenya half turned. "May I get my purse?"

"Sure," Vargas said. As soon as Zhenya began to walk down the hall, the detective nodded toward Jack, and they followed their suspect, not taking any chances. Zhenya noticed but didn't complain. They marched through the dining room and back to the living room, with its couch where Jack and Zhenya had first made love, its glass door onto the balcony where they had sat and drunk and enjoyed the sunsets over Brighton Beach. Zhenya went over to a desk in the corner and picked up her purse.

Jack swallowed. He turned to his colleague. "Linda, could you, uh, could you give me a moment here?" He lowered his voice. "I think I might be able to get some more information because I knew these people."

Vargas stared at him. Again, questions tumbled behind her eyes. But she shrugged and left the room.

As soon as they were alone, Zhenya came back toward Jack. She raised her hand and he flinched, expecting a slap. But she just placed it tenderly on his cheek. Her eyes were luminous and large.

"Poor man," she murmured. "I am so sorry."

He could barely talk. "I thought . . . I thought you were seeing him. You know, *seeing him.*"

Zhenya just shook her head ruefully.

He raised his eyes to her face. "Just tell me one thing: why did you kill Daniel? For money?"

She bristled. "Is this what you think of me? That I will do such a thing for *money?*"

Jack frowned. "Why, then?"

Zhenya sank down onto the edge of the couch. She looked away for a moment. When she spoke again, her voice was tight and controlled. "Daniel is your friend. You think he is nice man, very—how you say?—*friendly*. He is this way with other mens. He is this way when he is not drinking. But with the alcohol, he is like Dr. Zhecko."

Jack squinted. "Who?"

"Dr. Zhecko and Mr. Hyte. You know this book, yes?"

Jack nodded.

Zhenya frowned. "When he is drinking, he shouts. He is hitting me."

"Why?" Jack asked, then realized that the question was stupid. If the man had hit her, there could be no good reason.

She scoffed. "Why? Because he does not like the dinner. Because he does not like my clothings. Because he is zhealous." She touched the deep scar on her chin. "This was not bicycle. This was Daniel." She wrapped her arms around herself. "Sometimes he will not have sex with me. He calls me a whore. Other times, when I will not have sex with him, he rapes me." She looked up at him, bitterly. "You understand this? He *rapes* me. You are a man. Perheps you are thinking, a man cannot rape his wife. She is his property, no?"

Jack listened, thunderstruck. He thought of Daniel's jovial, hearty manner—but also of how closed off and sullen the man had seemed back in the hospital. Evidently, that first impression had been more accurate.

He stared deep into Zhenya's eyes. He had interviewed hundreds of suspects, and he could believe that the pain on her face was genuine. His heart twisted, but he fought the urge to sympathize. "You didn't have to kill him. Why didn't you just leave?"

Her eyes flashed with anger. "He told me he will call INS. He will say I am marrying him only for citizenship. They will deport me. I am afraid."

Jack ran a hand over his face. "Jesus." He swallowed, then asked the question he'd been dreading. "What about me? Were you just using me to get information about the case?"

Zhenya hung her head for a moment. When she spoke, he could barely hear her answer. "At first, I want to know if police will find me. But then . . . you was kind to me. I hev feelings for you." She looked up at him, and he was sure he saw some real love in her eyes.

He felt as if he had been punched again. He wanted to take her in his arms, to find someplace where they could go, away from all this mess, but there was nothing he could do other than to argue for lenient treatment of her, considering the domestic abuse.

He exhaled—he still had one more question. "What about this Balakutis crap? You were willing to send an innocent man to prison?"

She shrugged. "I never say he kills Daniel. I say they was in argument." She grimaced. "Anyhow, I think he is not so 'innocent.'"

Jack just shook his head, thinking about all the energy he had spent on trying to prove that Balakutis had killed Daniel. But then he thought of Andrei Goguniv's battered body and of a shopkeeper's bloody ear. Of strange transactions taking place in a doughnut shop and in a fish market. He would never have known about these things if not for her.

Zhenya stared forlornly at him. "The prisons here—they are bad?"

Jack knew she must be thinking about her childhood visits to her incarcerated father. "This is the United States," he said. "They're not so bad." He did his best not to wince at his own lie: a maximum-security prison was always a nasty place, even if it was a women's facility.

Zhenya read his face; she trembled.

He wanted to take her in his arms and kiss her one last time, but he was afraid Vargas would walk in. "Listen," he said. "Do you have a lawyer?"

Zhenya nodded.

"Does he know what he's doing?"

She nodded again.

"Good," he said. "Find his number and bring it now."

His ears perked up: some kind of commotion in the front of the apartment. A woman's loud voice, speaking in Russian.

"Find that number," Jack repeated. He went out into the hallway to see what was going on.

In the little foyer, arguing with Linda Vargas and the uniform, stood the grave neighbor Jack had seen in the apartment before—the woman who had reminded him of a little bishop. She spoke almost no English, but she seemed concerned about the police presence.

"Take her outside," Vargas told the patrol cop.

The officer did his best to gently steer the woman back out. "Don't worry," he said, as if speaking to a child.

Vargas turned to Jack and lowered her voice. "You wanna tell me what was going on back there?"

Jack frowned. He knew he'd have to open up about his personal relationship. His colleagues would spend lots of time interviewing Zhenya, and the truth was bound to come out.

He sighed. "Can we talk about it as soon as we get her back to the station house?"

Vargas frowned but nodded.

The detectives heard a sound like fingernails scraping on

a blackboard, coming from the back of the apartment. They looked at each other, then ran for the living room.

They were too late. Out on the balcony, Zhenya Lelo had pushed the little side table against the railing and used it to step up. Jack and Vargas reached the doorway just in time to see her stand and balance for a precarious second on the rail itself. Her fine blond hair glowed in the morning sun; the sky stretched out before her like an endless open field. She raised her arms and then, without looking back, she launched herself out into the light.

CHAPTER THIRTY-THREE

Three nights later Jack sat on his couch in the dark, an opened but unsipped beer clutched in his right hand. Outside the windows, below the streetlights, summer trees swelled and bowed in a night breeze, sending shifting shadows across the walls of his front room.

In the past few days, he had been rocked with too many emotions to count: jealousy, surprise, anger, disappointment, surprise, surprise again, and grief. Now he just felt drained, too tired to think of much of anything, though he couldn't help picturing Zhenya's sad eyes and wishing he might have done something to help her while her husband was still alive. As he puzzled over how things had played out, though, he couldn't really see what he might have done differently. He was a good detective, and he had done his job; he couldn't have let her just walk away from a homicide. He just wished he had never left her alone, that last fateful minute.

He set down the beer; he had no taste for it. He lay back on the couch, remembering her girlish joy during their jaunt along the boardwalk, her sadness in the middle of the nights, the taste of her sweet mouth. And he remembered their final talk. She had not betrayed him, not really, not even with that last forceful jump.

Ironically, she had even freed him from his job troubles. Before the paramedics arrived, he had started to explain the situation to Linda Vargas. They had worked together for a decade and learned to trust each other more than most married couples, and he couldn't bear for her to think that he was abusing that trust. But Linda looked at him, standing there so stricken, and she raised a hand to stop him. "I'm going to ask you just one question," she said. "Did you have anything at all to do with either of these deaths or with covering anything up?"

He could have gotten huffy, but he had no right. He just shook his head.

"All right, then," Vargas said. "It's over. Whatever happened, it's over." She put her hand on his arm. "Don't beat yourself up for this. If it wasn't for you, we might never have closed this case." And then she left him alone.

Now he lay in the dark, musing. He had been a detective for many years, but the true mystery was never really the whodunnit or the how. It was why it was so hard for people to really *see* each other, and why they inflicted so much absolutely unnecessary pain. The world offered some real external troubles, from famine to hurricanes, but violence based on hatred, greed, or jealousy was a purely human creation.

(Of course, if people *did* manage to stop killing each other and get along, he would be out of a job. . . .)

He got up and picked up a DVD. He inserted it into the player and pressed the remote.

Bright digital letters flashing time code in the corner of the screen: 4:27 A.M. From a recently planted surveillance camera, a grainy view looking down: a room with bare metal walls. In the background, three men wearing bulky jumpsuits to protect themselves from the freezing cold. Two severe-looking strangers and a third figure, unmistakably Semyon Balakutis. In the foreground, a big fish company employee, standing behind a massive tuna laid out on a table. The worker picked up a circular saw and applied it to the belly of the fish, which gleamed dully in the low light. He made a deep, careful incision, then set the saw down and pried up a segment of the fish's heavy flank. Balakutis, wearing long rubber gloves, stepped forward, reached into the fish, and started pulling out white packages bundled heavily in plastic wrap.

After a few seconds, the room suddenly flooded with people wearing jackets marked NYPD.

Jack turned off the DVD player. That was why poor Andrei Goguniv had died, that deadly powder. He thought of Balakutis's face as he had been led, handcuffed, toward a waiting police van. Just before he'd been pushed in, he had turned and seen Jack standing there. The man had done his best to maintain a proud, scornful expression, but it didn't quite reach his eyes, which were weak with fear.

Now Jack lay back down on his couch. He should have been feeling more satisfaction, but he didn't. He had put two bad guys away; tomorrow two more would spring up in their place. Angry, brutal men seemed to be one of the world's great renewable resources. He thought of his son, Ben, and of the ways in which he had failed as a father to the boy, and he resolved to try harder.

After a few minutes the angry faces faded from his mind, but another took its place. He thought again of what he had seen in Zhenya Lelo's eyes in her final moments. There was a weight deep in his chest, a pool of Russian sadness. The clock ticked on, and the night grew long, and gradually he felt another emotion taking hold, a surprising warmth, as if he had drunk of some smooth and very powerful liqueur.

Zhenya had given him a parting gift, with her last look of love, and he would carry it with him to the very end of his own days.

ACKNOWLEDGMENTS

I am greatly indebted to Reed Farrel Coleman and Peter Blauner for their wise counsel about the penultimate draft of this book. Thanks, guys!

I'm also grateful for earlier helpful critiques by Lise Mc-Clendon, Katy Munger, Rob Reuland, and SJ Rozan. Many other people gave me invaluable assistance, including Roxanne Aubrey, Tim Cross, Brooklyn North Homicide lieutenant John Cornicello, Michael Epstein, Erika Goldman, Carrie Grimm, Peter Grinenko, Ian Hague, Eileen Lynch Hawkins and Dennis Hawkins, Dinah and Bob Kerksieck, Sylvia and Lenny Pervil, Isabelle Redman, Jay Shapiro, former chief of the Rackets Division at the Brooklyn D.A.'s office, Helen Suby and her wonderful mother, and Elly Sullivan.

Thanks for fascinating medical information and for sharing their remarkable work to the present and former staff at the NYU Hospitals Center's Tisch Hospital and Rusk Institute of Rehabilitation Medicine, including Dr. Jung Ahn, Tara Kornberg, Evan Cohen, Bev Divine, Debra Shapiro, and Heather O'Brien. Thanks likewise to Peter Hisle and Elise Carney of Bellevue Hospital Center, and to Dr. Gregory Fried, former executive chief surgeon of the NYPD.

Thanks again to all of the good people at Thomas Dunne Books and St. Martin's Minotaur who helped make this book possible.

And thank you for reading it!